INSTANT
TEMPTATION

INSTANT TEMPTATION

JILL SHALVIS

KENSINGTON PUBLISHING CORP.

www.kensingtonbooks.com

Prologue

If you asked TJ Wilder to choose between a warm autumn night in the Sierras or a warm woman, he knew that most people would put money on him taking the woman.

And while that might have been true in his wild, unchecked youth, tonight they'd have been wrong.

Not that he didn't love women. He did. Short or tall. Willowy or curvy. Sweet or hot-as-hell sexy—actually, make that *especially* hot-as-hell sexy. Over the years he'd loved plenty.

Yet he loved the Sierras, too. While it was true that the tall, rugged, remote mountain peaks could be deadly dangerous to both life and limb, the mountains couldn't break a man's soul.

At least not without permission.

TJ no longer let anything break him. He didn't let anything break him or get to him, period. He was cool, calm, and prepared, always. Cam and Stone had long ago accepted, that as the oldest brother, TJ just knew things, like which direction to go on the mountain whether on skis or a bike, or in the helicopter. He knew which of their outdoor expedition clients would be a pain in the ass, and he could sense trouble a mile away.

Usually.

But, as he walked through Moody's Bar And Grill after a quick dinner with Cam and Stone, feeling full and surprisingly content for the moment, something plowed into his chest with the force of a cyclone.

Not something. Someone.

Harley Stephens—the one source of trouble he'd never managed to avoid.

Absorbing the impact, he prevented them both from tumbling to the floor, and as his brain registered how warm and soft she felt in his arms, she lifted her face, the scent of her filling his head. That's when something else hit him, too, the same inexplicable sense that he always got with her, the déjà vu feeling that he'd been there before. Not there in the doorway of Moody's with the fiery Indian summer sun setting behind her and the sound of the dinner crowd behind him, loud and rowdy . . . but there, as in having her practically wrapped around him.

Which made about as much sense as the head-buzzing physical reaction he got from the feel of her against him.

Wishful was a small mountain town. TJ knew every person in it fairly well, and Harley was no exception. He knew her layered blond hair, silky and straight and not quite touching her shoulders, even as a strand of it caught on the stubble of his jaw. He knew her face, always soft and pretty, though tonight it held more than a hint of fatigue and anxiety as well.

And just like that the sexual punch faded, replaced by concern. "Harley? You okay?"

Twisting free, she turned from him so quickly he was barely able to catch her hand. "Hey. *Hey*," he murmured when she fought him pulling her back into him. His hands were on her arms as he bent to look into her face, which did him little good. Her eyes were covered by reflective sunglasses.

He pulled them off, exposing her warm chocolate eyes, but whatever expression he'd caught a quick flash of was gone, carefully and purposely gone.

"Did I hurt you?" she asked, staring at his throat, always so tough on the outside, yet so soft on the inside.

"No, I'm fine. You?"

She wasn't. He could feel the tension of her body against his, in the quick quiver of her limbs, though that might just have been the same unwelcome erotic awareness he'd felt.

Still felt.

With Harley, he'd *always* felt it, though he'd gotten good at ignoring it since they subscribed to two very different philosophies in life. His being to live as uncomplicated as possible, including romantic entanglements. Hers being the opposite. She was complicated as hell, and she played for keeps.

"I'm fine, too," she murmured, flexing her shoulders beneath his hands. "Really."

He wasn't surprised at her statement. She was proud and she didn't need anyone. Just ask her. But he took a second, longer look at her, saw the exhaustion in the paleness of her skin, and the worry in the tight lines of her mouth. God, he loved her mouth. She wore gloss on a pair of lips that had given him more than a few dirty fantasies over the years. Then there was the milk chocolate depth of her gaze, which could warm anyone else's soul but sliced right through his. She wore faded, snug Levi's low on her hips and a pretty stretchy knit top that hugged the curves she was so often forced to hide beneath her mechanic overalls when she was working. "Harley, what's wrong?"

"Nothing."

A bullshit answer and they both knew it. Once upon a time, they'd been close enough that he could have called her on it. She was still close with his brothers, but TJ had never been able to put his finger on exactly when things had changed between them.

"Sorry about the collision," she said.

Wow. Four whole words, willingly given. "No problem. Watch out." He pulled her back up against him to let a customer move through the door, and for the second time in as many minutes he felt an undeniable . . . zing. And for the *first* time, he saw the mirror of it in Harley's gaze before she could mask it.

For a deliciously long beat she stayed plastered up against him, and he began to think she was enjoying the connection, but proving the ridiculousness of that, she snatched her glasses from him and turned to walk away.

"You telling me you didn't feel that?" he asked her back, having no idea why he pushed, or why he cared. Since when did he push for anything, especially something as nameless and intangible as what he might want from Harley Stephens?

"Feel what?"

"The thing that happens when we get too close."

She froze, then slowly turned to face him. "It's Indian summer, TJ. We're all a little overheated. It's natural."

"Is that right?"

"Yes." She broke eye contact, her gaze skittering away. "It's Wishful, you know. High altitude. And it's hot, it's really, *really* hot. It's normal to feel so . . ."

"Hot?"

She bit her lower lip. "Yes."

"So is that what happens when we get too close then, Harley? You get really, *really* hot?"

Her eyes jerked to his, clearly realizing she'd just given away far more than she'd meant to. "What are you even doing here anyway?" she asked. "You're usually in Alaska, or Wyoming, or anywhere other than here."

True. He took all the long treks for Wilder Adventures, which usually had him gone for weeks, even months at a time. He liked it that way. Always had. "I'm in between trips. So do you get really, *really* hot with Nolan, too?"

Nolan being Nolan Lightner, the owner of the car and truck garage where Harley wrenched part-time. And Wishful, being Mayberry-With-Attitude, loved its gossip mill, which meant that everyone knew she'd gone out with Nolan twice.

Not that TJ was counting.

"Yes," she said firmly even as a blush bloomed on her cheeks. "Nolan and I get . . . hot." She crossed her arms, as always, ready and willing to do battle when backed against a wall. "Is that what you wanted to hear?"

Hell, no. But TJ watched her fidget, and suddenly he felt a whole hell of a lot better.

Because she was lying.

"In fact, if you must know . . ." She stabbed a finger into his pec for emphasis, "there are so many sparks between me and Nolan that our clothes catch fire every time we're near each other."

He registered the abrupt change in the pitch of her voice and her overly defensive stance and grinned. Yeah, he was feeling *much* better, and leaned in close enough to whisper in her ear. "Liar."

A low growl of temper escaped her and once again she pushed clear of him, heading toward the pickup counter, bad attitude spilling from her with every swing of her sweet hips and sweeter ass.

Feeling a mixture of amusement, at himself, at her, he let her go.

Stone came up behind him. "You're supposed to ask them out, not scare them off."

TJ turned to his brother, standing tall and lean and tanned from long days on the mountain, his stark green eyes flat-out grinning, looking like what TJ knew was his own mirror image. "You think I scared her?"

"No, I think you do something else to her entirely." Stone shook his head. "Though I have no idea what she sees in you, man. You're ugly as sin."

Ignoring that, TJ twisted to look at Harley again.

"You going to run off on yet another long trip to get away from her again?" Stone asked. "'Cause that's only a temporary fix and we all know it."

"Stone?"

"Yeah?"

"Shut up."

Stone clapped a hand to TJ's shoulder and didn't shut up. "Face it, man. You're as drawn to that woman as you're drawn to the mountains. One guess as to which is more lethal."

CHAPTER 1

Late the next afternoon, Harley sat at her kitchen table staring at her bank balance, but no matter how long she sat there or how much she squinted, the balance wasn't going to cover her rent.

That is what happened when one took two part-time jobs, only one of them paying, and not all that well.

She shut her laptop, then thunked her head down on the table a few times, enough to scatter some papers and make her Canon digital bounce, but that didn't help either. After six years of night school, she'd recently completed her degree in wildlife biology. Six *long* years of wrenching cars and trucks during the day and staying up all night studying, and she still couldn't make ends meet.

But there was a silver lining. Thanks to her brand-new shiny degree, she'd been granted a part-time internship as a research biologist for a federal conservation agency, and if she impressed them, she had a shot at the lone full-time research position in their Colorado branch in the spring.

Since that job—unlike her internship—came with an actual paycheck, impressing them had become Harley's biggest goal.

Her duties involved putting together data and analysis on a species indicator report, which was seeking to answer questions about western coyote populations. It sounded a lot more impressive than it actually was. In truth, there was almost no funding for the project, and the staff consisted of two wildlife biologists located in Colorado, and a few lowly, unpaid interns like herself scattered throughout the states of California, Nevada, Idaho, and Wyoming.

But for Harley, it was a foot in the door, because she intended to get that job in Colorado.

When her belly rumbled, reminding her she'd skipped lunch, she got up to look in the refrigerator. Unfortunately, the food fairy hadn't paid her a visit, so her choices were questionable cottage cheese, an apple, or the last of her emergency stash of double fudge brownie ice cream. She'd been saving that for an extreme disaster, but the possibility of getting evicted for not paying her rent seemed pretty extreme.

She'd just stuffed a large bite into her mouth, and was moaning over the sweet chocolate melting on her tongue when her phone rang.

She looked at it with the same caution she'd give a piqued rattlesnake. It was probably her landlord. Or maybe it was her mom wanting to bring her some tofu concoction in thanks for helping her meet her mortgage this month. Or her father wanting to crash on her couch, since the fun-loving hippie had probably pissed off his latest lover and had nowhere else to go. It could be her sister Skye wanting to mooch food and/or cash, which—no surprise— was in shockingly low supply. Harley loved her family, she really did, but she couldn't seem to master their carefree, no-worries attitude.

Not when the worries kept piling up.

The phone stopped ringing before her machine picked up.

Blowing out a relieved sigh, shaking off her sense of impending doom, Harley looked down at her coveralls. It was a good day, relatively speaking, as she had only one grease stain streaked down a thigh and another on her bare arm. Not bad. She could probably get it off with fingernail polish remover. Lifting her spoon, she used it as a mirror. She wasn't vain. She knew she had an okay shape thanks to a decent metabolism, but seeing as she wasn't all that into makeup or fashion, she rarely did anything to accent her attributes. She took a quick inventory of her face and realized she'd spoken too soon about not being all that filthy, since she had another grease streak over her forehead.

Good thing she didn't have a date tonight.

Hey, look at that. Another silver lining to the crap that was her life.

The sorry truth was, she'd had only two dates in recent memory. Both with Nolan, her friend and boss. True, one of those dates had been more of an accident than anything else when she'd had to change out his alternator and drive him into South Shore for a meeting. But still, it was two dates more than she'd had in at least six months.

Tonight would have been their third night out, which would have been great because it was his turn to buy dinner, except he'd gotten stuck in Placerville and wouldn't be home until too late.

But if things were as really, really hot between them as she'd claimed to TJ, "too late" wouldn't have been a problem, a little voice inside her said.

There are so many sparks between me and Nolan, our clothes catch fire every time we're near each other.

God. She'd actually said those words out loud to TJ, who'd smiled that smile, the one that gave her goose bumps, as he'd whispered "liar."

Arrogant, cocky ass.

But he was one *gorgeous* arrogant, cocky ass.

She let out a shuddery sigh, the kind only good chocolate or a good-looking guy could cause and continued to eat her ice cream. When the knock came, she stared at her door, then slowly moved to look through the peephole.

Damn.

It was the *gorgeous ass* in person, looking a little hot and tired, as if, like her, he'd just come in from a long day. She remained still in indecision, blowing out a sigh when he merely arched a brow at her.

She said nothing when she opened the door, which wasn't polite, but she wasn't feeling polite. She was feeling out of control, unnerved, and off balance—three things that TJ Wilder probably never felt.

Something else he apparently didn't feel—the need to fill a silence. Instead he stood there, well over six feet of hard muscle and testosterone, doing what he'd been doing all her life without even trying—affecting her brain cells, turning them to mush.

Yes, just looking at him turned her from an educated biologist into a drooling imbecile. It wasn't her fault he'd been blessed by the gene gods. He had a lot of sun-kissed brown hair, wavy and unruly, falling over his forehead, and deep-set, assessing, sharp green eyes that missed exactly nothing. He was tanned from long days in the high-altitude sun spent trekking and guiding across trails that would make a city guy's bowels go weak. And then there was his body, honed to solid, ungiving sinew wrapped in a healthy dose of *male*.

"Why are you here?" she asked. Not exactly as friendly a greeting as Nolan would have received, but her reasons for not being comfortable with TJ were as complicated as everything else in her life at the moment.

His eyes said he'd registered her tone and was thinking about smiling. "You going to invite me in?"

Ah, he speaks. But no. Hell, no. That would be like inviting in the big bad wolf. She shook her head and simultaneously swallowed another bite of ice cream, which naturally went down the wrong pipe, and as the cold ache exploded behind her eyeballs, she choked.

Stepping in close, way too close for comfort, TJ ran a hand up her back, patting her between the shoulder blades as she coughed and gasped.

"Brain freeze?" he murmured, his hands still on her, which was disconcerting enough, but added to that, he brushed against her with all those tough muscles, the ones that could make a nun ache to touch him, and in spite of her current and regrettable lack of a sexual life, she was certainly no nun. If she were, she'd be excommunicated for the thoughts she was having.

Yeah, she had brain freeze, and not just from the ice cream. "Back up," she wheezed. "Give me space."

He obligingly took a step clear of her, managing to get inside her apartment as he did, because after all, he was a slippery, wily-as-a-fox Wilder. Their ancestors had created the wild, wild west, emphasis on the wild, wild. In fact, it was rumored that the Wilders were responsible for the addition of the second "wild." That tendency had carried down through the generations, each subsequent Wilder doing his best to live up to the name, most ending up in jail or six feet under. Somehow though, the current generation had escaped the worst of the bad genes, or at least outgrown them.

For the most part.

Didn't mean he wasn't up for taking advantage of a situation. "I didn't invite you in, TJ."

He just smiled.

He was built as solid as the mountains that had shaped his life, and frankly had the attitude to go with them—the one that said he could take on whoever and whatever and you could kiss his perfect ass while he did so. She'd seen him do it, back in his hell-raising, misspent youth.

Not that she was going there, to the time when he could have given her a single look and she'd have melted into a puddle at his feet.

Had melted into a puddle at his feet. Not going there.

Unfortunately for her senses, he smelled like the wild Sierras; pine and fresh air, and something even better, something so innately male that her nose twitched for more, seeking out the heat and raw male energy that surrounded him. Since it made her want to lean into him, she shoved in another bite of ice cream instead.

"I saw on Oprah once that women use ice cream as a substitute for sex," he said.

She choked again, and he resumed gliding his big, warm hand up and down her back. "*You* watch Oprah?"

"No. Annie does, and once I overheard her yelling at the TV that women should have plenty of both sex *and* ice cream."

That sounded exactly like his Aunt Annie. "Well, I don't need the substitute."

"No?" he murmured, looking amused at her again.

"No!"

He hadn't taken his hands off her. He still had one rubbing up and down her back, the other low on her belly, holding her upright, which was ridiculous, so she smacked it away. She did her best to ignore the fluttering he'd caused, and the odd need she had to grab him by the shirt, haul him close, and have her merry way with him.

That was what happened to a woman whose last orgasm had come from a battery-operated device instead of a man, a fact she'd admit, oh *never*. "I was expecting your brother."

"Stone's working on Emma's 'honey do' list at the new medical clinic, so he sent me instead. Said to give you these." He pulled some maps from his back pocket, maps she needed for a field expedition for her research. When she took them out of his hands, he hooked his thumbs in the front pockets of his Levi's. He wore a T-shirt layered with an opened button-down that said WILDER ADVENTURES on the pec. His jeans were faded nearly white in the stress spots, of which there were many, nicely encasing his long, powerful legs and lovingly cupping a rather impressive package that was emphasized by the way his fingers dangled on his thighs.

Not that she was looking.

Okay, she was looking, but she couldn't help it. The man oozed sexuality. Apparently some men were issued a handbook at birth on how to make a woman stupid with lust. And he'd had a lot of practice over the years.

She'd watched him do it.

Each of the three Wilder brothers had barely survived their youth, thanks in part to no mom and a mean, son-of-a-bitch father. But by some miracle, the three of them had come out of it alive, and now channeled their energy into Wilder Adventures, where they guided clients on just about any outdoor adventure that could be imagined; heli-skiing, extreme mountain biking, kayaking, climbing, *anything*.

Though TJ had matured and found success, he still gave off a don't-mess-with-me vibe. Even now, at four in the afternoon, he looked big and bad and tousled enough that he might have just gotten out of bed and wouldn't be averse to going back.

It irritated her. It confused her. And it turned her on, a fact that drove her bat-shit crazy because she was no longer interested in TJ Wilder.

Nope.

It'd be suicide to still be interested. No one could sustain a crush for fifteen years.

No one.

Except, apparently, her. Because deep down, the unsettling truth was that if he so much as directed one of his sleepy, sexy looks her way, her clothes would fall right off.

Again.

Wasn't that just her problem. The fact that once upon a time, a very long time ago, at the tail end of TJ's out-of-control youth, the two of them had spent a single night together being just about as intimate as a man and a woman could get. Her first time, but definitely not his first. Neither of them had been exactly legal, and only she'd been sober.

Which meant only she remembered.

Not going there . . . never going there again. "Thanks for the maps," she said in a clear invite to leave.

Instead he reached for her spoon and stole a bite of her ice cream.

Bastard. She'd bet her last buck—if she had one—that *he* wasn't orgasm deprived. Only the orgasm deprived got her ice cream!

"I wanted to talk to you." He licked the spoon with his tongue, flashing straight white teeth, and she remembered what else he liked to do with that mouth.

She dragged her eyes off it and up to his eyes. "About?" she asked suspiciously.

"Not here. I'll buy dinner."

"I don't go out to dinner with the big bad wolf."

He grinned. "Sometimes, Harley, you have to take a risk."

She wasn't real big on risk. Risk tended to end badly for her. Such as staring at her insufficient bank balance. Such as holding two jobs, neither of which was satisfying her. Such as waiting on Nolan to make his move sexually, when she was so overcharged she'd probably explode during her next shower.

Or the next time she leaned against the washer during the spin cycle.

Unable to explain any of that, she turned and started to walk into her kitchen. TJ hooked a finger into the back of her coveralls and halted her progress.

"Let go," she said.

"In a minute. You're off to Desolation Wilderness for a few days."

Her back was plastered to his chest, and it was a damn fine chest. Strong. Broad and warm. "I have to check on the tracking equipment. Several cameras aren't transmitting. Also I'm hoping to catch sight of any of the three core coyote groups that we're tracking. I've got a red, a blue, and a green group scattered through Desolation."

"*Hope* to catch sight of them?"

"Well, honestly, they're so slippery, even with the GPS system in place I'll settle for signs. DNA."

She heard his smile. "You mean you're going looking for coyote shit."

She sighed. "Why do guys think anything to do with bodily functions is amusing?"

"Because it is."

She rolled her eyes so hard they almost fell out of her head.

"Desolation, Harley? At this time of year?"

His mouth was disconcertingly close to her ear, and his voice, low and husky, had a terrible habit of bringing her deprived body to life. "I have to impress," she said. "I want that research job in Colorado. And besides, it's September. It's the best time of year to go. Only a very small chance of a snowstorm, and not quite hot enough to fry an egg on a rock."

He said nothing to that, and not being good at loaded silences, she squirmed free. "I don't know what the big deal is. You take treks like this all the time. You just got back from two months in Alaska."

"It's my job."

Right. She was just a mechanic and a part-time research biologist, used to being either under a car or behind a computer. She got that.

But she wanted a shot at being more. She wanted to say good-bye to coveralls forever, good-bye to needing a degreaser in the shower. She wanted to be excited about something, passionate. Dammit, she wanted to stop feeling like a hamster on the wheel and *live*.

Unfortunately, most of her internship consisted of staring at a computer screen. Hell, *all* of her internship consisted of staring at a computer screen. "All I have to do is fix two cameras," she said. The cameras were vital to the study. Luckily, coyotes were creatures of habit, and territorial for life. They made a den and tended to stay in a very careful ten-mile radius of that den, even taking the same path of travel along a fixed route on a daily basis. This allowed the remote cameras to give humans a slice of coyote life.

When the cameras were functioning, that is. Which meant *field trip*. She'd be hiking into the northwestern slope of Desolation, a hundred-square-mile federal wilderness area west of Lake Tahoe. True, it was some of the toughest, most rugged, isolated land in the country. Most of it was roadless, trail-less, and devoid of logging and grazing.

But she'd be getting out from behind her laptop.

"I get why you've been asked to do this," TJ said. "You're a cheap resource."

"Hey."

"You're also sharp, intuitive, and probably the best intern they've ever had."

While she processed that, both the compliments and the warm

fuzzies it sent skittering through her, he went on. "The question is why do *you* want to do this? Why not just skip the internship and apply directly for the job you want?"

"Because there's only going to be *one* opening, and only one of us interns is getting it."

"What about somewhere else then?"

"There is nowhere else hiring wildlife biologist researchers."

"And you're tired of wrenching."

And tired of being alone. And lonely. Her best friend Selena had met the love of her life, sold her pastry shop, and moved to New York. Her sister was busy most of the time, or preoccupied in a way only a twenty-one-year-old could be. And Nolan . . . well, if he moved any slower he'd be going backwards. "Beyond tired."

"Is it Nolan? Is he pressuring you in some way, or—"

"No." She wished. "Nothing like that. I just . . . I just need to make this change. Working at the garage was a necessity, never what I wanted to do. I need more."

She knew he'd understand that. He'd come from nothing himself, and he'd worked his ass off to get his "more."

Now she was doing the same.

"We're trying to hire another hand at Wilder," he said, watching her in that quiet, pensive way he had. "We'd hire you in a hot minute."

"Thanks, but I want *this* job."

A long inhale was his only answer, but it was enough to remind her of his past and a certain tragedy that he'd faced that might be making her pending trip difficult for him to accept. "I'm going to be fine out there," she said softly. "Nothing's going to happen to me."

"I know."

"I'm not Sam."

A tightening of his jaw was his only reaction. "I know that, too." He was quiet a minute, then shook his head. "You're right, you'll do great."

That brought her some unexpected surprise. Her dad had run a small holistic vitamin store before he'd lost it in the current craptastic economy. Her mom was an artist and a chef who preferred to float from one job to the next. Skye worked the cash register at the Wishful grocery store while sometimes attending classes at a junior college when it suited her or if she had a "hot" professor. Collectively, the Stephens family didn't tend toward ambitiousness, and as a result, none of them understood Harley's yearning for more.

So it was ironic as hell that the single most frustrating, annoying, maddening person she knew would actually be the only one in her life supporting her. She wanted to thank him for that, but more than anything, she wanted him to leave before she asked him to take off his clothes and then hers.

Clueless, he sat down at her kitchen table and carefully shifted aside her camera to gesture to the maps. "Show me your plan."

TJ was the brains behind all the creating, organizing, planning, and plotting of the trips at Wilder. He was good at it—in large part thanks to his ability to be incredibly intuitive and doggedly aggressive, not to mention he was a master planner and a survival expert.

He wouldn't approve of her plan to wing it.

"I've got it handled, TJ," she said. "Besides, I'm really busy at the moment, so . . ."

He eyed the ice cream still in her hands and raised one brow. How busy can you be, came his silent question.

Dammit. "Maybe I have a date."

"Do you?"

When she sighed, he simply crooked a finger at her in the universal come-here gesture.

And just like that, her feet overtook her brain and took her straight to him.

CHAPTER 2

TJ kept his eyes on Harley's maps and notes as she moved reluctantly closer. She was dressed from a shift at the garage, but the cute dirt streak across her forehead and baggy coveralls didn't impair his imagination any.

She was still hot.

"I didn't realize you were going in by yourself," he said.

"It's a long story."

"Does it involve a sharp blow to your head?"

She sighed. "It's not that dangerous, TJ."

"Harley, *any* lone trip into *any* part of the Sierras is dangerous. Most especially Desolation Wilderness. Where are you going in?"

She didn't sit, he noted, but instead remained at his side. "West entrance."

In terms of sheer acreage, Desolation wasn't all that large, but it was isolated, remote, and contained over a hundred glacier lakes, making it a haven for wildlife. No hunting was allowed, and even hiking in there required a permit. The west entrance was the closest access but not the easiest, which didn't matter because once she was in, there was little that was easy about the hike she'd be making. "What else are you doing in there besides checking on the surveillance cameras?"

"Looking in on the known dens."

"You've never gone into the field before."

"No. But like I said, two of the cameras are down and not feeding data at all. I'm the only staff here right now. It wouldn't look good to the guys in Colorado if I can't get the data in, much less process it."

He considered what she'd said, and all she *wasn't* saying. Such as the fact that he'd noticed the empty spot where her TV used to be, and the pile of bills next to the maps. He could feel her desperation, and it killed him. "You could ask for help."

"I could. But whoever they'd send is competing for the same job as me."

"Competing."

"Yes, competing. Like when you and your brothers race like a bunch of idiots down The Face on your dirt bikes to see who can kill themselves—er, get to the bottom first."

He slid his gaze up to hers in time to catch her mouth twitch and didn't bother to hide his smile. "Those are controlled test trips to ensure we can make the run safely with a client."

"Uh huh."

He kicked out a chair for her and waited until she sat. She thought this trip was no big deal but he disagreed. Vehemently. He'd seen too many causal hikers and campers get into trouble on far less rugged terrain. He and Stone were members of the local Search and Rescue team, and they'd rescued more people than he cared to remember. And there'd been Sam, the one he'd not been able to rescue at all. "When was the last time you were in Desolation?"

She hesitated and he sighed. "Tell me."

"Years," she admitted.

"Shit, Harley."

"But with the maps and the GPS, I can't really go wrong."

He could think of a hundred things that could go wrong. Hell, he'd probably seen every possible one of them.

"Look," she said, sounding irritated. "I realize that those loaded silences of yours probably yield you all the information you could want from a woman, mostly because one look from you and they probably melt, but they don't work on me."

He felt the smile curve his mouth. "You think I melt women?"

"It's September," she said, ignoring that. "You and I both know there's no one even out there this time of year except the occasional wild animal. I'm prepared. It's perfectly safe."

"Not alone it isn't."

"So I'll scratch you off my short list of supporters."

He caught her wrist as she surged to her feet. "Harley—"

"I want this Colorado job," she said quietly, giving nothing away in her expression. "And . . ."

And she needed the money from it. That was plain as day. He no longer lived hand to mouth but he'd been there, and it sucked. "We're hiring," he said. "I wasn't bullshitting about that." Wilder Adventures was overwhelmed and overloaded, and they'd been trying to hire for weeks. It wasn't easy to find qualified people. "You'd be perfect for the guided hikes we offer, and with your photography skills and education, we could even tailor some of them toward wildlife education, stuff like that."

"If I finish this research project, I'll have a job."

"In Colorado."

"Yeah."

"You really want to leave here?"

She pulled her wrist from his grip and went to the sink, looking out the window. TJ knew her dad had lost his store, that her mom had a hard time keeping a job, that her sister hadn't gotten a scholarship, and as the only one working, they needed her, depended on her. Standing, he came up behind her.

Out the window in front of them, for as far as the eye could see, lay the glorious Sierra mountain peaks, blanketed in vibrant fall colors. The lack of concrete was soothing. No sidewalks, no other buildings, no traffic. Nothing but nature. It'd rained earlier, leaving everything fresh and clean and sharp.

"I never get tired of the view," she murmured, reading his mind.

"Me either. Annie framed that shot you took of Granite Flats.

She's hanging it in the lodge reception room. It's an amazing shot, Harley."

"Thanks."

Taking her hand, accepting the little frisson of awareness that zinged through his body, he tugged her back to the table. "Show me your route."

"So you know where to find my body?"

He shot her a level look, and she flashed him a smile. He loved her smile, it was wide and warm and rare, and he found himself smiling back helplessly. "Take someone with you."

"Who? You?"

"Why not?"

"Don't you have another big trip coming up?"

"I do. A four-week trip across the Canadian Divide in about ten days. But I have time for this. All you have to do is ask."

She was silent, either too proud to ask, or hell, maybe she really didn't want his help. He ran his thumb over the pulse point at the base of her wrist and felt it leap. "I've spent a lot of time being baffled by your prickliness with me, but not, I don't think, enough to wonder why. Until now." He met her gaze. "Why, Harley?"

"I'm prickly with everyone."

Maybe. But beneath his fingers her pulse had picked up speed. Behind that irritation she wore like a coat, he *did* affect her, maybe every bit as much as she affected him.

"I'll ask someone," she said quietly.

"But not me. You don't want it to be me."

"No."

His lips curved. "Another lie," he murmured. "You're racking them up. Your nose is going to start growing."

She pushed free of him and paced the length of the kitchen, which meant she got about five feet before turning around and smacking right into the hard wall of TJ's chest. He stood there, filling the kitchen with his larger-than-life presence, making the room seem even smaller than it was.

"Want me to tell you what I think?" he asked.

"Are you going to agree with me about the trip?"

"No."

"Then no."

He smiled, laugh lines fanning out from his sharp green eyes. "Still stubborn."

"And you're still . . ." She couldn't think of an insult. With an annoyed huff, she moved toward the front door and opened it for him. "Thanks for coming. We'll have to do it again sometime. Buh-bye now."

TJ smiled, reached over her head, and shut the door. "Let's do it again now."

She thunked her head against the wood. She felt him lightly run his fingers down her spine, which caused a sensuous shiver, but when he spoke, the amusement was gone from his voice, replaced by a gut-wrenching gentleness. "Harley, why didn't you tell me you needed money?

Oh, God. "I—"

The phone rang, saving her pride, and she leapt for it, then hesitated, standing there in front of the answering machine.

At the third ring, TJ raised a brow. "You going to get that?"

"I'm trying to decide."

The machine clicked on and Harley's voice invited the caller to do their thing at the beep, and then her landlord's voice filled the small apartment.

"Harley Stephens, you're avoiding me."

Crap. Harley hit the volume button, but not in time to avoid her landlord's next line.

"You are ten days late on rent, missy. I need—"

Harley smacked the volume again and again, until the voice could no longer be heard.

Gaping silence.

Her back was still to TJ, so she closed her eyes and wished for a nice big hole to vanish into. "Don't say it." Without meeting his gaze, she tried to move around him, but once again his hands came up to hold her in place. She could snap at him or shove him, but the truth was, she liked his touch.

Too much.

Which told her just how bad off she was. She really needed some one-on-one naked time with a guy. Preferably someone who didn't make her think too much, didn't have the potential to obliterate her heart, and who wouldn't expect anything from her.

Nolan.

"Harley," TJ said softly, interrupting her thoughts, something more in his voice than she wanted to hear.

"Look, as fun as this has been—"

"*Harley.*" He paused, and she heard him take a deep breath before continuing. "If you couldn't tell me, then why not Annie, or Stone, or Cam? You know how much they care about you."

Her throat felt tight, far too tight to talk. "It's temporary."

He pulled out his wallet and emptied all of his cash onto the counter. "Not temporary."

"I don't need—"

"Consider it an advance. We need an assist on upcoming trips. There's three this weekend. Take your pick; a biking trip, a kayaking trip, or guiding a group of hikers up Eagle Falls to jig for halibut and cast for salmon. Your choice. Hell, for that matter, get your feet wet on one of those, and then come with me on my next long trek."

"Those treks take you at least a month." A month of thirty long nights. Given her entirely inappropriate and extremely annoying habit of yearning and burning for him, God only knew what would happen.

Reading her mind, he let out a wicked smile that made her nipples harden. Firmly, she put one finger on the money and pushed it back across the counter at him.

"You don't think you can control yourself," he said, sounding amused again.

She gritted her teeth. "I have enough jobs."

"Yes, but this one pays good." His gaze touched hers, oddly tender and gentle, and it just about did her in.

"I'll think about it." Then, because she couldn't seem to forget her manners, she added a soft but genuine "thank you." She busied herself flipping through the maps. "Hey, where's the top of the northeast region, just beyond Sioux Hill?"

"It's there."

"No, it's not."

TJ reached around her to fan out the maps himself. "Shit, I must have left it on Stone's desk. Sorry." He took her hand in his. "Let's go get it now."

"I can get it later."

"Sure. But if there's a God, Annie's lasagna will be done by the time we get there."

Besides being his aunt, Annie was the chef at Wilder Adventures. Her lasagna was legendary, the best lasagna in the history of all lasagna. Just thinking about it had Harley's mouth watering.

"Five-cheese," TJ murmured as if recounting a long-lost lover, "and three-meat lasagna. A restaurant-sized tray of it."

Oh, God. She let out a small involuntary moan.

His eyes dilated. "There'll be homemade bread, too. French loaf. Crusty on the outside, soft and gooey on the inside."

"I'm not hungry," she said weakly.

Her stomach made a liar of her by rumbling loudly.

TJ's lips twitched, but he was wise enough to hold the smile back. "If you don't come with me, I'll inhale the entire loaf myself." He rubbed his flat belly. "And possibly all the lasagna, too."

She thought about the questionable cottage cheese in her refrigerator. "Well, if you need saving from yourself . . . I guess I wouldn't want you to get any more . . . you know."

"No, I don't."

"Extra around the middle."

He arched a brow. "Extra around the middle?"

She poked his rock-solid abs. "Don't worry. It happens to everyone."

He lifted his shirt and bent his head to look at himself.

His jeans were low riding, revealing lean hips and a set of abs etched in sinewy ridges. Heat slashed through her and she began to sweat in places she hadn't even realized had sweat glands.

Not good.

She tried to picture Nolan in her head. Sweet, kind, adorable Nolan. She couldn't do it. She told herself not to panic. It was only because she hadn't seen Nolan without a shirt.

"You're right." TJ let his shirt fall back into place. "You should definitely come with me and save me from myself." He walked into her kitchen and made sure her back door was locked. He flipped off the kitchen light, then turned and faced her, stopping when he found her staring at him.

"We don't even like each other," she said, confused.

"I like you just fine. Sure, you're as difficult and grumpy as Chuck, but no one's perfect."

She choked out a laugh. Chuck was the Wilder mascot, a disheveled stray that they'd hardly recognized as a cat at first sight. He'd shown up last winter, scrawny and half a heartbeat from starvation. He'd been neglected and terrified.

Annie and Katie had taken him under their wings, fattening him up, loving him so thoroughly that he'd had no choice but to learn to accept them as his family.

And then Emma had determined that not only was Chuck missing a penis, but that *he* was pregnant. Now they had three kittens running amok in the lodge, three wild, lovable little miscreants with none of their mama's innate mistrust and all of her penchant for trouble.

But what was it he'd just said? That he liked her just fine? *What was that?* Just when she thought she'd gotten used to the odd push/pull of their prickly relationship, he was changing the rules and hadn't given her a copy. "What's going on here, TJ? Usually, you never talk to me without a frown on your face."

"Don't you have that backwards?"

She stared up at him, having to concede that he might have a point. She usually was on edge with him, but it was because they had a past, one that was significant to her.

One that he didn't even remember.

There were other reasons, too. Like the fact that no matter how dirty and grubby he got on *his* job, he still looked hot, while she wore her grease like a poorly chosen accessory. "I have to get out of these coveralls."

"You know you can go like you are."

"I know." She'd known Cam and Stone and Annie forever. Annie's husband Nick, too. They were warm and accepting and cared about her as much as she cared about them. She could show up in a sack and it wouldn't matter. Changing was for *her*. "It'll only take a second." Now that she'd agreed to lasagna, she was nearly shaking with hunger. She unzipped her filthy coveralls and began to shove them down, but at the low, rough sound from TJ, she glanced over. "I'm dressed under here, you know." She kicked free of the grimy coveralls. Beneath she wore a stretchy black tank and micro bike shorts.

"See? Full coverage."

Her jeans were on the back of a chair. She grabbed them and slid them on, hopping up and down a little until they reached her hips.

TJ made another sound deep in his throat as she buttoned them up, and she sent him a questioning look and found his gaze so scorching hot she nearly caught fire.

Holy smokes.

"Is it really, *really* hot in here?" he asked ironically, voice silky, green eyes holding hers prisoner.

She was completely and utterly startled. "I'm dirty."

"So?"

"Sweaty, too."

"I repeat. So?"

Oh boy. "I have a boyfriend," she whispered.

He just smiled one of the big, bad wolf smiles, took her hand and led her outside, locking her front door, walking her to his Jeep.

"I'll drive myself," she said.

"You'd rather drive yourself all the way out to the lodge than be in the same car as me?"

"Well, those awkward silences *are* so much fun."

"We're *never* silent. We're usually arguing."

"Hence the separate rides."

He let out a breath. "I'm trying to save you the gas and the trouble, Harley."

"I don't want you to have to drive me all the way back."

"I don't mind."

"But—"

"Jesus." He swiped a hand down his face. "Just get in the damn Jeep."

She looked into his eyes. He was looking a little irritated and also a little amused—at the both of them.

And still *smoking* hot.

It was a problem. *He* was a problem. "I'm not sure I trust you."

Or me.

He let out a small smile. "Well, then, it's a good thing I'm not your boyfriend."

CHAPTER 3

They drove in silence, which suited TJ just fine. It seemed to suit Harley, too. She wasn't giving much away as they drove through town. Wishful had been around since the 1800s, once upon a time making a name for itself as the wildest corner of the wild, wild west. It'd survived the gold rush, the lumber boom, and now, thanks to sitting at 6,000 feet altitude, was an outdoor enthusiasts' tourist stop on the way to Lake Tahoe—something TJ and his brothers had made full use of with Wilder Adventures.

At the end of town, he turned onto the highway, and then onto the narrow, private three-mile road that led to the Wilder lodge. Harley continued to stare out the window away from him, doing her best imitation of someone who didn't give a damn—which TJ knew was yet another big, fat lie. He affected her, and he had no idea what to do with that. "You're really good with moving to Colorado?" he asked.

She turned her head and met his gaze. "You think I'll get the job?"

"Yes."

She looked surprised.

That made the second time today he'd surprised her by offering support.

He knew her parents, both sixties throwbacks, who were

equal parts proud of their daughter and confused by her. The support system went from Harley to them, not the other way around. Same with Skye. It was doubtful Harley ever was on the receiving end of the same level of support she gave.

She kept busy looking at the thick, lush woods on either side of the narrow, windy road that led to Wilder Adventures. The trees were pine, most well over a hundred years old and a hundred feet tall. "I figure Colorado won't be all that different from Wishful," she said.

"What about the boyfriend?"

"Nolan?"

He slid her a look. "You have more than one boyfriend?"

"Why do you keep saying it like that, like you're putting quotes around his name?"

"I'm not. Nolan's a good guy."

"But?"

"I didn't say but."

"Yes, but there was definitely a but at the end of that sentence. It was a silent but implied but."

"Jesus," he muttered. "Can't you just answer my question?"

"Fine. What exactly is the question again?"

"Why isn't Nolan going out to Desolation with you?"

"I didn't ask him. Listen, I realize that in your eyes I'm only a mechanic, but—"

"You're more," he said quietly, then met her gaze for a beat to let her see he meant it. "Far more."

She was silent a moment, absorbing that. "I grew up out here, TJ, same as you. As the only tow truck driver in town, I've been called out at all hours. Alone. I've faced all sorts of things."

He'd known that. He'd always hated that. Letting out a breath, he pulled into Wilder Adventures. He parked in front of the three-story lodge that he and his brothers had built, the late afternoon sun illuminating the stone and wood accents harvested from the property itself.

Home, for better or worse. He spent a lot of time away from there, and yet he always came back.

"I forget how beautiful it is," Harley said quietly, and looked at him. "You ever think about it? Where you started out, and where you ended up?"

"Since we started out in the gutter and somehow ended up here, no. I try not to go there."

"You didn't *somehow* end up here. You guys worked your asses off. You deserve this." With that shocking statement, she hopped out of the Jeep.

The sound of whining engines rent the air around them. Cam, Stone, and Nick—their pilot and mechanic—were racing on quads.

They'd had a lot of rain in the past few afternoons. The ATVs were churning across the yard, mud from the tires flinging up through the air in high arcs.

Annie stood off to the side, Chuck at her feet, the kittens nowhere in sight, but most likely in the lodge, creating utter destruction. Annie wore her usual dark jeans, vintage rock T-shirt, and chef's apron. This one said: COMPLAINTS TO THE CHEF MIGHT BE HAZARDOUS TO YOUR HEALTH. She had her hands on her hips, and given her expression, she'd clearly rather be riding than watching, but Nick had set the law—no riding while pregnant. TJ was just glad Nick had told her that, since no one else could tell Annie what to do and live.

TJ set his hand on the small of Harley's back and nudged her closer, just as Cam whipped past Nick and skidded to a stop right in front of them, the apparent finish line. Cam pulled off his helmet, hopped off the quad, and grinned. "I've still got it."

Nick pulled in right behind him and shook his head. "You cheated. The finish line's around the back of the lodge."

"I'd have beat you there, too," Cam said, eyes on Harley, a smile curving his lips as he pulled her in for a tight hug, affectionately rumpling her hair.

Right in front of TJ's eyes, Harley softened, hugging Cam back, looking quite cozy while doing it.

"You're not running clean," Harley murmured to Cam about the ATV. "May be a carburetor problem." She gently hugged Annie as well, rubbing her belly. "You feeling good?"

"I'd feel better if we could come up with a baby name." Annie accompanied this with a long look in Nick's direction.

"Hey, I've offered a bazillion names," Nick said in his defense. "Ashley, Emily, Madison, Olivia. You vetoed them all. Even Abigail."

"*Not* Abigail."

Nick threw up his hands and looked at TJ. "She's right, man, your quad is sluggish. It needs work."

"Can't be," TJ said. "I just went over it."

"Really?" Harley lifted a brow and moved toward the quad, inspecting it with a sharp eye. Not that TJ was noticing anything besides how her Levi's were nice and tight across her ass as she bent down for a better look. "When?"

"Last week," he told her.

"Huh." She crouched at the quad and looked it over with a critical eye. "You did a pretty shitty job." She said this so sweetly it took TJ a moment to process her words.

Cam grinned. "If I'd told him that, he'd have kicked my ass." He pulled her up for a smacking kiss. "God, I love you. If I wasn't already getting married, I'd ask you to marry me."

TJ rolled his eyes. Cam looked just like Stone and TJ, but slightly leaner. TJ could kill him with one snap of the neck and make the world a better place, but he'd probably feel bad about it later.

Maybe.

Nick handed Harley his helmet. "Take it out for me? Tell me what else is wrong with it."

"There's nothing wrong with it," TJ said.

"Ride it hard in the turn," Cam told her. "You'll see what I mean."

"I can already tell you what's wrong with it. You have a carburetor problem, and maybe a failed spark plug." Harley slipped into the helmet, then looked at Nick, who was preparing to follow her on his quad. "Around the back of the lodge?"

"Yeah."

"What do I get if I win?"

Nick's gaze slid to TJ's. "I'll hold TJ down so you can beat on him."

She actually turned and looked TJ over as if that might be satisfactory to her.

TJ arched a brow, and she let out one of her rare smiles. "Deal," she said.

Before TJ could react to that, she threw a leg over the quad and kicked started the thing with an ease that was incredibly sexy.

TJ shoved Nick off his quad and replaced him. "If I'm the prize, then I'm sure as hell doing the racing." He revved the engine, shot both Nick and Cam a long look, then nodded to Harley.

They took off. The wind hit his face and cut right through his clothes. It felt great. Harley was about twenty yards ahead so he floored it, his quad agreeably leaping forward, coming up neck and neck with her. She was leaning low over the handlebars in her black tank top and jeans, her legs hugging the machine like he wished they were hugging his hips. Oh, yeah, now *there* was an image . . .

Taking advantage of his momentary loss of concentration, Harley took the sharp right at the lodge and vanished.

TJ turned, right on her tail, content to stay behind her for the view alone, especially when she stood up, leaning hard into the turn, her ass looking damn fine.

The wind kicked up, but he still heard her laugh, and it caused one of his own. It felt good to play, even better to play with her, something they rarely got to do because though she was warm and fun and open with just about everyone else, with him she put up that damn brick wall that he hadn't figured out how to break down.

Not that it'd mattered. None of it did. He was gone more than he was there anyway. And if he didn't get his head out of his ass, the muddy, laughing, screaming Harley was going to win the race. She was good, damn good, but luckily he was better. He caught her on the back side of the lodge and neatly cut her off.

In tune to her swearing, he hit the finish line a nose ahead of her. He stood up and turned to face her, grinning.

She turned off her engine and pulled off her helmet. She flipped her hair free and looked at him. She was mud splattered, and her tank and jeans were plastered to her. "Fine," she said, flashing him a rare but gorgeous smile. "You win. I don't get to beat you up."

"Maybe another time," he murmured.

"Count on it."

He knew she was only half kidding.

She shivered, and drew his attention downward. Her nipples were two hard points, pressing against the thin stretchy material of her tank.

"They're just a regular old pair of breasts," she said. "Half the population has them."

Not that perfect, they didn't.

She crossed her arms over herself. "I'm feeling cold."

That wasn't what he was feeling. But he shrugged out of his outer shirt and wrapped it around her, using it to tug her up against his broad chest.

"I'm muddy," she said in protest.

"Makes two of us."

She tilted her head up to meet his gaze warily.

"I won," he reminded her.

"Yeah. So?"

"So now there's something you can do for me."

"Let me guess. Something sexual." Her tone suggested complete disinterest. The pulse fluttering wildly at the base of her throat suggested something else entirely. "God, you are such a guy."

He held his silence, and finally she sighed. "Okay, what? What could you possibly think would be okay to ask of me?"

"For you to admit Nolan's not your boyfriend. At least not yet, he isn't."

She stared at him, then let out a breath. "Bite me, TJ."

"With pleasure."

Instead of looking pissed, she let out a low laugh. "What's gotten into you today?"

He had no idea, but he knew it was something he wanted to explore. Did she? He figured he had sixty seconds tops before his family made it around the side of the lodge on foot. He wanted those sixty seconds, so he stepped even closer, until their muddy boots were toe-to-toe. Reaching out, he rubbed at a spot of mud on her jaw.

Her breath caught, and unguarded desire crossed her face.

Yeah, they were definitely on the same page. "Nice riding."

"Hmmm." As if she needed balance, she set her hand on his chest. He liked the feel of her touch. A lot. She looked at him, her hand lightly dancing back and forth on his pec as if she didn't even realize it. Leaning in so that their mouths were only a whisper apart, he breathed out a soft, "Harley."

She looked up and met his gaze. He could see the swirl of desire and hunger, and the air escaped his lungs. "Harley," he said again, a little hoarsely now.

"I know." Her eyes drifted closed. Their thighs bumped. Heat and affection and need warred for space in his head as he laughed softly and pressed his mouth against her ear. "How about now? Are you really, *really* hot? 'Cause I sure am."

Her eyes flew open and she stepped back, spell broken just as Cam and Nick came around the corner.

"Who won?" Cam called out.

TJ didn't take his eyes off Harley. "She did."

Harley blinked, then shot him a look filled with an intoxicating mixture of confusion and desire.

Yep. Definitely on the same page.

CHAPTER 4

"And that's how I ended up making a fool of myself," Harley said to Skye after recounting the events of the quad race the night before.

Her sister had come by to bum breakfast before heading to class. Breakfast, and cash. She needed books for the new quarter.

"So let me get this straight," Skye said with a smile, eating a bowl of Frosted Flakes. She was the same five foot five that Harley was, but unlike Harley, she was willowy and dainty and model pretty. "You, Queen of Need No One, begged him to kiss you."

Harley sighed. "I don't know why I'm telling you this. You have a big mouth."

"I do not!"

"You told everyone when I locked myself out last week. I fielded calls on that one all day long."

"Yes, well, that's because you were wearing only your towel, which you dropped when you climbed in the window, mooning Mr. Kletzy across the street. Word is he hadn't seen a naked woman in fifty years. He's now requesting that next time you lose your towel at high noon because the light is better."

"It wasn't a complete flash, I caught the towel before it hit the ground, and I was just trying to get the damn newspaper."

"Focus, Harley. The begging."

Harley pictured herself leaning into TJ, all muddy and turned on, staring at his mouth as she touched his chest . . . "It's embarrassing."

"Walk me through it. You begged him to kiss you. And he didn't."

"Yeah. Pretty much."

Skye looked at her for a moment. "Harl, you don't ever ask for help on anything. I just don't see this happening."

"This was more of the silent type of begging." And worse, it hadn't been the first time. She flashed back to all those years ago, to that one night she and TJ had shared.

The one he didn't remember, the ass.

She could still feel his warm hands on her back, the pleasure those hands had brought her, how she'd been reduced to begging then, too.

Damn it. Damn him. She sighed. "Okay, so the begging was mostly done with my eyes. I might have leaned into him. And set my hand on his . . . chest."

Skye's eyes narrowed thoughtfully. "In the center of his chest, or did you touch nipple?"

"What does that have to do with anything?"

"A lot."

Harley blushed beet red. "Maybe I got nipple. But I didn't mean to."

"Doesn't matter. You took the casual touch to the next level."

"Involuntarily!"

"You put up a red flag. You might as well have announced you weren't wearing any underwear."

Harley groaned and covered her face. "Nothing happened!"

"Which reminds me—how does anyone resist *any* of the Wilders? They're all so hot. TJ especially. He's the biggest and the baddest, and when those sharp green eyes land on you . . ." Skye sighed. "He's something."

He was something, all right. "I'm dating someone else."

"Oh, for God's sake. Stop saying that. It's not even true."

"Yes, it is. Nolan and I have gone out twice."

"But one of those times was an accident!" Skye sighed. "Look, Nolan's great. Okay? He is. He's just not great for *you*. I mean, he's cute and smart and has a job, the major three requisites, but . . ."

"But . . . ?"

"The two of you are too much alike. Sweet, kind . . ."

Harley narrowed *her* eyes. "Beta?"

"Well not alpha, that's for sure. Get back to the begging."

"Hellooooo, didn't you hear my story? He leaned in, and I . . . touched him and closed my eyes and *begged* for the kiss."

"Silently."

"Yes, but he knew. He even laughed."

"Laughed—or chuckled?"

"What's the difference?"

"Laughing would imply he was a tease and an asshole. Chuckling softly would imply that he was as thrown as you, and is possibly just proceeding with caution since you're not exactly an easy woman to deal with."

Harley blew out a breath. Hard to dispute the truth. "Okay, maybe it was just a chuckle."

Skye gave her a smug smirk.

"We're so done talking about this."

"Look, if you wanted a kiss, why didn't you just grab his ears and make him kiss you, mud and all? You could have hosed each other off, and then moved to his shower, and then let the *real* begging begin."

Harley, who'd just taken an unfortunate scoop of cereal, choked on it.

Skye smiled. "Look at you, all aflutter. Who'd have thought, you and badass TJ, circling each other."

"See you're not listening at all. We don't even like each other."

"Oh, I've been listening. But I don't think *you* are. You like your comfort zone, I get it. We all get it. You're a creature of habit, and keep your own counsel. Well, guess what? In that single thing, you and TJ are two linked souls."

"Huh?"

Skye shook her head. "Let me simplify. You need to get laid. He's hot as hell. By the way, he's the opposite of beta. Honey, that man is *allll* alpha. There's so much tension between the two of you that the air sizzles and crackles when you're within a hundred yards of each other. Just *do it* already."

Harley had spent much of the night imagining exactly that, remembering how he'd looked after he'd shrugged out of his outer shirt and wrapped it around her, leaving him in just a mudspattered T-shirt, which had clung to his shoulders and abs. If it hadn't been for the threat of Cam and Nick coming around the corner, she'd have jumped him right then and there. The only thing worse than knowing that was the fact that *he'd* known it, too. "If there's any 'doing it' to be had," she said. "It'll be with Nolan."

Skye grimaced.

"What?"

"Stop hiding behind the fantasy of being Nolan's significant other. He's like . . . Clark Kent, okay? He'll never be your Superman. He'll never match your passion."

"Okay, no more Lifetime movies for you."

"I'm serious."

"Me, too," Harley said. "Passion fades. How many times have Mom and Dad proven that?"

Skye shook her head. "Honey, you have been too long without a man in your bed if you're already willing to concede passion in your life."

Harley sighed.

"Come on, you'd walk all over Nolan and we both know it. If you're looking for a man-made orgasm, my bet is on TJ."

"Oh for chrissake." Harley stood up, grabbed both their bowls, and moved to the sink. "I'm the older sister. How do you even know all this stuff?"

"We went to different high schools."

"We went to the same high school."

"No, you went to the Actually Learn Something High School,

and I went to the Boys Are Awesome and Party Hearty High School."

Harley laughed but Skye was right. She didn't want to live without passion. She *had* lived without passion.

"Whatever you're thinking," Skye said, coming to her side, smiling at her. "Go with it."

"Go to class, that's what I'm thinking. I'm paying too much for you to be late."

"Okay, but one more thing." She pulled a couple of well-read paperbacks from her purse. "Pick one and take it on your hike into Desolation. Read it by your campfire. If you can tell me that Nolan makes you as hot as some of the scenes do, I'll try to believe you."

"What are they?"

Skye grinned. "Really hot romances. Contemporary or historical?"

"Huh?"

Skye shook her head and tossed one onto the backpack that was half packed and against the wall. "Just read. And report back to me when you get home. Thanks for the cash. I'll pay you back."

"Good."

Skye hugged Harley hard. "Thanks for believing in me, Harl."

"Always."

Wilder Adventures sat on thirty acres of Wilder land, surrounded by 75,000 more acres of national forest. The compound consisted of the lodge, two equipment garages, and a series of eight smaller cabins. Their guests, if they'd arranged for overnight accommodations, stayed in the main lodge, which was run efficiently by Annie. All of the business equipment, of which there was a mind-boggling amount including bikes, quads, skis, snowmobiles, kayaks, boats, snowcats, and a helicopter, was handled by Nick. Each of the Wilders had claimed one of the cabins for themselves.

The start-up capital had come from Cam's earnings as a pro snowboarder. Stone had contributed the required construction expertise. And TJ, through his years of trekking before they'd gone into business, had brought in the high-dollar clients and business knowledge.

The three of them had grown up fast and hard and without much hope. There'd never been any doubt in TJ's mind that they'd end up dead or in jail just like the rest of the men in their family. But it'd never happened. Somehow they'd come out on top. So much so that they were pretty much paid to play for a living. Yet beneath that so-called play, Wilder Adventures was also a lot of hard work.

The offices were housed on the second floor of the lodge. At the moment, they were in Stone's office for their weekly meeting. As usual, it was more a family gathering to bitch and tease than anything else. Stone was at his desk with Emma standing behind him, rubbing his shoulders. She was dressed for work at her medical clinic, wearing her doctor's coat and looking official with her stethoscope around her neck, which clashed with her just-had-sex glow. Stone had the same glow as he sent her a slow, warm, lazy smile over his shoulder.

Cam was slouched in a chair in front of Stone's desk, and he was also looking pretty damn loose, no doubt thanks to Katie, their receptionist and Cam's bride-to-be, who was plopped in his lap.

Nick was in another chair, flipping through the latest mechanics' magazine. Chuck was under the desk, no doubt hoping someone would drop something good to eat.

Chuck lived for food.

Her kittens were winding their way around people's feet, having fun with shoelaces and each other.

Stone tugged the magazine out of Nick's hands, revealing what Nick was *really* reading—a book of baby names.

"What," Nick said in his defense. "Kid needs a name."

Stone tossed the book to the desk.

Startled, Chuck ran out from beneath it, ears back. Katie

cooed to her, picking her up and cuddling her while giving Stone a reproachful look.

At the cuddling, Chuck went still as stone. She still wasn't crazy about being held, but she didn't like to insult her human, either, so she endured Katie's snuggling with a resigned expression, hoping she'd be rewarded with a snack.

"How about Tude?" Stone asked Nick. "Short for Attitude, 'cause any kid of Annie's is bound to have it."

"Can we get to business?" TJ asked.

"Sure," Stone said. "I've got both good and bad news. Bad first. Goddammit." With a pained grimace, he peeled a solid gray kitten off his leg. He lifted the little thing by the scruff of her neck and looked her in the eyes. "Watch the claws."

The kitten batted at Stone's nose.

Stone sighed and put her on his shoulder, where she curled up and began to purr. "TJ, your Canadian trip just got cancelled. The clients had some work stuff come up and can't take the month off. But they forfeited their deposit with the last-minute cancel, so we're still getting paid." Stone grinned. "Guess you're stuck here with us for a while."

"Shit," TJ said.

Stone looked at him, smile fading. "Yeah, now see, I sort of thought that'd be the good news."

"Seriously, man," Cam said. "You've done nothing but trek after trek this past year. Thought maybe you'd want to hang around."

"You can help us with wedding plans," Katie said as if that was actually some kind of bonus. "Instead of showing up at the last minute like you'd have to do if you left."

Which is exactly what he'd been hoping for.

Annie arrived, looking harassed. "I'm late."

No one dared agree with her. She was temperamental in the best of times, and pregnancy wasn't one of them. No one wanted to risk their neck, not when her apron said it all: K*SS MY *SS—*Would you like to buy a vowel?*

Nick pulled her onto his lap, where she snuggled in, harassed look gone, replaced by a soft smile. "How are you feeling?" Nick asked her.

"Great, but Not-Abigail would be doing better if I hadn't eaten all the brownies I made earlier."

Nick rubbed her belly and smiled as Annie looked around. "What's up? I miss anything?"

"You almost missed TJ telling us what his problem is," Cam said.

Everything looked at TJ.

"I don't have a problem," TJ said.

"Really?" Annie asked. "'Cause you don't seem like yourself."

"Of course I'm myself. Who else would I be?"

"I don't know," Stone said. "Maybe some guy who's really good at shoving all his shit into a box and not dealing with it."

"What shit? I'm fine."

Stone coughed into his hand and said, "bullshit" at the same time.

TJ ignored him.

Annie sighed. "Told you," she said to Nick, who nodded sagely.

"Told him what?" TJ asked.

"That you're still on that whole don't-care, let-nothing-penetrate campaign."

"That's ridiculous," TJ said. "I care about plenty."

"About us, yes," Annie agreed. "But what about outside us?"

"Hell, there's so many of 'us' to worry about, why do I need more?"

"You used to need more. You used to have a huge wide circle of people you cared about. Then Sam died."

They sucked in a collective breath. Except for TJ. He didn't breathe. Samantha James had been his college girlfriend. Supporting herself through college as a river guide, she'd brought him into her world. Unfortunately, she'd been wilder than he'd ever even *thought* of being, and had lived more on guts and luck than actual skill.

She'd gotten herself killed on a river trip, and though it hadn't been TJ's fault—hell, he hadn't even been on that trip—it'd hit him hard because it'd been an unnecessary tragedy. If only she'd followed her brain instead of her gut, if only she'd been better prepared, if only . . .

He really hated if only's. When he'd decided to stay in the world that Sam had introduced him to, he'd promised himself that he'd never put himself in an *if only* position. As a result, he was a far more careful, more controlled guide for it. Stone and Cam called it anal. He called it smart. "This has nothing to do with Sam."

They all looked at him with varying degrees of concern. In general, they weren't an overly demonstrative family, which wasn't a surprise when one considered their childhood. Annie had done her best to help, but the truth was, she'd been barely out of her teens herself, and they'd needed a jail warden far more than they'd needed a caregiver. Still, she'd somehow pulled it off, getting the three of them into adulthood without any jail time. She hadn't done it by being a softie. "This has nothing to do with Sam," he insisted. "What happened to her sucks, and yeah, I think about her, but me needing to get out of here has nothing to do with her, nothing to do with any of you actually, and everything to do with me." He just needed to go, to get as far away from that daily dose of overwhelming love and happiness soaking the entire lodge. "Until another big trip comes along, I'll just lighten the load around here with the shorter trips, I guess."

"Fine with me," Cam said. "We're overbooked, and so far the only response to our ad has been either crazy, adrenaline-rush junkies or people who lied on their app and don't know a snowcat from a snowmobile. But now that we have you sort of captive for the next few months . . ."

"We'll definitely take advantage," Stone finished. "In fact, we have a new client, some CEO who met you on your glacier trip. He wants to take his VPs on a memorable seven-day trek out to Weststar Peak, and by memorable, he means he wants to kick the VPs' asses. He's asked for some video to see the landscape before he decides for sure. Cam was going to go out there today, but you can do it."

"Fine."

"Which leaves me free this afternoon." Cam waggled a brow at Katie, who grinned.

Stone pulled up the schedule on the computer and they spent the next half hour reworking it, taking trips from Cam's and Stone's queue and loading up TJ. When they were done, TJ looked at both of his brothers. "So whose idea was it for Harley to go to Desolation Wilderness alone?"

"Alone?" Cam raised a brow. "She didn't say anything about doing it alone when she asked for the maps." He looked at Stone, who shook his head.

"Bad idea," Stone said.

"Agreed," TJ said.

"You should go with her," Stone told him. "You're the one looking to get out of here."

Cam laughed at that. "Are you kidding? They'll kill each other."

"I'm not going with her," TJ said. "She doesn't want me to."

Cam looked at him for a beat. "You still have a secret thing for her?"

"I don't think it's so secret," Stone said.

"Well, me either," Cam replied. "But I try not to give him an excuse to pound me into the ground. In fact"—he carefully scooted out of reach of TJ—"here's what I'd do. Find a way to go with her, then wait until it gets dark. Let her get spooked by something, and when she gets scared and crawls all over you, comfort her. Then suddenly she's no longer irritated at your presence."

Kate was staring at him like he'd grown horns. "*Let* her get spooked by something? You do realize this is Harley, our close and dear friend?"

"What? He's going to *comfort* her."

"Not to mention," Katie went on, "that the whole getting-scared scenario sounds like some cheesy made-up *Penthouse* 'Forum' fantasy."

Stone smiled wickedly. "Honey, those things aren't made up."

Jesus. TJ stood up. "You're all insane." He shoved his fingers through his hair. "No one knows better than us exactly how dangerous it can get out there." Hadn't they just brought up Sam? "Things pop up, where nothing short of experience will save you." And Harley was far shorter on experience than Sam had been.

"You know," Cam said, watching him. "You could just tell her the truth. That you have a thing for her. Maybe she'd *want* you to go with her."

Yeah, that's not going to happen.

Annie stood up and gave TJ a long look that had him bracing for a lecture or a smack to the back of his head as she came close. One never knew with her. Instead, she pulled him in for a hard, tight hug that he endured with a sigh.

"We think you want out of here because we're all so disgustingly happy," she said.

"Well, you have the disgusting part right."

"Oh, TJ." She pressed her face to the crook of his neck and squeezed him tight, adding a little sniff that terrorized him.

"Annie," he said helplessly. "I'm fine. I'm glad you're all happy. You all deserve it. Christ, please don't cry."

"It's the baby," she said, muffled against him. "Not-Abigail makes me feel like crying."

"Okay," TJ said, carefully pulling free. "I get that you've all decided that *love* is the path to go, just don't expect me to follow."

Annie eyed him. "You're laughing at love?"

"Yes."

His aunt shook her head. "You know you just tempted fate right? Dangled a carrot in front of that bitch karma?"

TJ patted Not-Abigail. "You have *way* too many hormones

going on. Listen, I get that you're all in a different place than me, but I like my place just fine."

When he left the office, there was a beat of silence.

"Idiot," Stone said affectionately.

"And to think," Cam said thoughtfully. "I always thought he was the smart one."

CHAPTER 5

TJ was hiking down Weststar, the video footage for their new client safe in his pack, eyeing the wall of dark clouds coming over the east summit, when he saw the figure far below. He stepped to the edge of the cliff for a better look, surprised because he'd been out there for three hours and hadn't seen another soul. As always, his breath caught at the sight of the jagged Sierras sprawled out in front of him. To the north, the land carved upward past the tree line to ancient granite peaks, to the south flowed the Squaw River.

In between were glassy alpine lakes, weather-beaten slopes, and colorful meadows, as far as the eye could see. The sun filtered through the clouds and a thick umbrella of pine branches, creating dappled and lacy patterns at his feet, but something about the person far below had him pulling out his binoculars. When he focused in on shiny blond hair and a sweet, curvy body, he went still.

Harley.

She was on a trail below him to the southwest, several miles away, heading toward the western entrance to Desolation Wilderness.

A day early.

* * *

Harley had just passed the trailhead marker for the entrance into Desolation when she heard a series of familiar yet eerie yips.

Coyotes.

She checked her GPS. Seemed as if some of her blue group were on the move. The yelping didn't signify a hunt like sharp barks would have, nor was it a territorial howl of "I am claiming my area." Nope, the loud, mischievous yelping usually meant some sort of play amongst a pack.

Still, she made certain to make plenty of noise as she walked. She didn't want to surprise them. Tipping her head back, she eyed the dark clouds gathering and churning to the east. The air was still midday hot and unusually damp, and around her the forest pulsed with the oncoming storm. Kamikaze squirrels screeched at each other, racing frantically from branch to branch. She could hear the thumping cry of a group of tree frogs, looking forward to the impending rain.

The fire road she was on continued through White Wolf Woods. She had a drop of about sixty feet off to her left. To her right was dense forest. As she climbed, the fire road narrowed into almost nothing. She took a moment to consult her maps and the GPS. It looked like she was on target to the two malfunctioning cameras.

The survey she was working on for the conservation agency had several goals. The biggest was to nail down how many coyotes were indigenous in the Sierras, and whether the population was stable or growing. They wanted to figure out the best management strategies for the coyote population to coexist with the growing—and spreading—human population. There was plenty of room for both humans and coyotes out there, but for most places in the state, that wasn't the case.

Clouds rolled. Above her, the sharp report of thunder cracked in the distance. She jumped but kept going. It felt good to be out. Sitting at her laptop doing research didn't exactly promote health. Sometimes she jogged in the evenings if she felt that her jeans were too snug, but overall she skipped any organized form of exercise. But she liked hiking.

She'd been at it for several hours, and was as comfortable as she could be with the unaccustomed weight of the backpack. She wore a pair of hip-hugging cargo pants, a white stretchy tee, and hiking boots. So far so good, but then she heard an odd sound behind her. "TJ!" she gasped, whipping around, taking a quick step backwards—*too* quick, because she tripped over her own feet and fell to her ass.

"Christ." He dropped to his knees in front of her and reached out. "Are you okay?"

Pissed, heart pounding, she smacked his hands away. "No, I'm not okay!" It was the damn backpack. Feeling like a beached whale, she had to roll to her hands and knees to get to her feet, but before she could, TJ got his hands beneath her and tugged her up.

"You need a bell around your neck, you know that?" She brushed her hands over her butt and glared at him. "You scared the crap out of me."

"Bears don't wear a bell."

She sighed and shook her head, knowing he was right. "I'd have seen a bear. You move more stealthily than that, like a cat, a big, sleek, *stupid* cat."

"You should look around once in a while. Be more aware of your surroundings."

She *was* incredibly aware of *him*—of his big, tough body, of his gaze on hers, of how her body was reacting. He wore a baseball cap, dark sunglasses, and a pair of old Levi's, battered and beloved, the denim snug over hard thighs and probably his perfect ass, too. His light blue T-shirt stretched taut across his shoulders, biceps, and upper chest, looser over his zero-fat stomach. Bastard. "Yeah, well, chalk it up to a rookie mistake," she said. "Why are you here?"

"Saw you from Weststar." He pointed to the peak above them.

"You expect me to believe this is a chance meeting?"

"It is. I was hiking back after taking video for a client when I saw you."

"How could you tell it was me?"

"Binoculars."

"Wow. Good thing I wasn't having wild sex against a tree or something."

He arched a brow. "By yourself?"

She blew out a sigh. Sex with herself was all she had lately. As if she'd admit that.

He grinned, making her realize her thoughts were all over her face.

"Okay, look," she said. "You've seen for yourself I'm fine. So thanks for the concern, but feel free to continue on your merry way."

"I thought maybe you'd want company."

"Yours?" she asked.

"No, the Tooth Fairy's. Yes, mine."

Above them, clouds bumped and exploded in a burst of lightning, and she tipped her head up to look at the churning sky. *Huh.* That storm had moved in quickly. "Are we supposed to count one-Mississippi, two-Mississippi, or just—"

The sonic *boom* of thunder shook the ground beneath their feet, and she jumped. *Holy smokes.* Without meaning to, she shifted a step toward TJ, who looked like he was thinking about smiling again.

"Are you scared?" he asked.

"Of course not." She was far closer to terrified.

"Are you prepared for rain?"

"I'm prepared for anything, TJ." Theoretically, anyway. "I'm also wearing my Supergirl panties. So really, you can go home."

"You're right." He scrubbed a hand down his face. "You have a way of taking care of yourself. I have no idea why I feel the need to do it for you."

"You could just stop."

He pulled off his baseball cap and shoved a hand through his hair. "It's not that easy. I . . . think about you."

This made her blink. "You do?"

"Well, yeah. Don't you think about me?"

Far too often. She thought about why he was always gone, she thought about what made him need to be gone, and wondered if it was the same restlessness that sat low in her gut, the same nameless ache. Probably it wasn't. Because her ache was for him to touch her the way he had that long ago night, the night he didn't remember. "But we're nothing to each other," she whispered.

"I don't believe that." He shook his head. "And I don't think you do, either. You've been a part of my life since high school."

"Yes. I know. I remember. In fact, I wish I could forget as easily as you."

"What?"

There went her brain running away from her mouth again. "Nothing." She turned away to start walking again. "It's nothing." *Let it go. Please just let it go.*

He grabbed her wrist and pulled her back to him. "It's something."

"Okay, it's something, but nothing I want to get into right now." Or ever. "Go home, TJ. Please?"

He pulled off her sunglasses to see her face. "Maybe later." As he continued to tug her in, she set a hand to his abs for balance and her fingers brushed the hard ridges of his six-pack. Make that an eight-pack. She could have pulled back, but her fingers suddenly weren't listening to her brain any more than her mouth had. Not good.

In fact, this was bad. Very, very bad. He wasn't going anywhere. She got why, she really did. She'd inadvertently triggered his protective nature, and thanks to what he'd suffered through with Sam, there was no easy way to get rid of him.

But that didn't mean she wouldn't try. She had to, because she knew herself. She wasn't strong enough to fight off the asinine, juvenile attraction she had for him, and she wasn't in the mood to make a fool of herself. "I have to make a phone call."

"Okay," he said. "Go ahead."

"It's private."

When he didn't budge, she walked off, not exactly sure of which she hoped for more, that he'd go home . . .

Or follow her.

* * *

TJ watched Harley vanish up the trail, then pulled out his cell phone as well. He had a new text from Nick.

> Warning—you're Annie's new Worry Obsession. Fix it so she doesn't worry herself into early labor.

TJ called his client first. He had the video to show him, but he rescheduled their late afternoon meeting so that he'd be free to stay with Harley.

He called Stone next. "Today's afternoon meeting's cancelled. I'm with Harley."

Stone let that sink in. "When she kills you, tell her to call me. I'll help her hide your body. I know this great spot just off—"

With a sigh, TJ disconnected, then called Annie. "I'm fine."

"Promise?"

"Promise."

"Good. Because if you're planning on going off the deep end, I'd need to schedule it in, that's all."

"No need."

"You're still restless as hell."

"I'm always restless as hell. You're only noticing now because for the first time in forever, you're truly happy. Everyone's happy. I stick out like a sore thumb."

"Oh, honey. We can fix this. We'll—"

"Annie," he broke in gently. "I'm okay. Really."

He heard her blow out a breath. "Sure. I know that."

"Then stop worrying."

"Who me? Worry? Ha."

He smiled, and let her hear it in his voice. "You have other things to concentrate on. Like Not-Abigail, who'll be here before you know it. So stop giving Nick gray hairs and relax. If he knows you've been wasting your time worrying about me, he'll try to kick my ass, and then I'll have to kick his ass, and it'll be a whole ass-kicking thing, and you'll get pissed."

"Okay, fine. You're fine, we're all fine. I'll just go back to the kitchen, where I'll be barefoot and pregnant and a useless piece of fluff."

Annie had never, ever, not once, been a piece of fluff, and as a result, he and his brothers had their lives to show for it. He laughed. "You promise?"

She disconnected, and he grinned. She was no longer worried, she was pissy. He texted Nick.

Mission accomplished.

As he slipped his phone away, he looked up with a frown, realizing Harley had been gone for at least five minutes. He scanned the trail as far as he could see, which wasn't far with the overgrown landscape blocking the way. He listened but heard nothing more than the usual Sierra sounds.

A pinecone falling a hundred feet from a tree, then hitting the ground.

Squirrels chattering.

The rush of a creek not far off.

But no footsteps indicating Harley's movements, no rustling of her clothing.

Nothing. More than nothing, an utter lack of a sense of her existence at all.

She was gone.

Fuck. He whipped out his cell and called hers, but it switched right over to voice mail. Either she'd turned it off or hit IGNORE. Both options sucked.

It took him a surprising and uncomfortable quarter of a mile before he came around a corner and caught up with her.

She'd been hauling ass, hoping to lose him. In spite of the quickly cooling afternoon, a few damp tendrils of hair were stuck to her face, and she was breathing hard. Her eyes were flashing with heat and not the good kind.

He understood that perfectly. He felt the heat of a rare temper himself. "How was your phone call?"

She had the good grace to blush. "Great. Fine."

"You could have just told me you didn't want me to come with you, Harley."

"Helloooo, I *did*!"

"Is my company that bad?"

She hesitated, and her gaze skittered away. He might have conceded the battle right then and there, and faced the fact that she'd really rather be alone—except for one thing.

Actually, two.

The pulse at the base of her neck was tattooing a frantic beat. And her nipples were hard.

Since he doubted very much she was cold after that run she'd just taken, he got his first flash of satisfaction for the day.

Harley knew that TJ was a tracker at heart. What she hadn't known was just how good he was. It'd taken him less than five minutes to find her, and when he did, she'd nearly swallowed her tongue. She was trying to be cool, when in reality, she was sweating, huffing for breath, and very close to nervous laughter. "It actually took you longer to catch up with me than I thought it would," she said. "You must be losing your touch."

"You lied to me."

Oh boy. His eyes were glittering dangerously, which seemed in direct opposition to the slight quirk of his mouth, as if she was amusing him almost against his will. "I *omitted*," she corrected. "Big difference. Though to be honest, I was thinking about lying to you. I was thinking about telling you that I hurt my ankle and that I needed you to go back down and get help."

"You'd do that?"

"Yes, but Cam said that wouldn't work. I called him to complain about you, but he wasn't too sympathetic. He said there was a pool going, to see who would kill who first. I put a ten in on me. Killing you."

She had no idea why she was baiting him. Except it was giving her a rush she hadn't felt in a long time.

"I wouldn't have left you," he said. "I'd have carried you out."

"Yeah, that was con number one."

"What were the others?"

"Having you hold me again."

"Again? What—" He gritted his teeth as his cell phone vibrated. "Search and Rescue." He looked at her as he dropped his pack. "I have to take this."

"So take it."

"If you take off on me, I'll find you and I'll—"

She arched a brow, having no idea why the words sent a dark thrill through her instead of sparking her temper. Probably the aforementioned lack of orgasms. "And?"

"And . . . Jesus. Just stay," he commanded. "Or I'll . . . *something*."

It was a desperate, empty threat, and worse, they both knew it.

TJ had to move back down the steep, narrow path about fifty yards to get clear enough reception for his cell conversation. The Search and Rescue team was shorthanded, so he agreed to be on call for the next two days. He then made his way back to where he'd left Harley, holding his breath.

She'd dropped her pack and was sitting on a rock, eating an apple. She laughed at the expression on his face.

Laughed.

He supposed it shouldn't turn him on to be standing there while she mocked him, but it was Harley. She'd been turning him on, upside down, and every other possible way for so damn long, he was at a loss as to whether he wanted to strangle her or kiss her.

She looked up then and met his gaze, seeming to read it perfectly, because her own went bright with intelligence and wit, and something else.

Awareness.

In that beat he knew *exactly* what he wanted from her, and it would only start with a kiss. Walking right up to her, he pulled her to her feet, tugging hard enough that she hit his chest with a little "oomph." He stared down into her face, so close to his.

The grimness of her mouth conveyed annoyance rather than the easy amusement she wanted him to believe she felt.

She was pissed.

Well, get in line, because he was pissed first. She had no reason for not wanting help this weekend, and it scared him. All the things that could happen to her scared him. "You let me think you needed privacy, and I fell for it hook, line, and sinker."

"Yeah, you should really work on that."

He just stared at her.

She opened her mouth to say something, probably to rip him a new one, but then she seemed to realize that they were practically in each other's arms, and suddenly her arms wound around his neck.

Worked for him. He gripped her hips hard.

She stared at his mouth. "God, TJ. You make me so . . ."

"Yeah." His arms tightened on her. "Ditto." And then, even as he said it, she shifted her body to his and he felt his frustration and anger melt into something far more dangerous. "Harley."

Her eyes were twin pools of ravenous hunger. She licked her lips, and he couldn't help it, he groaned and bent his head, until their lips were gently, almost sweetly touching.

"This is insane," she whispered in one beat, and in the next they were kissing, hard and wet, and just a little bit desperate.

She moaned her pleasure into his mouth and then sank her fingers into his hair and let out a soft, sexy, demanding little mewl. He shifted so he could press her back against a tree, freeing up his hands to thread into her hair, to draw her in deeper.

Jesus. He was out of control, unaware of their surroundings, completely gone, lost in her, until two loud birds squawked at each other right over their heads, fighting over something. Harley jumped and pulled back, slipping down the tree trunk a few inches as if her knees had gone to Jell-O before she locked them into place.

He took his hands from her and braced them on the tree, on either side of her shoulders, as he tried to draw air into his lungs and tighten the tenuous grip on his sanity.

It wasn't easy.

"So I'm guessing all is forgiven," she said, her voice a little ragged.

He pressed a finger and thumb into his eyelids and took a deep breath.

"You look like you're torn between kissing me again and spanking me."

He dropped his hand and stared at her. "Good idea. How about both?"

Her eyes widened, then he hauled her up and kissed her again.

For a beat she was utterly still, then met him halfway, melting into him, over him, fisting her hands in his shirt as things went instantly wild. She came up for air first, but even then her lips clung to his before she slowly pulled away.

Looking as completely perplexed as he felt, she stared at him. "What the hell was that?"

A category-five hurricane. "A hell of an adrenaline rush."

"And?

"And"—he finally went with total honesty—"I have no idea. You drive me fucking crazy."

She let out a sound that managed to convey frustration, amusement, and temper all in one. "Same goes."

"You should probably slap me the next time I do that."

"Yeah." Her gaze dropped to his mouth again. "TJ . . ."

Ah, hell. He was going to do "that" again, slap or not, and they both knew it.

In fact, they lunged at each other.

But instead of wild, this time the kiss was deep and soulful, and devastatingly necessary as air. He felt her knees give, and gliding his arms around her, supported them both as her fingers wove into his hair at the back of his head. It felt so damn good he groaned into her mouth, sucking on her lower lip, biting it, kissing it again. He could feel the heat of her body, the soft cushion of her soft curves pressed up against him, and his brain clicked completely off, instinct and need taking over.

When they broke apart, she pressed her face into his neck and he felt her draw his scent in, as if maybe she couldn't get enough of him, and his chest ached, physically ached.

God. He had no idea what was happening, but suddenly he wanted to know he wasn't alone in this. *Needed* to know he wasn't alone in this. Fisting his fingers in her hair, he gently tugged until she tilted her face up.

Her eyes were closed. "Harley, look at me."

It took her a minute, as if she was trying to get it together before she did, but when she opened those seductive eyes, the truth was there for him to see.

He wasn't alone in this.

That wasn't necessarily a comfort.

The silence was as heavy as the humid air around them, and was broken only by their accelerated breathing. Then a branch cracked overhead, falling through the trees to hit the ground near them.

Harley jerked.

TJ didn't move a muscle, not knowing what to say. Rare for him.

Harley finally gathered herself first, turning away to get moving again, leaving him to follow.

Or not.

He knew what she was hoping for. She wanted him far, far away. Hell, on that they were in perfect accord. But what he wanted to do and what he needed to do were two very different things. He needed to know she was safe.

So he followed.

CHAPTER 6

Harley walked hard and fast, but still couldn't outpace her demons. Or the fact that her body felt so . . . alive. Every nerve ending hummed and pulsed, and little electric zings of sheer lust randomly fired from erotic pulse point to erotic pulse point.

She had no one to blame but herself. She'd *known* the minute that TJ's lips touched hers she'd be in big trouble.

Lord, the man could kiss.

He knew just how to work that warm mouth of his, too, how to hold a woman, how to pull her in and make her purr. Hell, she was *still* purring.

He was following her, of course. Keeping pace but letting her lead, leaving her to her thoughts.

Thoughts she could do without, so she slowed until he was at her side.

Even more devastating than his mouth were his eyes. They were a deep, velvety green, and mirrors to his soul. She turned and looked into them. He had a few fine lines fanning out from the corners. Not from age, but from his easy smile, from squinting into the bright high-altitude sun, from planning and thinking about his clients' fun and safety, from worry and concern about those he loved.

From following her up a mountain out of that worry and concern.

All those little things he did were just pieces of the puzzle that made up the boy she'd once loved, the boy who'd grown into a man. A good man. A solid, strong man.

A man, despite everything her common sense screamed at her, she was incredibly attracted to.

With a long exhale, she stepped off the narrow trail and up on a huge boulder overlooking the wild, open forestland and jagged mountain peaks for as far as the eye could see. And there, surrounded by three hundred and sixty degrees of glory on earth, she could secretly admit one more thing—she'd never gotten over him.

And it was unlikely that she ever would.

She felt him step up to her side and take in the view as well, still silent.

She'd thought this trip would be easy. Fun. Exciting. She'd spend some time just . . . being. She could ruminate on her favorite TV shows. She'd talk herself out of her addiction of chewing on her thumbnail. She'd think about her life and how she wanted to move outside her comfort zone and really live it.

Passion included, please.

But she couldn't think about any of that because TJ was with her like white on rice, the poster boy for Distraction. When she tugged off her pack to dig through it for water, he simply pulled a bottle from a side pocket of his annoyingly organized pack, the scrumptiously defined muscles in his back and shoulders working as he twisted off the lid and handed it to her.

He waited in silence under the churning sky while she drank, a low breeze playing with his hair, the sun reflecting off his aviator sunglasses. The wind gusted harder, playing with the hem of his shirt, lifting it briefly to reveal his abs, making hers clench. He drove her crazy, too, she realized. Crazy with lust.

She closed her eyes and downed some water, which did nothing for her parched throat and out of control, not-been-laid-in-far-too-long body. Huh. Seemed she was out of her comfort zone already, without even trying.

At the next rumble of distant thunder, she started walking again, not bothering to wait to see if he followed. She didn't need to, she couldn't have lost him if she'd tried. He'd been born and raised in those mountains and knew them like the back of his hand. He could probably track her coyotes better and faster than she could.

They climbed another mile before he spoke. "Going to rain soon," he said.

She looked up at the still churning and ominous sky. "That problem will have to get in line."

He slid her an amused glance. "You have other problems?"

Yes. Not the least of which was that they'd come to a fork in the trail, with three possible directions. Two veered right, and she wasn't sure which she was supposed to take. She looked down at her map and at the little GPS unit Stone had given her, and she *still* didn't have a clue.

"Want help?"

Hell, no, she didn't want help. It was one thing to sit at her laptop and interpret data, but—as she was beginning to realize—it was another entirely to be in the field. "Give me a minute." She grimaced. "I'm talking myself into not being stupid, into accepting help from one of the smartest, sharpest, best guides in the country." She eyed her map again. Yeah. She was going to need his help.

Dammit.

"All you have to do is ask," TJ said quietly, all mocking and signs of humor gone.

She kept her eyes on her maps rather than him because looking at him was doing funny things to her insides. "How much will it cost me to keep you from saying I told you so?"

"We'll work on a payment plan."

Lightning lit the sky, followed by another sharp crack of thunder that made her jump again.

"You have raingear?" he asked. "We're going to need it."

"Yeah, but I don't want it right now." She was still overheated from their kiss. Not him, apparently, because he removed a waterproof shell from his backpack and pulled it on. And damn if he didn't look good in it, like he could be on the cover of *Outside*.

Or the centerfold of a different magazine altogether.

"Let me hold your stuff while you gear up," he said.

"I'm fine for a minute. Here's where I want to get to tonight"—she said, pointing to the map—"which is where the first malfunctioning camera is set up. I think the best route is this far right trail. You?"

He leaned over her shoulder to take a look. She could feel the heat and strength of him seeping into her, and she had the oddest urge to press into him, sink against him.

"This one drops you in right above Mystic Flats." His arm came around her as he pointed with a long finger. "And this one ends at Big Oak Flats. They'll both get you there, but yeah, Mystic Flats is the easier way in."

She searched that statement for an insult but decided there was none. Even more interesting, he was leaving the decision to her, not taking charge. It defused her, and honestly, also completely charmed her.

So they took the far right trail and she did her best to keep the pace up, wanting to get there before nightfall.

At the next burst of thunder and lightning, the drizzle began, the light mist feeling cool and delicious against her heated skin.

"You want to stop and wait out the storm?" he asked from behind her.

She knew it was stupid to let herself get wet, but it felt so wonderful. *Intoxicating*. She turned to shake her head and he pulled off his sunglasses to eyeball her.

"What?"

"Nothing," he said. "I like the look, is all."

The look? That's when she realized she was smiling from ear to ear. It was just that lately she'd been so damn stressed all the time, awake or asleep, and it'd gotten to her. It'd been slowly sucking the energy and life from her.

But it'd all faded away to nothing when he looked at her like that. "You're getting wet," she pointed out.

"No shit, Harley. It's raining."

She laughed. "I like it out here."

His gaze touched over her features, a small smile on his lips. "I know the feeling."

Common ground.

It was unexpected, and like everything else in regard to him, arousing. They just looked at each other, the moment more intense than the kiss they'd shared. She let out a breath, and they started walking again.

A quarter of a mile later, the skies opened up and dumped on them. Walking became tricky, their feet slipping on the thick carpet of pine needles shedding from the trees all around them. "Here," TJ said, pulling her under the protection of a tree as the sound of the rain hitting the ground in large, golf ball–size drops deafened them both. They dropped their packs, which felt like a nice relief.

"It's a little too late for this," Harley said wryly.

"Yeah." He stood next to her, hands on his hips, watching her from behind those reflective glasses. Shell zipped, hood up, he was completely dry.

Unlike her, who thanks to her own stupidity, had gotten drenched while being pelted by the big drops.

She shivered.

"Harley," he said on a barely expelled breath. He sounded almost pained.

Yeah. She knew. In a matter of three seconds, her clothes had plastered themselves to her body. She pressed her spine to the tree, dropping her head to study her muddy shoes. "I might have made a tactical error not putting on a jacket when you did."

"Wait here. I want to check out the distance from the cliff."

While he was gone, another burst of lightning hit, and then

the shuddering boom of thunder so close it rattled the ground beneath her feet. The rain hadn't let up, and she took a moment to be impressed in a sort of distracted way. Like most things out there in the Sierras, thunderstorms were oversized and amazing to behold.

A set of boots came into her vision, attached to a pair of long denim-covered legs. A single finger, warm and callused, lifted her chin, and two sharp green eyes held hers. He had a five o'clock shadow going, which only upped his sexy factor, giving him a dangerously alluring appeal that he didn't need. "You look like you could use an umbrella," he said.

"Umbrellas are for sissies."

"How about jackets?" he asked. "Are they for sissies, too?"

"No." The truth was, she knew her shell was shoved in the very bottom of her backpack. Somewhere. She was a lot of things, but organized wasn't one of them, and she really wasn't anxious for him to see the state of her pack.

Especially since his was perfect—obnoxiously so. "I like the feel of the rain on my skin." Or she had, up until she'd gotten chilled to the bone, a fact she involuntarily gave away when she let out a full-body shiver.

"Harley." He waited until she looked at him, which she didn't want to do because she didn't want to see him laughing at her. His eyes were dark, and full of lots of things, but he wasn't laughing. "On my first solo trip, it snowed. In July. I walked in it for three hours in a T-shirt. I thought I was in heaven."

Again their gazes held for a long beat, and as always when he gave her his undivided attention, heat slashed through her stomach. "What happened?" she whispered.

"When I got home, I had pneumonia." He turned them so that he was the one backed up against the tree. He unzipped his shell, then pulled her into his arms. She leaned into him as he tucked her inside his jacket, allowing her to absorb his body heat.

Heaven, and hell. Heaven, because he smelled . . . yum, and felt even yummier, and hell because being up against him like that after avoiding contact for so long brought up memories she tried to only visit in the deep, dark of her dreams where secret fantasies reigned.

"You okay?" he murmured, his mouth to her ear, his breath a warm caress on her skin as he rubbed small circles on her back.

Was she? She could feel the steady beat of his heart beneath her cheek, could feel the lean hardness of his muscles, the way his hand was infusing her with his warmth as he stroked her. Startlingly, she realized she was *so* much more than okay. Forcing herself to shake off the haze of desire, she stepped free. "Yes. Thanks."

His gaze dropped from her face to her T-shirt, then swept back up again, blazing with heat.

She looked down. Her nipples were two tight little dark points pressing against the white material as if begging for attention.

Perfect.

"Is this the part where you tell me that they're just breasts?" he asked a little thickly. "Because I've got to tell you, Harley, they're pretty fantastic breasts."

"It's not like you haven't seen them before."

He stared at her while the shock reverberated through her. Why had she said that? God. She whipped around to grab her pack but he snagged her by the back of the shirt and reeled her in like a snared fish.

"Look," she said. "I have to—"

"Talk to me."

"Yeah, that's not what I was going to say." She struggled against him uselessly. "*Let go.*"

"Goddammit, Harley." Shrugging out of his shell, he wrapped her up in it.

The warmth from his body infused her and she sighed. Okay, she'd needed that. "Thank you."

Not responding, he pulled out another shell from his pack and put it on himself, proving how much smarter than her he was. He wouldn't let himself get wet and cold. He was too good for that. Then before she could grab her backpack and put it back on, he once again effortlessly pinned her to the tree, his face in hers. "For years you've avoided me or been pissed off at me. But now you keep saying things that give me the impression I'm either stupid, or missing something."

She closed her eyes. "The latter."

"Now we're getting somewhere. And I'm not moving, *you're* not moving, *no one's* moving until you talk," he said.

He wasn't kidding. He'd completely immobilized her, which meant that once again he was plastered up against her and that meant her brain was functioning at less than ten percent. Far too low for rational decision-making processes.

The rain was still falling all around them, splattering on the ground with an oddly musical sound. The tree provided a good amount of relief. It was their own little cocoon, enclosing them, providing protection, creating an intoxicating sense of intimacy.

An intimacy that was increased tenfold by TJ's gentle but firm hold. "This is ridiculous," she said. "We can talk later. At home."

"What's *ridiculous*," he said, enunciating her word, "is the fact that we've been tiptoeing around each other for forever now, and I want to know why. Whenever I get too close, you either snap at me or get all flustered, and if I touch you, we're so combustible, we just about burst into flames." He bent his knees a little to better see into her face. "I'm completely willing to go up in flames, by the way." His smile was tight, his eyes dark. "But this first."

Her breath caught. "This?"

"Yes. Let's start with why you treat Cam and Stone like they're blood, and me like the redheaded bastard stepbrother."

"Well, I wouldn't exactly use the word *brother* . . ." she muttered, drawing a breath. Not easy when she was plastered to him, chest to chest, belly to belly, thighs to thighs, and everything in between. "Please, TJ . . . just let it go."

He dropped his head close, so close that his jaw brushed hers. The stubble there scraped gently across her skin and gave her a shiver. The good kind, dammit.

"Tell me," he said in that quiet voice that tended to make people do exactly as he asked.

She curled into him. He smelled so good. So good that she maybe, sort of, kind of by accident, pressed her nose to his neck.

"Harley."

His low voice rumbled from his chest, a soft warning she didn't heed, and when she moved against him again, his grip went from gentle to something far more dangerous as he breathed her name again.

Unable to help herself, she pressed her mouth to his neck and felt him stir against her.

"You're trying to distract me," he whispered roughly.

Distract him, herself . . .

And before she gave too much thought to it, she opened her mouth on his throat, scraping him with her teeth, absorbing his rough groan.

And then . . .

And then he abruptly yanked himself free of her with a soft oath, pushing her behind him. "TJ? What—"

He strode from beneath the protection of the tree to the center of the clearing, his head cocked as if listening for something.

"What?" she said.

"Someone was standing right here, watching us."

"Who?"

"I don't know." He turned and pointed at her. "Stay."

And then he vanished down the path.

CHAPTER 7

Harley waited a few minutes, but when TJ didn't come right back, she went after him. He was a hundred or so yards down the trail, and when he saw her, said nothing.

Fine with her.

Speaking, sharing, emoting . . . all *waaaaay* overrated.

Finally, hands on his hips, looking torn between frustration and acceptance, he spoke. "Nice job on the staying thing."

"Did you see who it was?"

"No, just a flash. A guy though."

"The forest service told me I was the only one who pulled a permit for this weekend."

He was quiet as he absorbed that, not looking happy.

"Back there, at the tree," she said, "when you realized we weren't alone, you pushed me behind you."

"Watching your back."

"Just my back?"

"I'll watch whatever you want me to." His eyes were smiling but his mouth was not. He was done playing. "Harley."

"Let me guess. You're sticking to me like glue."

At that, his smile did meet his eyes. "The better to watch your back."

They'd put their packs back on and had gone a few hundred yards when he spoke. "You still owe me a story."

"Once upon a time there was this big, bad wolf who—"

"You know which story, smart-ass."

Yeah. She knew. What she didn't know was how to tell it to him.

TJ waited, but Harley walked in silence. He gave in to her silence because he could see that she wasn't ignoring him on purpose. She was thinking.

"Why now?" she eventually asked. "Why did you kiss me now after all this time?"

The truth was easy enough. She was warm, funny, attractive. But she was also scary as hell. So though he'd wanted her, and had for as long as he could remember, it'd also been far easier on him to stay away.

Something he was going to have a hard time remembering now that he'd had a taste of her.

"TJ?"

"You want to play twenty questions, Harley? Because I believe you're up on deck first."

He took her next silence to mean a resounding "no thanks." His cell phone vibrated, and he pulled it out of his pocket.

"What's up?" Cam asked him.

"You called to ask me what's up?"

"No," Cam said. "I called to see if there's anything you want to tell me."

"About?"

"I don't know. The weather. The Angels game. Or wait, I know. How about the client you cancelled on to follow a certain sexy blonde? Want to talk about that?"

TJ moved away from said sexy blonde for privacy. "No."

"Everything okay?" Cam asked after a moment of contemplative silence.

"Yes."

"You haven't done anything stupid with the one woman in town that hasn't fallen under your charms or between your sheets, have you?"

TJ gritted his teeth. Define stupid, he thought "No."

"Do I need to come up there and show you how to catch her, then?"

More gritting of his teeth.

"Okay, then, glad we could clear all this all up."

TJ shook his head. "Do you have a real reason for calling, or are you just running up the minutes for the hell of it?"

"We switched over to unlimited. And yeah, I have a reason. I wanted to see which of us back here at base have won the bet. See, we're divided on whether you'll come back with a just-laid expression on your face or if you'll be bleeding."

"Since clearly you don't have enough to do to keep busy," TJ said over Cam's soft laugh. "Do the research on that new climbing gear we were looking at. And I need a detailed mapping for that Yosemite trip Stone wants to pass off on me. Oh, and then there's a stack of paperwork on my desk—"

Cam stopped laughing, but the smile remained in his voice. "Ah, man, it's been a long time since you've resorted to pussy threats to shut me up. So . . . you ready to admit you're crazy about her or what? Inquiring minds need to know."

TJ closed his eyes. The rain had stopped, and he tipped his head at the quickly clearing sky. "What you need to know is that I'm going to kick your ass when I get back."

"Admit it. You're gone over her. You've got it bad."

"Fuck you."

"Hey, it's your own fault," Cam said. "You laughed at love. Like Annie said, you tempted karma."

"*Sideways,*" TJ told him.

Unperturbed about his impending death, Cam laughed out loud.

TJ disconnected, shoving the phone back in his pocket as he turned and came face-to-face with Harley.

"What was that about?" she asked as he pulled off his shell, rolled it up, and stuck it through an outside webbed pocket of his pack—because suddenly he felt quite warm.

"A question for a question, Harley. One hundred percent honesty at all times, no exceptions." He was fairly confident she wouldn't dare.

She looked at him for a long beat. "Fine."

Well, if that didn't surprise the hell out of him. He dropped his pack and she did the same. "Okay," he said. "Tell me why you're always mad at me."

She drew a deep breath. "Maybe it's because you talk to me in that voice, that low, husky, sexy voice that makes me feel like you'd like to sleep with me."

"I would."

Shoving her fingers in her damp hair, she turned in a slow circle. She couldn't be more drenched, and she couldn't be more beautiful, with her small, tight little body so perfectly outlined in nothing but that white tee and thin cargoes, both plastered to her like a second skin. "Harley—"

"See, that!" She pointed at him. "That voice right there, the one that says you want nothing more than to be inside me." She turned away from him and so softly he could barely hear her, murmured, "When you already were."

He couldn't have been more shocked if she'd hauled off and hit him.

She let out a low sound that might have been a laugh but also sounded dangerously close to a sob. He recovered enough to grab her, turn her to face him, and haul her in close.

It wasn't easy. She had temper and frustration all over her, in the stiffness of her body and the fierceness of the set of her mouth, but it was the shame and humiliation burning her eyes and cheeks that tore at him. "What?" he repeated hoarsely. "What did you just say?"

"Nothing. I said nothing."

"Harley."

"Oh, God. Please don't make me say it again." She closed her eyes and dropped her head to his chest.

He ran a hand up her spine, wrapped his fingers in her hair, and gently tugged her head up until she met his gaze. "We slept together," she whispered.

Stunned, *gutted*, he could only stare into her liquid brown eyes.

"Although," she said with great irony, "it should be noted that there was no sleeping involved."

"What are you saying?"

"Long Lake," she said. "The summer after your graduation."

Vague images of being seventeen years old hit him, vague because he'd been stoned or drunk just about his entire senior year of high school. "What about it?"

"Remember that big camping party, the one everyone had to four-wheel up Pioneer Slate to get to?"

"Still not ringing a bell."

"July Fourth," she clarified.

He slowly shook his head, thoughts racing. He'd been wild and out of control, *especially* that summer. No mom and an abusive father did that to a kid. That summer had been the last of a long, misspent youth before he'd left for college in Colorado, where he'd studied as little as possible, met Sam, traveled extensively, and had gotten his first taste of the great, big world outside of the Sierras.

It'd been heaven on earth after the childhood he'd endured. "I camped and partied that entire summer," he told her. "It's all one big blur to me."

She nodded. He knew she knew that. She knew a lot about him.

Maybe too much.

He'd thought he'd known a lot about her as well, but he was beginning to think that might not be as true as he wanted it to be.

"You were with Chrissie," she reminded him.

Chrissie had been his on-and-off girlfriend through high school. Mostly off.

Actually, to be more accurate, girlfriend was a loose term for fuck buddies.

Good times.

"I went up there with Lance O'Brien," she said.

TJ remembered Lance. They'd played basketball together.

Lance had gone on to become some big hotshot sports announcer in San Francisco, but back then, he'd been into a different girl each week, slowly making his way through the entire student body.

Harley had been very shy and quiet in high school, and it had been an odd match.

"Yeah," Harley told him, reading his mind. "It was what you might call a pity date on his part." She didn't look happy to be recounting the story.

In fact, she looked uncomfortable and extremely embarrassed.

"Lance was an ass," he said.

She looked slightly mollified. "You and Chrissie were parked next to us, having a great time. I *wasn't* having a great time." She paused, then pushed away from him and walked a few feet off, staring into the wilderness, her shoulders straight but quivering slightly, as if they held the weight of the world.

And though he knew he wasn't going to like the story, he moved close. "Tell me," he said softly.

Harley had thought a lot about what had happened between her and TJ over the years, about her resentment, about him not remembering, but surprisingly enough, she'd never given any thought as to what it'd be like to tell him. She turned away from him and crossed her arms over her chest, staring into the woods, which were still echoing with the rain dropping from the trees.

TJ said her name, a quiet demand. "Harley."

She acknowledged the low timbre and roughness of his voice with a little nod. She wasn't being coy or annoying on purpose. She was just so nervous that her legs were shaking, but she'd started this, she'd finish it. It helped that she had her back to him, that he couldn't see her face. "Chrissie had stolen some of her dad's booze, and the two of you were sitting in the back of your truck sharing it." Closing her eyes, it was as if she was back there. Late, hot, dark night. No moon. No breeze. Just the sounds of the crickets, the water lapping at the rocks, and TJ and Chrissy laughing and enjoying themselves.

Oh, and her own misery.

"I was mortified," she went on quietly. "Because I'd been determined to lose my virginity that night, and you were parked right next to me. The whole time Lance was kissing me and copping a feel, I"—she shook her head—"I was wishing it was you," she whispered.

She could feel him staring at her, could practically feel his frustration.

"Christ," he said. "I don't remember."

"Chrissie asked you if her dress made her butt look fat and you didn't answer. She got pissed, threw the bottle of liquor over the side of the truck, and got out."

"Sounds like Chrissy."

"She came over to us and asked for a ride home. Lance was drooling over her halter top. She was . . . far more well-endowed than I was, and I was already over the evening, so I got out of the car and said he could take Chrissie, that I was going to party with the others." She paused. "I didn't."

"What did you do?"

"I climbed into the bed of your truck to sit with you." She closed her eyes again. "They drove off and I found you lying alone, watching the stars." He'd looked so damn hot all sprawled out. "You smiled and held out your hand, and I lay back with you to watch, too. You closed your eyes and drifted off. I did the same." She'd been glowing, a little toasted from the alcohol. Mostly she'd been glowing because she was lying next to the big, bad, wildly sexy TJ and he'd been holding her hand. "You turned to me and pulled me into you and told me I smelled pretty." He'd been so sweet, unexpectedly so, and warm. God, so warm. "You kissed me and . . ."

And here was the tough part to handle. "You . . . started touching me," she said. "I'd had this stupid, silly crush on you for so damn long, but you'd never treated me as anything other than a pesky little sister, and . . ." And he'd kissed so amazingly, like heaven on earth. Some things never changed. "You started touching me, and all our clothes sort of fell away, and then . . ."

And then he'd pulled her beneath him and she'd completely lost herself.

It'd been heaven, all of it, until he'd fallen asleep afterwards. She'd tried to rouse him and he'd pushed her away, muttering "Chrissie, shh. Tired."

She'd never forget that, staring down at him in confusion and utter devastation. Remembering it now brought a flush of embarrassment to her face, and she put her hands up to cover it.

TJ let out a long, slow exhale, his breath ruffling the wet hair at her nape, and then turned her to face him. His voice was different when he spoke, calm but the concern clear even with his tight control. "Did I hurt you, Harley?"

"No. God, no. You . . . you were . . ." Sweet. Loving. Hot. *Perfect*.

He pulled her hands away from her face and held them, waiting until she looked at him to speak. "Are you sure?"

"Very," she said weakly, and closed her eyes, swallowing hard. "And I'd really like it if we could go back to not talking about it now."

"We didn't talk about it because I didn't remember it," he said quietly. "If I had, believe me, we most definitely would have talked."

"It was a long time ago. It's done."

He let out a long breath.

"So . . . is this going to be uncomfortable now?"

"Does it feel uncomfortable?"

"No more than usual." With her eyes closed, she registered the sounds around them. The wind rustling the trees, the rainwater still in the branches falling to the ground. The chirping of birds . . .

Incessant chirping, actually, which wasn't a normal, happy sound. "Do you hear that?"

"Hear what?"

Shaking her head, she turned and followed the bird sounds, off the trail and through the thick brush.

"Harley—"

"Hang on, there's something wrong."

She found it at a full, majestic Jeffrey pine, towering at least a hundred feet in the air. At the base of the thick trunk sat a very young bird, squeaking, pathetically flapping its wings for all it was worth and getting nowhere. Above it was the nest from which it'd fallen, its frantic mom, and two more babies. "Oh, no, you poor thing." Harley carefully scooped up the baby and eyed the tree, trying to figure out how to climb it with the baby in her hands when TJ gently nudged her aside.

He reached for a branch above his head, using it to pull himself up with what appeared to be no effort at all. His T-shirt clung to all those flexing and bunching muscles as he straightened to a stand on the branch. He tested the branch above him, his jeans going tight and snug over his very fine ass.

"Here," he said, crouching low again to hold out his hand for the baby bird, and caught her red-handed staring at his hind end.

He said nothing but did raise a brow at her.

She shrugged, but figured apologizing was a waste of breath. Besides, he'd ogled her in her wet shirt plenty. Fair was fair. She set the birdie in his palm and watched in awe and not a little bit of envy as he gently settled the little bird back into the nest. In thanks, the mom viciously pecked at him.

He pulled his hand back quickly, chuckling as he lithely leapt to the ground. "I don't think she liked me much."

Harley took his hand and looked at the blood welling from the new hole between two of his knuckles. "Ouch."

"It's okay." He gestured to her to precede him back through the bush to the trail, where they'd left their packs. She started to open hers to look for her first-aid kit but he already had his out. "It's really nothing," he said. "Just want to make sure it's clean."

She took the kit from him. Since they didn't have running water, she took his hand in hers and used an antiseptic spray. They both had their heads bent over their joined hands, so close she could feel the warmth of his breath on her jaw. Looking up into his eyes, she winced for him. "Hurt?"

"Nah."

She smiled softly. "Now who's the liar."

Then she lifted his hand to her mouth and still holding his gaze, softly blew on the wound.

His eyes smoldered.

Later Harley would think she had no idea what the hell came over her, but she blew again, and he appeared to stop breathing. "If you're doing that on purpose," he said softly, his voice pure silk, "you should know, paybacks are a bitch."

Next, she dabbed antibiotic ointment on the wound, then covered it with a Band-Aid, struggling with her conflicting emotions over him. The need to run far and fast—versus the need to crawl up his body.

"I don't know what you're talking about," she finally said, innocently.

He let her get away with that. Or so she thought, but when she turned to walk off, he snagged her, pulling her back against him. "Are we playing, Harley?" he asked, his mouth against her ear.

She could feel him, hard and warm at her back. Were they playing? Tilting her head up, she looked into his eyes, dark and heated.

"Is that question going to take you awhile?" he asked, mouth slightly curved.

"The question's going to have to wait, since we're losing valuable daylight."

His slight smirk said he recognized a diversion tactic when he saw one, but he let her have it.

They had two hours left, she figured. She set the pace, and they walked in silence—which didn't mean she couldn't feel the weight of his thoughts, because she could. But he kept them to himself. It shouldn't have made her like him even more, but it did.

An hour later, they cleared a ridge and came to a stop while Harley consulted her maps and GPS. "There," she said, pointing to the next ridge over. "That's where the first camera is."

"Where did you plan on staying tonight?"

"There, or as close as we can get to it before dark."

From where they stood at the cliff, they were overlooking a wide meadow, which was abundant with plant and small animal life that her coyotes depended on for food. Some large elk were grazing, their impressive antlers glinting in the waning light. It would take an entire family of coyotes to bring down one of those beauties. "I'm hoping to get a visual on some of the tagged coyotes," she said, "if they show themselves. According to their trackers, most of the red group is in this area. There's six in their pack and—" She paused. "Listen," she said as the telltale buzzing of flies sank in, along with a sudden dread.

Stomach dropping, she followed the sound to a cluster of trees. At the base of one was a large burrowed hole in the ground, reinforced with a fallen log. A coyote den. Lying just inside was a far too still ball of fur. With an involuntary gasp, Harley crawled closer. "Oh, no."

TJ dropped to his knees beside her and leaned in to look at the coyote. His expression was grim when he sat back on his heels.

"Dead," she murmured.

"Not just dead." He looked at her, jaw tight. "Shot."

Her stomach dropped, but she brushed past TJ to look for herself, and felt her heart squeeze when she caught sight of the tag. Red. The coyote had been one of theirs. Throat burning, Harley consulted her GPS and her maps, and shook her head. "She was right where she should have been. She just got in some asshole's way."

TJ covered the mouth of the den with large rocks, making it a grave so that other animals couldn't get to it, but also marking the spot so that Harley could lead the authorities up there if she had to.

TJ called it in to the forest service, and then Harley worked on pulling herself together with sheer will as they hiked to the next ridge.

It was a challenging hike, and got more challenging as they climbed. The air was thin, and they were surrounded by peaks that had been formed more than 30,000 years ago beneath ice sheets and snowfields. Back then, the ice had piled more than

5,000 feet deep in places, and as it'd retreated, the meltwater had forced glacial troughs, forming the harsh peaks and outcroppings, creating a rugged, isolated, unfriendly land.

For humans.

But wildlife tended to thrive there. Especially coyotes—at least when no one was shooting at them. Proving it, Harley watched as a group of them moved as one through the meadow far below, bounding through the tall grass calling and yipping to each other.

She pulled out her camera and lost herself for long moments, taking pictures with her wide lens. The moist air rode out on southeasterly winds. Clouds were still sifting trough the trees like wood smoke. The weak sun hung as low as possible in the sky, seeming to perch precariously at the horizon line for a beat, then sank down in a blaze of glory. After that . . . utter darkness.

In that darkness, the air was heavy with humidity from the storm and fragrant with late autumn wildflowers and pine. It was gorgeous, and Harley felt a rush of excitement and adrenaline from all of it, the moon-streaked landscape, the wildlife's natural music.

The company.

"What now?" TJ asked when she'd put her camera away.

"Make camp." Which was really his expertise, not hers. She felt a little nervous pulling it off in front of his watchful eyes, but he'd let her lead all day long, and didn't seem in any hurry to take over.

She knew that was out of deference to her, that he wanted this to be her gig as much as she wanted it for herself. She appreciated it, more than he could know. Being out there, being in control and in charge, had fueled her soul in a way she hadn't expected.

Even with the unexpected emotional trip down Memory Lane, and finding the dead coyote.

Standing in the clearing where she'd planned on staying the night, TJ shook his head, pointing to signs of a recent campfire. She stared at it, wondering if whoever had shot that coyote had camped there.

Beneath the ambient moonlight, he took her hand. "Not here."

"A little higher?"

"Definitely." He squeezed her hand. "I'd like our backs up against the mountain and a good view in front of us."

She nodded, and for the first time all day, let him lead, which he did with expected efficiency, using his Maglite. He moved them along as fast as they could go in the dark, and in less than ten minutes, he'd found a better spot. It was higher and, as he'd wanted, had the added advantage of them being able to keep their backs to the wall.

As they stood at the new spot, Harley realized for the first time that they were going to spend the night.

Together.

Her body gave one traitorous little quiver of excitement, which her brain worked hard to shut down, though it wasn't entirely successful.

It's not like the last time you spent the night with him, she told herself. For one thing, this time, you'll be fully dressed.

No getting naked, she repeated to herself several times.

No getting naked.

CHAPTER 8

"Here, where the ground is dry." TJ used his flashlight to better reveal the spot in the clearing. He dropped his pack on the ground and looked at Harley, who nodded but didn't speak. She was hugging his jacket to her and seemed pale. He figured it was due to the combination of the shock of finding the dead coyote and being cold and wet. "I'm going to get wood for a fire," he told her. "You need to change into dry clothes."

"No," she said, and pointed to a fallen log. "*Sit.*"

He arched a brow. "Excuse me?"

"Yeah," she said toughly, ruining it by shivering. "You're going to sit. And stay. Just like you told me to stay before."

"But you didn't stay."

"Okay, true," she said. "But you've already walked through a rainstorm, climbed a tree, got a hole pecked into your hand, and dragged rocks for a grave for that coyote, all for me. Hell, you even gave up your warm jacket. So now you're going to sit and let me do the rest, as I would have done for myself anyway."

He wanted to argue, wanted to say he could get a fire going in three minutes flat, and that she needed to get warmed up quick. But those things were counterproductive to his plan, which was getting her back to relaxed and enjoying herself. He really wanted that for her, so he obediently sat. "You going to cook for me, too?"

They both knew damn well she could burn water with little to no effort, but she shot him a considering look over her shoulder. "You know what, Mr. Smart-ass?" she murmured. "I think I will."

Now he paled.

And she smiled.

Another mission accomplished, he thought, but as she turned her back to him to gather kindling for the fire, his smile fell away. Because he . . . was not relaxed. He had questions, lots of them. Most centering around the little bombshell he couldn't stop thinking about.

They'd had sex.

Jesus Christ, he'd had sex with Harley, his greatest fantasy come true, and he was too much of an idiot to remember any of it.

Harley came back with a load of twigs and branches in her arms. She kneeled in the center of the clearing and started with the small twigs, graduating up to sticks, crisscrossing them over each other so the hot air would rise through them and help them catch. Then she set a big log on top before she lit the kindling, and he opened his mouth to correct her.

But she was frowning, concentrating deeply, and muttering to herself as she worked, looking frustrated and chilled, and so fucking adorable he shut his mouth.

He'd had her. Naked. Beneath him.

And he didn't remember.

Yeah. That was going to haunt him for a damn long time to come.

In spite of not letting the kindling catch fire before she put the big hunk of wet wood on it, the fire actually smoked and flickered. He watched as she kneeled there in the dirt over the small flame, blowing on it, babying it along with soft coaxing murmurs that cracked him up, and then blowing some more, which didn't crack him up but made him hard.

"Look," she said triumphantly, turning to him, catching him staring at her mouth. "I got it."

"Nicely done." His voice was hoarse, and he cleared his throat. "You're going to change now, right?"

She turned back to her fire and watched it proudly.

"Let me rephrase," he said. "You *are* going to change now."

She shot him a look over her shoulder. "I knew you were too alpha to sit there and follow directions for long."

"I'm not all that al—" He stopped at her *get real* look. "Fine. Am I allowed to get up and move closer to the warmth?"

She smiled. "Sure."

Except just then, the fire died.

"Dammit," she said.

"Maybe you didn't talk to it enough."

She shot him a look and he let out a laugh. "It's not your fault, Harley. Everything's wet." He opened his pack and pulled out a bag of Fritos.

"Hungry?" she asked.

"Yes, actually, but not for food." Even in the dark he could feel her blush. "The chips are my emergency fire starters," he explained.

"Get out."

"I'm serious. All the grease makes them highly flammable." Crouching beside her, he removed the big log from her pile, then opened the bag and placed a chip beneath the stacked kindling. He lit a match and set it to the chip, which immediately lit.

"Wow."

He waited a few moments until the pile was really flaming before he added the log.

"Neat trick," she said.

He stared at the flames. "It was Sam's."

She was quiet a moment. "You learn a lot from her?"

"Yes. But mostly what *not* to do." He smiled because the ache from her death had dulled, leaving just good times and good memories. "I loved her, but she was wilder and more reckless than even me."

She raised a brow, looking amused. "That's saying a lot."

"Yeah." And it'd been the death of her, literally. She'd died due to her own negligence and not being properly prepared for the turbulent waters on the river. She hadn't been wearing the proper gear, and when she'd hit a rough rapid and gone under, she'd drowned.

For TJ, it'd been a senseless tragedy and an unwelcome wake-up call.

He'd been prepared, maybe overly so, for every single trip since. "She discovered the Frito trick by accident one night," he said softly, a fond smile curving his mouth. "We were out of food and it'd been raining buckets for days. We had one match left, and one bag of Fritos, which we used to build a fire. Afterwards, starving, we tried to convince ourselves that being warm was better than full, but truthfully it was a toss-up."

Harley smiled, but reached out and squeezed his hand. "So that trick was hard earned."

"Yeah." Leaning back, he looked up at the sky. Perfectly clear now, it was littered with stars like diamonds on a blanket of black velvet. Not a single cloud, which meant no more rain—and boded well for sleeping in the open. "You sure you're not frozen solid? You really should change."

"I will." Harley pulled out a can of soup. "I know you intended to be back home by now, so you probably don't have food. I've got chicken noodle."

"I'm okay."

"TJ, I'm not going to eat if you don't. And besides, I'm still in charge. You're eating." She'd been rifling through her backpack as she spoke. "Uh oh."

"What?"

"Might have spoken too soon. Can't find my can opener." She began to unload her pack, pulling out the maps, her GPS tracking unit, a bottle of lotion, a hairbrush, a pair of pink bikini polka-dotted panties that just about gave him heart failure, and a paperback. The cover was a scantily clad woman in the arms of a soldier, whose shirt was wide open.

"A camping handbook?" he teased.

"It's a historical romance, from Skye. She said I need to read it and broaden my horizons."

"Read it out loud and broaden both our horizons."

She eyed the cover. "You'd have to put me in chains to get me to read that out loud to you."

He held out his hand for the book. She winced, clearly not wanting to hand it over, but she eventually did. He read the back cover copy. "'He's been released from his bonds to the government, but she's only just begun her servitude—willingly.'" He looked up and grinned. "Turns out that chains might be the perfect accessory for this book."

"Ha." Face flaming, she yanked it out of his hands and stuffed the thing back into the bottom of her pack. "I'm sure I have a can opener in here somewhere."

TJ pulled out his utility knife, opened the can, and set it in the middle of the flames to heat up.

"You're good."

"Just practiced."

Harley eyed his backpack with envy. "What other magic necessities do you have in there?"

Condoms, he nearly said, but he was fairly certain she wouldn't consider that a magic necessity. He pulled out an apple, which they shared with the soup.

TJ had spent a myriad of nights just like this one, out in the open, a fire crackling, the wind rustling the trees, the night insects humming. It always brought him peace. Tonight, however, he wouldn't have labeled his mood peaceful. More like . . . revved up. "You warming up?" he asked, knowing she was because her cheeks began to go from pale to rosy.

"Actually, yeah, and it's making me tired. I know it's early, but I'm going to hit the sack."

He stood and added wood to the fire while she opened her sleeping bag and spread it on the ground. "Going to sleep now means you don't have to talk to me," he pointed out.

"And that."

Saying nothing, he watched as she crawled into her sleeping bag. He opened his bag and spread it on the opposite side of the fire. He'd just slid into it when Harley asked, "How come you even have your sleeping bag when all you were planning was a day trip?"

"I like to be prepared."

"That's pretty prepared. That's almost . . . overly prepared."

"I told you about Sam. You know there's a lot that could happen out here. Even a sprained ankle could lead to me being stuck overnight. Or a rockslide could hold me up, or having to go straight to a rescue, anything."

"Or a childhood acquaintance coming out here alone, making you feel that you have to keep an eye on her."

He said nothing to that.

"I imagine you've seen and heard it all, and rescued half of them," she said.

"Probably."

She was quiet a minute, then began rustling about like she was having a wrestling match with herself.

"Everything okay in there?" he asked.

"I'm fine."

Of course she was. She had "fine" down to a science. She was quiet for all of two seconds. Then he heard her swear softly.

"Problem?" he asked.

"Yeah." A bare arm appeared, her shirt dangling from two fingers. "This needs to dry." She tossed it to the log they'd just vacated.

Then she did the same with her pants.

He found himself holding his breath, hoping her underwear was coming next, *praying* her underwear was coming next.

But his luck wasn't that good.

Finally she seemed to settle down, and he spent the next few minutes picturing her in the sleeping bag in only her bra and panties.

He wondered if they were silky.

Or lace.

Maybe she wore a thong . . .

God. He had to stop the self-inflicted torture. "You okay now?" he asked, hearing the huskiness in his own voice.

"Yeah."

Her voice was husky, too, as if she knew what she did to him and maybe, maybe he did something to her, too.

"Good," he managed. "Glad you're okay."

Because *he* wasn't.

Not even close.

The mountains were never silent, and that night was no exception. The wind whistled through the treetops. Animals rustled. Crickets chirped.

But he got a big, fat nothing from the woman across the fire from him. After a long minute, he let out a breath and told himself she wasn't going to climb into his sleeping bag the way she'd climbed into his truck all those years ago.

Because apparently a guy only got lucky like that once in a lifetime.

CHAPTER 9

Harley tossed and turned, but no matter what she did, she couldn't get warm enough. "Dammit."

"What?"

"N—nothing."

"You're cold."

She sighed at TJ's low, knowing voice from across the flames. If she lifted her head, she'd be able to see him by the fire's glow, which would be a bad idea because he looked gorgeous by the glow. She'd been noticing all night. She'd been noticing other things too, like how the muscles of his chest and arms flexed when he tossed wood onto the fire. Or when he did things like wrap her in his jacket and slice an apple with his knife and offer it to her.

Hell, who was she kidding? He looked gorgeous when he breathed.

And they were alone up there, on what felt like the top of the world.

At the sound of movement, she lifted her head in time to catch TJ rise from his sleeping bag. He'd removed his shirt and wore only those faded, battered Levi's, disturbingly low on his hips. She watched as he cranked up the fire with minimal effort on his part, his body like poetry in motion, oozing testosterone and sex with every heartbeat.

"That should help," he said, poking at the flames with a big stick, those muscles she loved bunching in a way that made her mouth water.

He was edible all half naked like that. He could give a dead woman an orgasm.

And she was far from dead.

He added another log and crouched low, stick in hand, watching the flames. His hair fell over his forehead, curling at the back of his neck. He hadn't shaved that morning, and probably not the day before either, and he looked almost impossibly handsome as his eyes flicked to her. "Better?"

She blinked. "Um, what?"

Still hunkered down in front of the fire, he let out a breath. "You're still a popsicle, aren't you?"

"I'm still a popsicle," she whispered.

"I'm not."

Oh boy.

"You could come over here and we could share body heat."

Uh huh. And that wouldn't be all they shared either. Not with the amount of crazy chemistry they had.

There was a rock under her hip.

And she couldn't feel her toes.

She curled into a ball and told herself to ignore both the rock and the shivering of her limbs. She managed it, too, for at least half an hour after she'd heard TJ slip back into his sleeping bag. But then came a howl, long and eerie, and she jerked. Just a coyote. Probably one of hers. They don't attack humans.

Mostly.

Another cry, sounding more like a mountain cat. She gasped, leapt out of her sleeping bag, and in nothing but her bra and panties, dove into TJ's before she could take another breath.

Just as she'd known it would be, his sleeping bag was higher quality than hers, far cushier, bigger, and toasty warm.

TJ hissed out a breath when she pressed her icy feet to his, but otherwise didn't say a word, just wrapped his arms around her and pulled her in against him.

He'd stripped out of his jeans, but wore boxers, and was deliciously warm. "Cold?" he asked quietly. "Or scared?"

She tilted her head up and met his gaze. His hair was still over his forehead, almost in his eyes, pretty much inviting a woman to push it back for him.

To resist, she tightened her fingers in a fist against his pecs, which didn't really help since he was built like a kickboxer, all hard and lean and mind-bendingly *perfect*. She took a deep breath, which meant she inhaled his scent. Problem was, in spite of his being outside all day long, he smelled like rain and mountain and man, and so . . . *yum* it made her take a sniff, and then she couldn't seem to stop herself. She was breathing him in like he was her private stash of crack.

He ran a hand up and down her back. "Harley? You hyperventilating?"

"No," she said weakly, and dropped her forehead to his chest. Oh, God. Big mistake. Because her mouth was only a fraction of an inch away from his skin. If she so much as breathed, she'd have her lips on him—oh look at that, she breathed.

A lot.

TJ let out a long, shaky breath of his own. "You're shivering." He ran his large, warm hand down her arm until he reached her hand. "And your fingers are ice." He held them in his, gently rubbing his thumbs over her skin.

Harley closed her eyes. Getting into TJ's sleeping bag had been a bad idea. Such a bad, *bad* idea she moved to get out of the bag, but he tightened his grip. "Shh," he said, and giving up the resistance, she pressed her face into his throat and let her eyes drift shut. Her teeth were chattering and she was shaking, though honestly, she was no longer certain it was just from cold.

In fact, she was pretty sure it wasn't the cold at all, but him.

"Breathe," he murmured into her hair, rubbing soothing light circles on her back. "Breathe deeper."

She absorbed his calm, his strength, and best of all his heat, and after a few minutes, her jaw relaxed, and her teeth stopped chattering. Finally, the rest of her stopped shaking.

* * *

Harley woke up some time later, lying on top of TJ. If she pressed her knees into the ground on either side of his hips and pushed herself upright, she could ride him like a pony.

Yep, definitely out of her comfort zone. Her legs were entwined in his and her face was plastered to the crook of his neck. She didn't have to wonder if he was awake because his hands were slowly caressing her back, holding her in all that wonderful body heat of his.

Or maybe that was her heat. She certainly felt . . . *heated*.

"I know you're awake," he said. "You stopped breathing."

She still didn't move, incredibly aware of her hands braced on his chest for leverage, the muscles hard beneath her palms, his heart beating steady and sure beneath her fingertips.

Unlike hers, which was racing.

When he spoke, she felt the rumble of his voice, even deeper and huskier than normal. "We've played this your way," he said. "I didn't like it. My turn now."

Oh boy.

Cupping the nape of her neck, he urged her head up. His other hand slid down low, to the very small of her back, holding her in place for his kiss. At the first touch of his mouth on hers, her bones completely dissolved, and that was it, she was his for the taking.

Please take me . . .

She already knew that getting kissed by him was a full-body experience, but she hadn't expected to be rendered a quivering mass of lust before his tongue even touched hers—a huge miscalculation on her part because she knew, dammit she knew he kissed like heaven on earth. She braced for the onslaught of erotic, sensual heat, but when he lightly ran his tongue over the seam of her lips, she opened to him, softening in his arms, letting out a low moan. A sound he apparently took for acquiescence because he tightened his hold on her and deepened the kiss. Giving herself up to it, she sank her fingers into his hair, holding his head to hers as they devoured each other.

When he finally drew back and looked at her, there was warmth in his eyes and a smile on his face that promised all sorts of wicked things if she only said the word. And suddenly she became incredibly aware of how little she wore, how her nipples were boring holes in his chest, how his arm was low around her back, his palm sliding across her ass, skimming the thin silk of her panties.

Yeah, there was a word right on the tip of her tongue, and that word was *yes*! Her hands ran over his shoulders and down his sides—

That's when she remembered. She'd wanted passion in her life, but she'd planned on finding it with Nolan. Sweet, gentle, kind Nolan, who *would* remember their lovemaking, once they had it. "*Crap.*"

TJ pulled back a fraction, all sleepy and sexy-eyed. "That's not the reaction I usually get."

"I'm thinking of Nolan."

TJ's hands went still. "My kiss made you think of another man?"

She winced at the warning in his tone. "No, your kiss melted my bones."

"Like the sound of that," he murmured, rocking his hips against hers. Hers responded in kind before she stopped herself. Dammit. She rolled off the glorious mountain of heat to her side, which was as far as she could get in the sleeping bag, roomy and cushy as it was. Outside, it was still very dark, which was a good thing. She wasn't ready to see him.

"You're not *with* him," he said, tucking one arm beneath his head, resting his other hand on his belly. "Two dates—and one of them not counting—doesn't make anything exclusive."

"Why does everyone keep saying that? And how in the hell does everyone know we had two dates and that one of them didn't count?"

"Wishful is Mayberry, remember? Everyone knows everything." He rolled to face her, propping up his head with his hand, the other settling on her hip. "You had to save his ass when he should be saving yours."

"And what does *that* mean?"

"Nothing." He paused, then ran the tips of his fingers lightly up her spine. And damn if she didn't melt all over again. "You really think of him as your boyfriend?"

She wanted to nod but she didn't. Because the truth was, she liked the idea of Nolan being her boyfriend, but somehow it never seemed to materialize.

And she didn't know why.

TJ brushed a soft kiss to her temple before trailing more of those soft kisses along her jaw, and without thinking, her body arched to give him better access, which she abruptly stopped when she felt his smile against her skin. *Damn him!* "TJ—"

"Uh huh . . ." he murmured, making his way back to her mouth while his fingers slid across her belly. Goose bumps erupted on her skin. Then those fingers headed north, just grazing over her silk-covered breasts as his thigh slipped between hers.

He caught her gasp with his mouth, and the kiss went hard and demanding again, until finally they ripped apart, breathless. TJ looked down at her, his eyes dark and filled with hunger. "Tell me you're happy with him and we stop this right now."

"I'm . . ." She struggled for the words that would make her a big, fat, *turned-on* liar.

With shocking patience, TJ waited her out.

"I want to say yes so bad," she finally whispered. "But it's the 'with him' part that's holding me up."

"Because . . . ?"

"Because I'm not with him, am I? Plus, I just had my tongue down your throat." She shook her head. "Oh, God, this is bad. Very, very bad."

She saw his white teeth flash in the dark as he leaned in close. "Can I kiss you now," he asked huskily, "or is there any other guy in your head we need to discuss?"

At the thought of another mind-blowing kiss, her brain voluntarily shut down, giving her body tacit permission to take over. "Well, there's Brad Pitt," she murmured. "And—"

"Shut up, Harley." He nipped her lower lip.

"Shutting up," she murmured just as his tongue touched hers, and she began a slow and delicious repeat of the insta-melt thing. His hands slid up her body, and she crawled all over him again, but then *he* froze.

"TJ?"

He tightened his grip on her hips for a beat, indicating that she should stay as still as he. "Did you hear that?"

She hadn't heard anything but the blood rushing in her ears. "No, I—" Suddenly he slid soundlessly out of the sleeping bag.

Breathless, she ate up the sight of him by starlight, his hair tousled, jaw rough and in need of a shave, his chest bare, his boxers disturbingly low on his hips, his— "Oh my God. You can't go anywhere like that!"

Unconcerned, he moved to his backpack and pulled out . . .

His knife.

Then he slid into his jeans, pointed at her to stay, and vanished.

CHAPTER 10

Harley clutched TJ's sleeping bag to her body and strained her ears, but she could hear nothing. Well, nothing except the light wind, the occasional cry of a bird, and . . . crunching pine needles beneath someone's feet. "TJ?" she whispered, thinking *oh please let it be TJ*.

"Just me." He came out of the woods in nothing but those still unbuttoned, low-slung Levi's, hair a little wild—from her fingers, she realized with a bit of a shock—eyes cool and calm as they took in their surroundings. "I thought I heard someone, but I didn't see anything." He appeared to be at ease, but on second look, she could see that was an illusion, because in truth he was battle ready.

And she? She wanted to lick him from sternum to belly button and beyond, thank you very much. She realized she had other issues to be concerned with, but holy smokes.

Standing there by moonlight, he was all raw, sexual, barely contained power, and she felt a little ping in the region of her gut, another in her heart, and a third in a place where no one had given her a ping in a long time.

Including Nolan.

TJ dropped more wood on the simmering fire, then crouched at her side, all powerfully toned and tanned. He reached out and put a finger under her chin to close her mouth, which had been hanging open. "You're giving me ideas," he said very softly.

She slammed her mouth *and* her eyes shut.

"Are you warm enough now?" he asked, sounding amused.

Sure. If sweating in unusual places counted. She nodded jerkily and felt him rise. She opened her eyes and saw him go for her sleeping bag.

Wait a minute. "You're . . . going to sleep over there?" she asked.

He stopped and met her gaze across the fire. "Your choice."

She opened her mouth to say he should absolutely stay waaaay over there, maybe even move to the next ridge, but all that came out of her was expelled air.

He came back, once again hunkering at her side. His movements were slow, easy, and entirely uninhibited.

And God help her, she wanted to be uninhibited, too. He cradled her face in one of his hands, ran the pad of his thumb over her lower lip. "I'm going to need more of a sign, Harley."

Dammit. Couldn't he just be a he-man and take the choice away from her? She realized that the thought set women back a few hundred years, but she didn't know if she could verbalize the truth.

And that truth was that she wanted him against her. *In* her.

He pulled back his hand, but he remained crouched at her side, patient and calm. And with the firelight flickering over his bare chest and shoulders, unintentionally sensual as hell.

She felt fluttery and trembly. Being with him always made her fluttery, but the trembling thing was new.

This was more than a crush. Which meant that she was in way over her head. She knew this. But did she put up the white flag? Did she call the cavalry? Did she run like hell?

No.

Even knowing that despite trying to keep her distance, he'd gotten hold of her heart, even knowing that she couldn't entirely trust him to be careful with it, she lifted the edge of the sleeping bag in a clear invite. "For warmth only."

His lips curled into just a hint of a smile as he slid in. He leaned over her and kissed her softly, just a warm, gentle press of his lips that registered shockingly high on the intensity scale for having no tongue involved.

She shivered and found herself clinging to him. Good. Great way of keeping her cool.

He met her gaze, then closed his eyes and flipped her away from him. She had no idea if the emotion that rushed through her was relief or disappointment.

"For warmth," he said in her ear, pulling her back against his chest, spooning her. Her back was immediately infused with warm, sexy male, and she had to bite her lip to hold her moan in. One of his arms rested loosely on her hip, the other crooked up and behind his head, his elbow her pillow.

In spite of herself, she felt a shiver of sheer lust race through her and she squirmed.

"What was that?"

She shook her head. "I didn't say anything."

"No, you wriggled your ass against my—"

"I did not!" But she did it again, a completely involuntary movement that she couldn't control.

"Harley." He sounded a little rough. "You've got to stop moving, or—"

"You're too close!" *Stop moving or what*? a very bad part of her wanted to know.

"Keep rocking your hips and I'll show you just how close I can get."

She inhaled and went as still, caught between wanting him to follow through on that threat and wanting to run screaming into the night.

After a long silence, during which time she held herself so rigid she couldn't even breathe, he sighed. "Relax. You know I'm not going to jump you."

Yeah, that wasn't what she was worried about. She was worried *she'd* jump *him*.

"Go to sleep," he commanded softly in her ear.

Uh huh, like that was going to be possible with his delicious warmth and sexy bod cradling hers! She wasn't the only one affected if the rigid length poking her butt was any indication. "TJ, you're—"

"Ignore it. I'm trying to."

She snorted, and the hand lightly gripping her hip tightened. "You're laughing at me."

"A little. It's just that you're usually the one so in control."

"And you are?" he countered. "In control? Unmoved by the proximity?"

"Completely." She went still, waiting to be struck by lightning for the lie.

"Really." His fingers skimmed her belly; slowly, achingly slowly, stroking up and down, not quite reaching her bra or the edging of her panties, but coming close enough that she was breathing again. Or more correctly, panting.

Her nipples were hard. Between her thighs, she was damp.

"You're completely unmoved," he repeated.

She bit her tongue rather than lie.

"It's easy enough to check," he said in a raspy, sexy voice, his fingers just barely slipping beneath her panties, heading south.

With a squeak, she caught his wrist. "Okay, I'm not unmoved!" She threw his hand off her. "But it's not you. It's that I've not—it's been a long time."

"How long?"

"*Long.*"

At that, the bastard chuckled.

She rolled her eyes, not that he could see her. "Go to sleep!"

"I'll try, but if you crawl all over me again, all bets are off."

"I won't crawl all over you!" She hoped. She lay there for a long time.

"Harley?" His voice was husky low, as if he'd nearly drifted off.

"Yeah?"

"You think about me?"

"All the time," she murmured without missing a beat.

All the time? She wrestled with second thoughts over that little tidbit for a few minutes until he pressed his hot mouth against the nape of her neck. "Brad?" she murmured. "Brad Pitt, is that you?"

He gave a soft laugh. "I could make you pay for that."

Who was he kidding, she'd *willingly* pay for that.

"Why are you still awake?" he asked.

"Why are you?" she countered.

When he spoke, his voice was soft. "I keep going over it in my head."

"I'm not going to admit I'm not unmoved again, TJ," she quipped, pretending to misunderstand him, trying to keep it light. And talking about what had happened that long ago night at Long Lake wouldn't be light. Not for her. "That was a onetime confession. A gift."

"Not that." He wasn't playing. "I'm sorry. God, I'm so damn sorry for that night. If I could take it back, if I could grovel for forgiveness . . ." He paused, and she heard him swallow hard. "I can't get it out of my head, what it must have been like for you. Your first time. With a drunken idiot." He hugged her in a little closer, pressing his face into her hair. "In a fucking open truck bed." His voice was hoarse and filled with self-loathing. "With others all around us. Christ, I was such an ass back then."

"Back then?" she teased.

He said nothing to that. Okaaaaay, he was clearly not ready to find it amusing, and he was beating himself up to boot. Deep down, she could admit that's what she'd wanted from him for years.

Hurray. Mission accomplished.

Except . . . She rolled to her back to see into his face. Looking up at him, into his pained expression, she didn't suddenly want him to pay at all.

The fire was nothing more than a flicker, and she'd always loved looking at people by the firelight. Somehow it was so revealing, and let her see right through to the heart and soul of a person.

As she was seeing TJ.

Did she want to see through him, right to his heart and soul? It was a deep question, a difficult question, but the simple answer was yes.

His eyes were two dark pools, but his concern and regret rolled over her in waves. His legendary cool was gone. In another time and place, it'd be fascinating. "I told you that you didn't hurt me," she said quietly, watching a grimace twist his mouth at her words. "I meant it, TJ."

He said nothing to that, and she tried nudging him, a smile on her face. "But I wouldn't mind hearing more about the possible groveling."

He still wasn't playing and couldn't be distracted. "Your first time," he repeated so softly she barely heard him.

Her eyes drifted shut as she let memories wash over her. Between the wild crush she'd had on him and the time he'd spent stroking her body into a quivery boneless mass of bliss, the pain of his first penetration truly had been shockingly minimal.

In fact, if truth be told, the reality of that night had haunted her through her following sexual experiences. None of them had come close to measuring up.

Which of course, at the time, had only upped her resentment factor.

"If I didn't hurt you," he murmured, stroking his hand up her arm to cup her face, "why have you hated me all this time?"

Oh yeah.

That.

She was already sorry she'd turned to face him, and considered switching back around, but his hand went to her hip and held her still as he waited with that bottomless patience she knew he'd earned the hard way.

"I told you, it was fine. I was fine. You were fine, we were all fine. Can you let it go now?"

"Fine," he repeated, forcing the word out like she'd just insulted his manhood.

"Yes. *Fine*." Yet another big fat lie. Which settled it. She was going straight to hell in a handbasket.

Because the truth was, it had been amazing.

So.

Damn.

Amazing.

Not that she intended to share that *little* tidbit, no sirree. That confession just might kill her. "As for why I was mad," she went on, knowing he needed to know to move on, "I guess it's that I got to remember it all this time and you didn't. I know it's silly and juvenile, but there it is. So can we stop talking about it now? Or yesterday. Yesterday would be even better."

He was quiet a moment, and she let out a breath. Good. They were moving on. She began to relax.

"I was out of control," he said after a few minutes. "And we both know it. I slept with half the population of Wishful and I barely remember a fraction of it." He sighed, sounding disgusted with himself. "I've always said that the past is the past, and it's never bothered me much—until now."

She tipped her head up and met his gaze, his filled with regret and a softness that made her heart catch as he touched her face, running a finger over her temple. "I really hate that I don't remember that night, Harley."

"I know." And she did. But it was finally, somehow, okay for her. Besides, she remembered enough for both of them. "Close your eyes, TJ. Go to sleep."

He closed his eyes, his lashes dark and thick. "In the back of a fucking truck," he muttered to himself.

She closed her eyes, too, because looking at him made her want to do something stupid, like soothe him, which would be a bit like trying to soothe a wild mountain lion.

"Where it was," he went on, "apparently, *fine*."

She opened her eyes and looked at him speculatively. "Is all this self-flagellation because I used the word fine?"

His wincing expression said she'd hit a bingo, and she had to laugh. "I'm going to sleep now, TJ."

With that, she turned back over and was very careful not to wiggle. She tried to stay on her side of the sleeping bag, but he put a hand flat to her belly—*oh, God*—and tugged her back to him.

"For warmth," he murmured.

Right.

For warmth.

His fingers danced lightly over her skin, and her heart kicked into gear, leaping against her ribs. She couldn't help it, and she certainly couldn't control it. His hand was big and warm, his palm was callused, and it felt good.

Too good.

It took her another heartbeat to decide not to fight him, especially since it *was* warmer all spooned up against him, even if she was incredibly, shockingly, erotically aware of his hand spread wide on her abs, his thumb only a fraction of an inch from the curves of a breast, his pinkie finger actually touching the edging of her panties. She hoped to God that he couldn't feel her heart reverberating off her ribs and against him.

Exhaustion finally took over, but just as she drifted off, she'd have sworn she heard him mutter "*fine*" again, like he would an oath, and she smiled as she fell asleep.

Chapter 11

TJ was having an *excellent* dream. He was flat on his back, wrapped in a tangle of warm, feminine limbs, the owner of said limbs working her mouth down his neck toward his chest.

Oh yeah . . .

She paused to dip her tongue into the hollow of his throat, then sucked a patch of skin into her mouth.

"Mmmm," rumbled out of him and he rolled her beneath him, slipping a thigh between hers, making her gasp in pleasure as she rocked herself on his leg.

Christ, he loved this dream.

With one hand beneath her panties palming a sweet ass, he ran his lips down her throat, over a narrow collarbone and encountered a bra strap.

No problemo.

He simply nudged it down, and then the silk cup, following its path with his mouth to a warm curve of breast. He swirled his tongue over the tip and felt the nipple pebble. With another groan, he sucked it into his mouth just as two small hands fisted in his hair. Then he switched to the other side, and the warm, sweet body beneath his arched up with a soft cry, riding his thigh for all she was worth.

She was hot and getting wet. He could feel her dampness on his skin.

It was like a drug.

Needing more, his hand came around, slid down her stomach and into her panties in front now, finding hot, wet, silky flesh.

His dream lover's hands were on the move, too, gliding over his chest, toying with the buttons on his Levi's, which were damned uncomfortable now that he was hard as a rock.

She got the buttons opened, giving him desperately needed room, and he let out a rough exhale that backed up in his throat when she slid her hand home.

It was getting better and better.

He slid a finger into her, brushing his thumb over her center, and she cried out again, arching up as he teased her nipple with his tongue, then his teeth, gliding his thumb in the rhythm her hips demanded. He knew by the way she was panting and writhing that she was close, and by the way she was stroking him that he wasn't too far behind, and then suddenly she burst with a soft cry and a name on her lips.

His.

He let her down slowly, skimming his hand back up her warm, sated body, his still hard and throbbing.

That's when she said his name again, in a shocked whisper. "*TJ?*"

Well, who the hell else? After all, this was *his* dream. But the panic in her voice impeded into his dream and he opened his eyes.

It was still dark, but his body told him dawn wasn't too far off. He focused in on the wet nipple right in front of his eyes. His thumb was rasping back and forth over the other one, both breasts being offered up to him by the bra he'd shoved down.

He lifted his head and met Harley's startled, sleepy, and glazed-over eyes.

Oh, shit.

"We were dreaming," she said thickly, and then seemed to realize she had her hands down his pants. She yanked them out so fast he winced, and she covered her face.

Getting out of the sleeping bag without touching her, with his body still cocked and loaded, was an exercise in torture. Grabbing her shirt from the log near their heads, where it'd dried in front of the long-dead fire, he handed it to her.

While she pulled it on, he walked to the edge of the clearing.

He was still standing there mentally flogging himself when she cleared her throat.

Grimacing, he faced the music and turned to her, searching her expression for any signs of distress, fury, or more of that gut-wrenching humiliation and shame he'd seen yesterday.

Nothing. She was showing nothing. "Harley, I'm—"

"Sorry," she said softly at the same time as he did.

He stared at her. "Yeah."

"That was entirely my fault," she said.

He was educated. He helped run a successful business. People paid him shocking amounts of money to be good in any of a variety of dangerous, life-threatening situations. Yet when he opened his mouth, the only thing that came out was a brilliant, "*huh?*"

"I started it." She let her gaze drop over his bare chest before she caught herself and closed her eyes, pressing the heels of her hands against them. "God. I'm such a slut when it comes to you. You have no idea how much that pisses me off."

When she whirled away and headed toward her backpack, he stared at her back and felt a reluctant grin tug at his mouth. "You started it?"

He wasn't surprised when she didn't answer.

Even so, somehow knowing she felt that way made him feel a helluva lot better, even if it was possible he was going to die of blood loss from the hard-on he was still sporting. "You started it?" he repeated dumbly.

"I said so, didn't I?" She was ripping through the mess that was her pack. "It's almost dawn. I need my camera."

He moved closer, risking life and limb. "You're a slut when it comes to me?"

Her head whipped around so fast for a moment he thought she'd turned into the little girl in *The Exorcist*. "Don't you dare laugh." She paused and drew a breath. "Okay. I realize that there's possibly an etiquette here." She eyeballed his crotch and grimaced in guilt. "After all, you gave me an, um . . ."

He arched a brow. "Orgasm?"

"Yes." She blushed. "That. And I didn't . . ." She gestured with her finger in the general direction of his button fly.

"Do me in return?" he finished for her.

She closed her eyes. "I . . . owe you."

"Are you offering?"

Her mouth fell open, and he let out a low laugh. Her eyes narrowed and she shoved a toothbrush into her mouth, vanishing into the woods.

He shook his head, grabbed his own toothbrush, and made his way into the woods in the *opposite* direction.

By the time he got back, Harley was peeling an orange. She looked up at him, for a single beat, her gaze both soft and unguarded, and he felt an odd catch deep inside.

Then she blinked and the moment was gone. She handed him half of the orange.

"Thanks." He had no idea what she was thinking. "You okay?"

"Don't worry, TJ. I know what that was. Or rather, what it *wasn't*."

"Okay, good. Maybe you can explain it to me."

She shoved a piece of orange in her mouth. "We're going to be okay. All we have to do is get back to where we were."

"You mean home?"

"No." She gave him a *duh* look. "I mean metaphorically. We need to get back to basics. Back to ignoring each other. And/or bickering."

"I see," he said, when he really didn't see at all.

"I mean something *real* between us would never work," she said. "Knowing that makes it easier. Right?"

"Right." Christ, she was making him dizzy. Or maybe that was because most of his blood was still drained out of his brain and in his—

"It's not like you're even around to be a boyfriend," she said, still talking, still under the apparent illusion that he was following her logic. "You're gone all the time. You like women in your bed but not your life. Et cetera, et cetera." She sucked on a piece of orange and blew a few of his brain cells.

"So trust me," she continued. "I don't look at you and think relationship. Mostly I look at you and think I wish I had something to hit you over the head with."

He blinked. "So I should stay at arm's length then?"

"Eight to ten inches should do it."

She'd walked away by the time the laugh tumbled out of him, but he didn't remain amused. He'd just been thoroughly put in his place, dumped before he could even think about doing the dumping.

Even more disconcerting, he got it. He got her. Because he knew her better than she wanted to admit. He knew that thanks to her sweet, hippy-throwback parents, she'd grown up with an utter lack of tradition, and he knew she secretly yearned for exactly that.

She wanted a solid, stand-up guy, with a white picket fence and two point four kids. Which is what had drawn her to Nolan. Nolan was one of those solid, stand-up guys, one who'd absolutely give her what she needed.

Unlike him. "Harley—"

"Ignoring each other," she said. "Remember?"

Yeah.

Her eyes drifted to his bare chest, then darted away, but not before he caught the flare of heat.

"I'm going to have a hard time ignoring you when you're looking at me like I'm lunch," he said, reaching for his shirt.

"I'll work on that. Maybe you could get fat or ugly or something." Ignoring his laugh, she sat on the edge of the ridge as dawn rode in, banishing the last of the dark, bringing first a deep violet, then a lighter purple, and finally pink into the sky. TJ sat with her, and in silence they watched Mother Nature do her glorious thing.

As the sky lightened, far below a handful of coyotes moved through the meadow, looking for breakfast. TJ counted four coyotes and . . . "What the hell? That looks like"—he sat up straighter—"a badger?"

"You've never seen that?" Harley asked, looking through her camera lens. "The two breeds have a sort of symbiotic relationship when they need to. The coyote can run, but they're not good diggers. And the badger—"

"Can dig but not run." He grinned. "They're working together for breakfast. Amazing."

The only sound was the hum of insects and early morning bird chatter, since Harley's long-lens digital camera snapped silently. "Look," she murmured, leaning into him to show him her LED screen and a gorgeous shot of one of the coyotes up close, nose quivering in the air as the animals caught their scent on the morning air.

"You're good," he murmured, turning his face into her hair.

"It's the camera."

"It's more than the camera." He pulled back and looked at her. "Hell, Harley, you really should come work for us."

"Why?"

"Well, for money, for one thing. Our clients would pay big bucks for you to document their trips."

Standing, she pulled on her pack. "I'm going to try to fix the equipment on that west ridge."

He pulled on his pack also, and they headed out. Normally, being on the mountain in the morning was his favorite time. The air was crisp with a hint of the warmth the day would bring, and the residual dew made everything sparkle. Far above, the majestic peaks were still snow-tipped. The ground beneath their feet was soft and spongy from the rain, everything around them bursting with fall colors.

"So," he said after a few minutes. "Why exactly aren't we going to follow through with this thing between us?"

"There is no *thing*, TJ."

"Really? 'Cause it felt like a thing this morning when I made you come."

She tripped, and sent him a glare. "No-talking zone."

He grinned. She was walking with attitude, and she was sexy as hell. "You want me," he said.

"No talking."

"I want you back," he told her. "I think I've proved that. So what's the problem?"

"My problem?" She stopped so abruptly he nearly plowed her over when she whipped around to gape at him. "It's you! It's always been you!"

He raised a brow.

She blew out a breath and pushed him in front of her to walk in the lead. "You drive me crazy," he heard her mutter.

"Maybe, but you're watching my ass as I walk."

"Yeah, well, it's a great ass," she admitted, surprising a laugh out of him. After about five minutes, she sighed. "Okay, it's possible I overreacted back there."

"No. Really?"

"My problem isn't you, per se," she said. "But more the way I seem to react to you."

"Is that an apology?"

"For what?"

"For molesting me in my sleep."

"I was kind of hoping we could forget about that."

Normally that would be fine with him. After all, he never begged a woman to want him, and he didn't plan to start now. If she hadn't been interested, he would have let it go.

But she *was* interested. Interested enough to come all over him, panting his name as she did. It'd been erotic as hell.

Which left him confused. He glanced back at her. She was small and curvy, and walking with an attitude that was making him hot.

Oh, wait.

He was already hot.

Their little wake-up call might have cooled *her* jets, but his were still on and ready to go.

Halfway up to the impaired camera, they came to a natural gorge. Just on the other side, up about fifty more feet, was the ledge where the camera was placed. Between there and where they stood was what was normally just a low-lying creek. But the rain had it swollen and rushing like a raging river. It was a good twenty feet wide, knee-deep in the middle, and roaring over slippery rocks. Worse, on either side, the banks were muddy and unstable.

Harley was standing at the edge with a funny look on her face.

"What?" he asked.

"There are frogs."

"There are always frogs. Especially after a rain."

"Doing it."

He looked down at the rocks she was staring at. Yep, she was right. There were frogs doing it.

"Don't stare," she said, and made him laugh.

"Maybe there's something in the air," he said hopefully, and then it was her to turn to laugh.

She moved a little bit downstream and then closer to the edge of the water just as a fish leapt straight up into the air and then dove back under. With a startled gasp, Harley took a step back and caught her heel on a rock. She would have gone down, but TJ caught her.

Instead of pulling immediately free of him, she turned within the circle of his arms to face him, further surprising him when her fingers fisted in his shirt.

"You okay?" he asked, holding onto her. "Your ankle?"

"I'm good." And yet she didn't let go. Instead she stared up into his eyes.

TJ wondered what she saw when she looked at him like that, all soft and unguarded, as if maybe she saw things in him that he didn't, couldn't. And suddenly *he* felt unguarded, and before he could stop himself, he dipped his head and ran the tip of his nose along her jaw.

"Time to cross," she said shakily, and turned to stare at the water. Then, without another word, she started to step into it.

"What are you doing?"

"I need to get to the other side." She looked at him over her shoulder. "You can wait here if you want. Or—"

"Yeah, yeah, or head back. Just hold up a minute." He took her hand, and waited until she met his gaze. "Trust me?"

"With my life or my body?"

He shook his head and guided her farther up the mountain, out of their way. About a quarter of a mile later, the water slowed and narrowed, but more important they weren't near a sharp turn, with an unsteady and precarious hillside that looked as if it might go at any moment.

She looked at the new spot, then at him, conceding. "Your knife, your Fritos, your expertise. You're a handy guy, TJ."

"Handy," he repeated, and watched her expression change as she remembered just how "handy" he'd been in the sleeping bag.

"I didn't expect the water to be this high this late in the season," she admitted.

"Fall can be risky." He looked around and found a wrist-thick, chest-high stick with a natural fork at one end for wedging between rocks, which he handed to Harley. "Use this as a staff."

He searched the thick growth for another one for him, then grabbed her arm when Harley would have headed across. "Wait. Lose your shoes and socks first."

He kicked his boots off and attached them to his backpack by their laces, then rolled up his pants. "We'll have better traction in bare feet. Plus, having dry shoes on the other side will be a bonus."

She bent and untied her boots and pulled off her socks, stuffing them into her pack.

He smiled at her bright pink toenails, and knew it was yet another peek into the complicated psyche of Harley Stephens. She worked as a mechanic, a woman in a man's world. If she wasn't covered from head to toe in coveralls and grease, then she was behind a desk analyzing data by herself. The toenails seemed to be her concession to being a woman beneath it all. "Pretty. Come on." He went first, sucking in a breath as the icy water washed over his feet and halfway up his calves.

"Holy shit!" she squeaked, following him.

Grinning, he reached back for her hand and led the way.

CHAPTER 12

On the other side of the creek, Harley shivered as they climbed to dry ground. "Nothing like a refreshing stream to wake a girl up."

"Really," he said dryly. "Is that what woke you up, or was it when I—"

"Stop," she said with a low laugh, and shivered—and not from the cold.

TJ smiled at her, his eyes warm with approval as he handed her a chamois from his backpack to dry off her feet. "I've taken groups out here for fly-fishing in the streams, biking up nonexistent trails, rock climbing off the cliff. Tough, experienced clients in much warmer temps than this, and every one of them would have been whining at what we just did. Hell, even Cam would be complaining."

"So I'm tougher than Cam?"

He grinned. "Much."

His smile had the usual effect on her, meaning she was rendered momentarily stupid. She was sitting on a rock, pulling her socks from her shoes, when he sat next to her, thighs touching. And then his hands were on her shoulders, turning her, pulling her back to his chest to whisper in her ear. "Across the water, two o'clock."

A hundred yards over a black bear stalked the edge of the water, walking away from them, her shoulders moving powerfully with each step. Behind her rollicked two bear cubs, waiting for mama to catch breakfast.

Harley's breath caught in her throat as she slipped her hand into her backpack for her camera and started snapping.

They watched in awed silence as the bear charged into the churning water, splashing, pouncing, striking out with a plate-sized paw, coming back up with a large fish in its mouth. Fur dripping, she turned to her babies, who were far more interested in romping at the water's edge than eating. Mama admonished them with a nudge, and they wandered off.

When they were gone, Harley realized she was practically in TJ's lap, and his arms were around her. "Don't get much of that from behind my computer."

He watched as she put away the camera and reached for her shoes. "This Colorado job. It's a research position then? No fieldwork?"

"Almost all research, with very little if any fieldwork."

He didn't say a word. And she didn't either. But she thought maybe he was wondering why she'd chosen research instead of field study.

At the moment, she was wondering the same. Concentrating on that, she tugged her laces tight, and one snapped off in her hand. "Crap."

TJ went to his pack and pulled out the same pouch he'd pulled out the other night, the one that had held the smaller bag of Fritos. From it he withdrew . . . dental floss. "Shoelace."

She stared at it, then slowly took it out of his fingers. "I think I'm in love with your backpack."

"And my sleeping bag."

"Yeah. That, too."

"And my sexy bod."

She slid him a look. "What did I tell you about that?"

"You said not to bring up *your* sexy bod. I didn't do that. I brought up mine." He smiled innocently. "So what else are you in love with?"

When she didn't say a word, he smiled. "Let me guess. Me."

"Ha."

He went quiet a moment. "There are all kinds of love, Harley."

This stopped her. "How many kinds?"

"Well, there's the deeply affectionate kind," he pointed out. "Like you'd feel for family. Although sometimes it's more . . . murderous than deep affection."

"I'll buy that," she said.

"And then there's the love you feel for someone you're attracted to."

"You mean lust," she corrected.

"That, too, but I'm talking about more than one hot night. Like maybe you want to be with that person—for now."

She eyed him, curious. Was he talking about them? "Without the commitment."

"Yeah."

"For people who have a short attention span, or are afraid to go deeper."

"Maybe."

"Like every fling you've ever had?" she asked sweetly.

"Calling the kettle black?"

"Hey, I haven't had a fling in forever," she said.

"It's not the quantity . . ."

Knowing he was right, she held her tongue. For a moment. "I've never known you to be afraid of anything. I mean, I've seen you huck yourself off a cliff with your brothers with just a snowboard on your feet and live to tell the tale. I've seen you hanging off a rock that you free-climbed without a rope, nothing saving you from certain death except your own fingertips. Hell, I've even seen you face down a pissed-off rattlesnake."

His eyes never left hers. "Those are all physical things."

"You saying you're afraid of something as simple as an emotion?"

He didn't respond—which she supposed was answer enough. Who was she to press the issue, because when it came to that particular fear, they were in perfect accord. "So say you're right," she said, needing to lighten the mood. "And that there are all kinds of love.

"Yeah?"

"Then I guess it is entirely possible that I love you."

He tripped over his own feet, something she'd never, ever, seen him do, and she smiled. "In the way I loved watching those bears," she continued. "With a healthy respect and a good amount of distance for my well-being."

"Now who's the funny one?" he asked.

TJ followed Harley to the broken surveillance equipment on the ridge. She'd put on a pair of sunglasses and some ChapStick, both having taken her a good long time to find in her backpack, which made him shake his head.

But God, he loved to watch her.

"What?" she asked.

"Nothing."

"You're smiling."

"All right. Maybe"—he stroked a finger over her temple— "maybe I love you, too." He heard her breath catch. "In the same way that we both loved that hungry, *grumpy* bear."

She let out a low laugh. "So we're even."

"Even."

At the ridge, Harley sat next to the nonfunctioning camera equipment and got to work while TJ accessed his messages. Stone had two client calls for him to return regarding new upcoming winter trips. Good. Cam needed TJ to go for a tux fitting before Katie killed him—not good. And Nick had a question for Harley. "Nick wants to know if you've kicked my ass yet."

"It's still a possibility."

TJ grinned. "Do you want to check in with anyone?"

"Most definitely not." She shrugged at his unspoken question. "The joys of family."

There were plenty of times he and his brothers drove each other halfway to the insane asylum, but they had each others' backs, always.

Harley's parents weren't together, but they got along. They didn't get drunk and beat on their kids, they'd always managed to put food on the table, and yet he knew, sweet and kind as they were, that Harley absolutely did not get the same support from her family that he got from his.

Her parents let their whims drive them. Whatever happened, happened. Harley had always needed more than that whimsical existence, and her hopes and dreams baffled her family. They loved her but didn't understand her.

In spite of that basic lack of understanding and support, Harley had grown up incredibly strong, solidly grounded, and was the most softhearted person he knew. Not that she'd thank him for that assessment. She didn't like to be soft, and she didn't do need. Ever. "I know you're working so hard to help out your parents," he said. "And Skye. If you ever need—"

"I don't." She glanced over and sent him a smile to gentle her tone. "And you'd do the same thing if you had to for your family. You *have* done the same thing."

So she remembered. Remembered what it was like for him to be the oldest, to put everything in his teenage life aside to make sure Cam and Stone were cared for. "That was all a long time ago."

"You don't talk much about growing up," she said quietly. "Even though I know it was bad. Especially when your father was still alive."

Everyone in Wishful had known his father and his infamous temper. He'd been a pro bull rider who'd been rough on his animals and rougher on his sons. Mostly the youngest, Cam, who TJ had stepped in to protect whenever he could, usually at his own peril. "Like I said, it was a long time ago."

"And yet you make sure to spend as much time away from here as you can."

"I'm an expedition and adventure guide," he said. "By the very definition, I *have* to be gone."

"Your brothers are guides, too. But they don't do the three-month Alaska trips, one right after another. They don't traipse across Canada or wherever. They stick."

"And because they do, I go," he said. "Look, *someone's* got to do those trips. They're high-end, big-bucks trips that provide us with the majority of our income."

"TJ," she said with terrifying gentleness. "Now who's the liar?" She held his gaze, letting that sink in. "You and I both know that there's plenty of business right here. At home."

Since that happened to be true, he said nothing.

"So what are you running from?"

Well, hell. How she'd turned this around on him, he had no idea. "I'll tell if you tell."

"You will not."

"I will," he said, and waited while she gave him a long, considering look.

Finally, she blew out a sigh. "I'm running from the poverty on my heels and a possible lifetime of dirty fingernails." She flashed him a tight smile. "I don't want to be like my mom, always needing to depend on others, always in a bind, always unhappy. I want to have a job that fulfills me *and* pays the bills."

"Nothing wrong with that," he said.

She nodded her agreement of that, then gestured to him. "Now you."

"The camera . . ."

She patted it. "It's going to make it. It's motion- and air pressure–sensitive, and calibrated to allow for winds up to fifty miles per hour. But that windstorm we had last week, with the gusts up to seventy-five miles per hour, knocked it out of whack. I've reset it." She arched a brow. "Now you," she repeated.

Fuck. "Okay, it's like this. When I was young and I needed to escape, I'd hit the trail." He didn't go into what he'd needed to escape from. "Depending on the season, I'd grab my bike or my skis and I'd vanish." No drunk-ass father, no school, nothing but his own wits. "Now I no longer need to run from anything, but . . ."

"It's still your go to," she said softly, understanding in her warm eyes. "Your escape."

"Yeah." He let out a long, slow breath he hadn't realized he'd been holding and lifted a shoulder. "It's where I feel the most . . . alive," he said simply. "But now, lately . . ." He shook his head. "The lodge is all weddings and babies and *kittens*. I'm surprised there's not a fucking rainbow hanging over the roof. Cam took flowers to Katie at her office."

She laughed. "That's sweet."

"He's done it every day this week. It's some sort of an anniversary thing. You can't even see Katie at her desk anymore. It's like she's working in a florist shop. And then there's Stone. He's still trying to rope Emma in, so he's doing all this shit to impress her, and getting himself hurt so she has to treat him. The guy is a walking Band-Aid."

"It's love, TJ. Not some lesser degree of love, but the real deal."

"It's a little over the top."

She was quiet a moment. "You don't believe in the real deal love?"

"I didn't say that."

"Then what? What about the real deal love gets to you?"

How about it hurt like hell? "Like I said, there are all kinds of love," he said carefully. "Something different for everybody. This kind, this 'real deal' as you call it, I'm not sure it's for everyone, that's all."

She looked at him for a long moment. "I know this will shock you, but I happen to agree with you."

Once again he found himself letting out a long breath he hadn't even realized he was holding. He couldn't help it. She kept surprising him, kept worming her way into his heart.

And making him rethink his stance on just about everything, including the whole love thing. He took her hand and ran a thumb over her fingers, enjoying the contact in a way he rarely did with anyone else. "Did we just agree on something?"

"I think we did."

"I hope it's a trend."

"Ditto."

Cupping her face, he pulled her up against him for the sheer pleasure of it. "You were right before. You scare the hell out of me, Harley."

"Again," she said softly. "Ditto."

"You might have been the one with a crush on me growing up, but I've had a crush on you for several years," he admitted. "I don't know why. I think it was all that bickering we did, it always made me"—he flashed her a grin—"hot."

She rolled her eyes and made him laugh.

"Every party, every get-together, every pool game, it all drove me crazy," he said.

"You never said."

"I hid it behind a helluva lot of long trips." He smiled grimly. "And a lot of cold showers."

She stared at him, her eyes soft. "I never knew."

"I never meant you to. You're not the only one who can hide their feelings." He nudged her in even closer. "The truth is, Harley, what I feel for you could slip right past lust into uncharted waters if I let it."

She swallowed hard. "If you let it?"

"Don't worry. I'm working on it."

"Okay." She nodded, but then shook her head and closed her eyes. "Maybe we should go back to the bickering. Bickering was so easy."

"Think we can?" He nudged her with his knee, slid a hand up her back, and felt her practically melt into him, which was more than a little gratifying. "Really?"

She left her eyes closed and dropped her head to his shoulder. "We can try like hell." The doubt was heavy in her voice. "We're both tough, we're fighters. We can do this."

"Yeah." But a small part of him wondered if they were fighting a battle that had already been lost.

CHAPTER 13

"So what now?" TJ asked after Harley had finished with the camera.

"The next camera." She consulted the GPS and her maps. "I think I can hike to it and be back by nightfall." She looked up and found him watching her.

They were still sitting side by side. Their thighs were touching. Purely by accident, she decided. The log they were sitting on wasn't all that big.

But when he leaned close and offered her a bottle of water, there was nothing accidental about the zing that went straight through her body, making her thighs clench together. She looked up into his face to see if he noticed.

His eyes were on hers, deep and steady. And heated.

He'd noticed.

Fighting this, she reminded herself. Be tough. "Thanks," she said quietly and set the water down.

"You need to stay hydrated."

"I'm tired of peeing in the woods."

"It's not that bad."

"Says the guy who gets to pee standing up without exposing vital parts."

He slid her a look.

"Okay, so you have to expose *one* vital part." One *really* vital part. "Big deal."

He grinned and offered her dried mangoes and beef jerky from his pack.

"Thanks." She dipped her hand into the bag.

TJ leaned forward to grab another water for himself and the length of their thighs pressed together again. She could have pulled free but she didn't, and when he straightened back up, opening the bottle of water, his biceps brushed her arm and the side of her breast.

Her breath caught.

He drank long and deep, his throat working. He stopped when he sensed her staring at him and licked a drop of water off his upper lip. A small insect landed on his shoulder. Without thinking, Harley leaned in, pursed her lips, and blew.

TJ's eyes went to her mouth. "What was that?"

"You had a bug. I blew it away."

His eyes seemed to darken at the word "blew." "Do me a favor."

"I already owe you a . . . favor."

His eyes smoldered at that. "There's no debt between us, but don't blow on me like that again unless you mean it."

Okay, good to know. Suddenly parched herself, she drank some of her water, but not nearly as gracefully as he had, managing to dribble several drops down the front of her.

Both their gazes went to her chest. He made a noise, low in his throat as he exhaled.

"I'm messy," she whispered.

His eyes lifted back to hers, heated. "I like messy."

She took a gulp of air.

"What now?" he murmured.

Um, we forget the being tough thing and have wild sex against a tree? "We should find something to bicker about and fast."

He laughed softly. "I meant regarding your work."

Oh. Right. She struggled to concentrate. "East ridge."

"There and back before nightfall, and then . . ."

"And then I hike home in the morning," she said.

"You're not a you. You're a we."

Until they get back. While they were out here. After that, it was back to real life. Suddenly she wished all the cameras were down and she had an excuse to stay out there with him for longer.

"What will you do when you get home?" he asked quietly.

She lifted a shoulder. "Keep working the research internship until spring."

"And work long hours at the garage?"

"Yes."

"And worry about your parents. And your sister."

"Yeah, and stress about whether or not taking the Colorado job is the right thing to do. It's called life, TJ. *You* work long hours, *you* worry about your family. It's what we do."

"You're questioning taking the Colorado job?"

Trust him to anchor in on the one thing really bothering her. "No." She squeezed her eyes shut, then opened them. "Yes."

"Tell me."

"Maybe . . . maybe the research position is the wrong angle. Maybe being out here fulfills me like it does you." She met his gaze. "What do you think?" she asked, honestly wanting to hear what he'd do, even though a part of her already knew. He'd do what was right, not necessarily what was easy. Taking the job, if it was offered, was the easy route. Figuring out what would fulfill her, what would make her happy, would be better.

He looked at her for a long moment. "It's your decision to make."

"Thanks. You've been a big help."

"I think you already know what you want to do. I think you know you want to be out here and not at a desk, but you're worrying about everyone other than yourself. That, or you're scared."

"Of what?"

"Of admitting you don't always have the answers. Of disappointing yourself. Of making a mistake. Of taking a real risk. Hell, I don't know, Harley, pick one."

How about all of the above?

His smile was gentle. "Sorry you asked?"

"Hard to be, when you're right."

"I like being right." He reached for her hand and entwined their fingers. "Think of yourself, for once, Harley. Do what works for you."

Her throat went a little tight. "TJ?"

"Yeah?"

"Do you really think we can do this? Be friends? After all this time?"

He let out a low, deep breath, but surprised her by giving her an honest answer. "I want to think so."

Well, that was something at least.

"But you'll have to stop talking about blow jobs."

"All I did was blow away a bug!"

"I think it's the word blow." He shifted as he thought about it, then nodded. "Yeah. It is."

She rolled her eyes as his phone vibrated, then watched as his good humor vanished as he took the call. "What is it?" She asked when he was done.

"Search and Rescue. There are two people missing from Red Rock as of last night."

"Red Rock . . ."

"About three hours north of here by foot." He looked at her, clearly conflicted. He didn't want to leave her alone, but this was his job.

"Go," she said. "They need you. I'll be fine."

"You're just going out to that east ridge and back to the same spot for the night, yes?"

"Yes. And then home in the morning. I'll probably be back in town before you. I'll be fine."

Still he hesitated.

"TJ, go. Don't worry. You've taught me some good tricks."

He opened his pack and lifted his Maglite. "You have one of these?"

She rolled her eyes. "Yes."

"Extra batteries?"

"Uh huh." *Somewhere.*

"Enough food and water?"

"TJ, I'm a big girl. I won't be a responsibility to you."

"You're not a job to me, Harley," he said, his voice low and serious. "You're much more than that. Here." He handed her the magic goodie bag from his pack.

Her heart tugged hard, but she tried to hide it behind a quip. "Aw, your dental floss and Fritos. How sweet."

"Smart-ass." He went to take the bag back, but she grabbed it and hugged it to her. Then she shifted close. "Thanks," she whispered, letting him see that she meant it. Going up on tiptoes, she set her hands on his biceps and kissed his jaw.

At the contact, he closed his eyes, as if her touch meant something to him. His arms came around her hard, and he pressed his face into her hair. They stayed like that for a moment, frozen in time, and it wasn't until she finally pulled away that his eyes locked with hers.

And she froze again, barely breathing as his hand came up and trailed his fingers across her temple, over her throat, down her arm, where he took her hand and squeezed. "You're welcome," he said just as softly, then kissed her, his mouth warm as he lingered for only a second before pulling away. He reached into the bag he'd given her and showed her the mace. "Shake hard to activate it if you have to use it. And trust me on this—stand upwind."

"TJ—"

He handed her something else. "A stun gun. Although if you get close enough to a bear or a pissed-off pack of coyotes to need it, you'd better mean business." He showed her how to use it, then looked at her for a long moment. "Harley—"

"I'm going to be fine."

"Yeah, you will. That's not what I was going to say." He waited until she looked at him, until she could see the seriousness of his expression. "Don't be timid. If you feel like you're being watched, or your instincts start screaming about anything, have this in hand. Promise me."

She paused, then nodded.

"Give me your cell."

"Why?"

He just held out his hand.

Quandary. She had a feeling she knew what he wanted with it. He wanted to put his number in. Thing was, she already had it, and didn't really want him to see.

"Harley."

With a sigh, she caved and slapped the phone into his big palm.

He flicked it open. "I want you to call me if you have any problems."

"There won't be." She watched him thumb through her contacts and began to panic. He was going to see . . .

"Humor me." He narrowed his gaze on her screen. "You have Stone and Cam in here, but not me."

She winced and tried to grab the phone back. Better he think that than find the truth. "I'll add you."

But instead of handing her the phone, he punched in his number himself, then went to save it, only as she knew it would, it came up as an existing number. "Um—" she started. "I . . ."

Too late. He was staring at the screen. "I *am* in here."

Crap. She bit her lower lip. "Yeah."

He cut his eyes to hers. "Under *Sexy Jerk*?"

She finally managed to snatch her phone back. "Should have seen it last month when you brought that leggy brunette chick into Moody's for a game of pool," she said with a defensive jerk of her shoulder.

TJ was looking at her, eyes unfocused as he tried to remember, because apparently he knew too many leggy brunettes. Then suddenly, he smiled. "She was a client."

That hadn't seemed to matter. What *had* mattered was that they'd clearly just been riding mountain bikes, and still in their gear, they'd been all hot and sweaty and laughing. "You were listed as *Butthead*, then."

His lips twitched. "Good to know I'm moving up in your world."

"I'll change it again."

He didn't look excited about that. "Yes, but to what?"

Good question.

CHAPTER 14

TJ caught up with Stone and the rest of the Search and Rescue team at Red Rock. Stone handed TJ a bag of gear and TJ dropped his pack and crouched down to reload. "What's the story?"

"Two teens." Stone's expression was grim. "Vanished at first light two days ago. They were camping with their parents and another family."

TJ grunted in acknowledgement as he worked. "They take anything with them?"

"Daddy's flask."

Shit. "Okay, let's get this the hell over with." When he looked up from preparing his gear, he found Stone staring down at him. "What?"

"Get this the hell over with? You love this stuff. Plus you weren't even on a job. What's the matter, we pull you away from something good?"

Since Stone knew damn well what TJ had been doing, he didn't bother to respond.

In spite of the seriousness of the situation, Stone crouched at TJ's side and took a moment out to give his brother some shit. "Would it have anything to do with a certain research biologist we both know and love?"

When TJ didn't answer that either, instead just continuing to switch his gear from one pack to the other, shoving things in without taking his usual care, Stone grinned. "Aw, man, look at you all flustered. You're really in a hurry to get back."

TJ surged to his feet and shouldered his pack. "Shut up."

Stone barked out a low laugh. "No can do. Plan of action?"

"Securing your big, fat mouth."

"You mean keeping me from telling Emma, Annie, Nick, and Cam that you're so caught up with a certain hot sexy blonde that you didn't organize your backpack with meticulous care?"

TJ flipped him the bird and walked away.

Stone easily caught up, a stupid grin on his ugly mug. "Oh, I'm going to enjoy this even more than I thought."

"The rescue?"

"Watching you make a fool of yourself over a woman."

"Never going to happen."

"There you go, tempting karma again."

Harley made it to the east ridge and back by early evening, with an hour or so of daylight to spare. She'd had no surprises along the way, for which she was grateful, and had been able to replace the bad battery pack on the camera.

It'd been another warm Indian summer day. When she got back to where she and TJ had spent the night before, it took her about one minute to decide she wanted to bathe in the creek. Stripping felt a little brazen, but she hadn't seen or heard signs of another soul, so she decided to brave it.

When she was done, she sat at the cliff to watch the sun set, hoping to catch a glimpse of the coyotes. As dusk fell, she heard the yips and watched breathlessly as first one, then two, then three coyotes appeared in that last motionless beat between daylight and nightfall.

As they tipped their heads up and began their nightly howls, goose bumps rose on her skin at the eerie beauty. She took as many pictures as she could until the light was completely gone, and then suddenly the coyotes were gone, too, and she was utterly alone.

And that's when it hit her, when she realized that she had an entire night to get through by herself. Time for a rip-roaring fire.

But to her frustration, she couldn't get it to light, not even with one of TJ's magic Fritos under the kindling. Chip number two didn't work either, nor chip number twelve.

So she sat in the growing dark and ate them. She ate them all, and when they were gone, her stomach hurt.

And it was really dark.

What now? She'd never been the girl to call for help. The path of needing someone had always irritated her. It reminded her of her mom, much as she loved the woman. Harley liked to depend on no one but herself.

But that path seemed like a cold one tonight. She blew out a breath, pulled out her cell phone, scrolled through her contacts for the Sexy Jerk—she really needed to change that—and called him.

"Miss me already?" he asked in a quiet voice, as if maybe he wasn't alone.

Which reminded her—he was in the middle of a rescue, and she was interrupting. "I'm sorry, I didn't think—never mind."

"Are you okay?"

"Yes, but I can't get a chip to light. What am I doing wrong?"

"Try a pile of chips, not just one."

She hesitated. "I ate them."

She could almost hear his smile. "Did you eat the bag, too?" he asked.

She blew out a breath. "No."

"Then light that. The oils are still in it."

She kept the cell in the crook of her shoulder as she held a lit match to the bag and *whoosh,* she got fire. "Thank you."

"Anytime."

"You keep giving." *And giving.* "I'm running up a tab here."

"I told you, no tab. Ever." His voice lowered. "So . . . about that missing me thing."

"What about it?" she asked warily.

"What are you wearing?"

She rolled her eyes and hung up. She used his utility knife to open another can of soup, and set it near the flames to heat.

She hoped TJ had a spare knife on him.

Which was ridiculous. Of course he did. And why was she wasting energy worrying about him? She'd never met anyone better equipped to take care of himself. Crouching in front of the fire, she held out her chilled hands. The night wasn't that cold, it was more nerves than anything else. Because while she'd planned for this trip, had wanted this trip, had even looked forward to this trip, the reality of being alone out there was suddenly a little daunting.

You were lucky you weren't alone last night, she told herself. So get over it. She got into her sleeping bag fully dressed and ordered herself to sleep.

It took a very long time.

She had no idea how much time passed before she came suddenly wide awake, blinking like an owl. She could see nothing but complete blackness, no stars, no fire, nothing. Panic licked at her and she struggled for a minute before realizing she was completely engulfed by her sleeping bag. Clearing her face gave her fresh air and some meager light from the stars. She peered at the cell phone she was still clutching in her hand.

Four a.m.

She'd done it, she'd made it, with no problems. Or almost, anyway. She smiled at that, then went still at the odd noise in the woods behind her. Not the harmless hum of an insect, or the hoot of a bird, but the snapping of a twig.

Crap.

She slowly crept out of the bag and pulled the mace and her flashlight from her backpack. Feeling far too out in the open, she backed into the woods on the opposite side of the clearing from where she'd heard the noise, and vanished into the dark.

Then, eyes straining, she circled around, hoping to catch sight of whoever was watching her. Her heart was pounding in her ears, her blood pumping through her veins as she shoved the flashlight in her waistband and pulled her phone from her pocket. She had her thumb on her contact list, ready to hit TJ's number, when she saw a shadow walking through the woods about ten yards from her.

Coming right at her.

Little gray dots danced in her vision. She talked herself out of fainting and reviewed her options at the speed of light. Plan A— she could run. Run like hell. Problem with that was she didn't have her pack, which meant she didn't have the GPS or her compass, and in the dark she'd get lost for sure. Plan B—she could scream. That wasn't going to work either, as she doubted the bears and coyotes were going to do anything to help her. Plan C—she could simply go up to him and demand to know why he's spying on her. No. Not big enough balls for that.

Plan D—stun gun. Yeah. That was her best option, and she lifted it at the ready.

He was tall. Built. And . . . and he had familiar unruly hair, a stubbled jaw, and piercing green eyes. "*TJ.*"

He came to a stop before her and looked at the stun gun. "Huh. And here I thought you'd be happy to see me."

"You are so not funny." She pressed a hand to her thumping heart and shivered.

"Cold?"

"No." She shivered again. Fear. Excitement. Maybe going to pass out. "You scared me half to death."

He reached out very carefully and relieved her of the stun gun. "You're shaking."

"I know. Dammit."

He nudged her up against a tree and pressed his body to hers. "It's adrenaline. You need an outlet for it."

"Gee, let me guess." She meant to sound sarcastic, but it was hard to pull that off when she was trembling so hard she was stuttering almost to the point of being unintelligible.

TJ had his hands and forearms flat on the tree, bracketing her head. He was warm, and though his voice had indicated a certain level of frustration, exhaustion, and that bafflement she always seemed to cause in him, she didn't feel threatened.

The opposite.

Which meant that it was official, she was crazy. Certifiably so. Because she wanted to curl into him, wanted to wrap herself up with him and lose herself. Which is *exactly* what would happen if she let her guard down. She had no doubt that a relationship with him, fleeting as it would be, had the major potential to shatter her heart into a thousand pieces.

But God, she wanted another TJ-induced orgasm.

Tipping up her head, she looked into his face. His jaw was dark with almost three days' worth of stubble. His eyes weren't giving much away other than hunger. Hunger for sleep? Hunger for food? Probably.

And hunger for her. No question, she thought, a little shaken at the deep, raw look of desire in his gaze.

Helplessly reacting to that, she shifted against his body, seeking to ease an ache from deep inside.

He let out a low sound. "If you're not doing that on purpose, Harley, you need to stop."

She had no idea what came over her, but she did it again, and felt him respond.

He was hard.

Everywhere.

She dropped her gaze to his mouth, and he groaned as he shifted his hands from the tree to her face, gently cupping it, stroking her jaw with his thumbs. While staring into her eyes, he angled her head to his liking and kissed her. It started out slow, but progressed to holy shit pretty quickly, and then without warning, he lifted his head and looked at her, all sleepy eyed. Before leaning in close again, pressing his mouth to the spot beneath her ear, then her throat as he fisted his hand in her hair to turn her face, exposing the other side of her neck.

She felt his open mouth there, and just the tip of his tongue touched her skin as his other hand slid across her stomach, slipping beneath her shirt.

"I'm starting to forget why this is a bad idea," she said, her own hands making themselves at home on his chest, gliding them back and forth for the sheer delight of feeling the play of his muscles.

"Me, too," he murmured, heading for her mouth again, but she pulled back a fraction, breathing hard.

"I think I have a handle on myself now," she said, knowing that wasn't quite true.

He merely redirected his mouth to her throat, nibbling wet, hot kisses that made her knees wobble. "I've got something else you could get a handle on."

She choked out a laugh.

"Sorry." He grimaced and pressed his forehead to hers. "I'm so fucking tired. I say really weak shit when I'm tired."

She dropped her head to his chest and realized she was still touching him, beneath his shirt, making her no better than him.

He lightly skimmed a warm finger up her spine and made her shiver. "Let's go back to your sleeping bag."

She gave a full body shiver. "Oh, God."

His voice sounded strained. "Is that oh, God *please?*"

Yes, said her body.

What happened to hanging tough? asked her brain.

Stupid, logical, careful brain. "Why were you spying on me?" she asked.

"I wasn't. I didn't see you by the fire and didn't want to scare you into stunning me."

"Where did you think I was?"

"Checking on your equipment, peeing in the woods, I don't know. But I'd armed you myself, and was being cautious." He grinned. "With good reason." He pulled the stun gun from his pocket. "Except you didn't have it on."

"I was working up to that part."

He laughed. "Glad I wasn't a hungry bear."

"You're more dangerous," she muttered, and pushing free, walked back to the fire in tune to his soft laugh. It sounded hollow, and she took a closer look at him. His eyes were lined with exhaustion, his mouth grim. "How did the search and rescue go?" she asked. "You find your missing people?"

"Kids. They are barely teenagers. They'd gone up the Red Rock cliff on a dare and one of them stepped off the cliff. It's a sixty-foot drop."

She gasped. "Are they okay?"

"Yeah. With the ground and slopes so wet and loose, the kid set off a mud slide, which is what saved his life. He caught a roller-coaster ride like no other, though. It was hell to get to him without finishing him off with another slide over the top of him."

Above them, the sky had gone from black to . . . a slightly paler black. Dawn was coming. She looked up and found TJ watching her. Was it her imagination, or was he not looking so tired anymore? Suddenly, she wasn't feeling so tired either.

Uh oh.

His eyes darkened, and she felt the hitch in her breathing. Damn, she really needed to work on her self-control.

"You don't trust yourself around me," he said.

"Not even a little."

"Smart woman," he said softly, with something else in his voice, a quality that said he was proud of her, and also . . . hurt? She'd had absolutely no idea she had that power, and reaching out, she lay a hand on his arm, which was rigid with strength and warmth.

And bloody. "Oh my God. You're hurt."

CHAPTER 15

"It's nothing," TJ turned to tell Harley, pulling his arm back. "Trust me, I've had worse." And he had.

"It's more than nothing." Harley grabbed his hand and tugged, and because he liked her touch, he let her. She squinted against the harsh glare of her flashlight as she tried to see. "You're all cut up. Come sit down." She pulled him to the fire pit and pushed him to a log, putting her hands on her hips as she stood over him. "Are you hurt anywhere else?"

"If I say yes, will you strip-search me?"

She rolled her eyes and pulled out her first aid kit. "We need to wash off the dirt so you don't get an infection."

"I like the 'we.' You can bathe whatever part of me you like."

She laughed, a sweet magical sound that he didn't hear often enough from her. "You wish."

"Aw, you're no fun."

She'd dropped to her knees at his side and stared at him. "I wasn't aware that we were having fun."

"We've had our moments," he said silkily, then laughed softly at her blush, knowing she was remembering yesterday morning, and how he'd made her come.

"Take off your shirt," she commanded softly, wielding antiseptic and gauze.

"I like it when you get all bossy." He yanked his shirt over his head and smiled as her nipples hardened and pressed against her white, long-sleeved T-shirt. *Nice view.*

She ignored him and once again made the antiseptic her friend, going for the largest cut on the underside of his forearm first. He hissed in a breath and she winced as if she hurt for him. Then she lifted the gauze, bent her head, and blew softly.

Good Christ. "What did I tell you about that?"

"That wasn't foreplay. I'm nursing you."

"Yeah, well, my brain's fuzzy on the difference."

She shook her head, probing at the cut. "This one looks deep enough for stitches, TJ."

"Butterfly me up. I'll have Emma look at it when we get back."

"Speaking of Emma, why didn't you go straight home?"

Good question. It was one he'd asked himself more than a few times during his not so pleasant, hard-as-hell middle-of-the-night hike back there. Stone had flat out laughed his ass off at him for skipping the helicopter ride home to come there instead. "I wanted to make sure you were okay."

"According to you," she said, "you already knew I would be. So the question stands. Why?"

Because he cared about her. He might as well deal with that. She cared, too, in spite of trying to keep her distance. She cared deeply, and they both knew it.

In a world where he was often the one in charge, where he was the one doing all the caring, it felt good.

"It's almost dawn," she said softly when he didn't answer. "I want to watch the meadow as light hits."

"From the ridge?"

"Yeah."

He grabbed his pack. "I'll meet you there."

"Where are you going?"

"To the creek to clean up."

Her eyes tracked the length of his body, which seemed to affect her breathing.

"Not too late to soap my back," he told her.

She backed up a step. "I think you can handle it."

"Keeping your distance?"

Her eyes were filled with heat and hunger. For him. Of that, he had no doubt. But there was also a healthy amount of worry and self-preservation there.

And just a tinge of something that stopped him cold.

Fear. He understood it, though he hated it. He'd hurt her once before, all those years ago, and no matter what she said, she hadn't forgotten. That he hadn't known, that he would have done things differently if he *had* known, didn't change the fact that he'd caused her pain.

"That's what the instincts are telling me," she whispered.

He stood up, looking down at her. She'd bowed her head so he couldn't see her expression. "Harley." When she tipped up her face, he ran a gentle finger over her jaw. "Always go with your instincts."

While TJ was gone, Harley sat before the fire pit and tried to think clearly. Here's what she knew. She'd alternately resented TJ and crushed on him for years. But the resentment was gone.

And that, she was discovering, was dangerous.

So damn dangerous.

Because it left only the crush.

Unable to sit, she got up and walked. She'd only meant to pace around the fire pit, but her feet took her to the creek.

Bad feet.

TJ stood at the creek's edge, his back to her. He'd clearly just gotten out. His hair was wet, and a few scattered drops of water dotted his broad, sinewy back.

Even knowing it was rude, she couldn't take her eyes off him. No shirt, jeans riding low on those narrow hips, hair wet and messy, he sat on a rock to tug on clean socks. The muscles in his back bunched and worked as he pulled on his shoes.

Heat slashed low in Harley's belly and spread to all her good spots, and she quickly turned back the way she'd come, back to where she'd slept. She plopped onto the log and was still huffing and puffing when TJ silently and suddenly appeared at her side.

Nearly leaping out of her skin, she jumped up and put a hand to her chest.

He smiled. "What are you doing?"

"Nothing. I was just . . . nothing."

A soft laugh said he'd made her as a liar. "I heard you go running like a bat out of hell. What's the matter, Harley, see something that bothered you?"

Yes. Yes, she was bothered. Hot and bothered. "The big bad wolf."

He laughed again. "Should have stayed and let me show you what big . . . teeth I have."

His hair was still damp and he smelled like soap. He'd pulled on a Wilder Adventures hoodie sweatshirt. He crouched at her side, his arms resting on his thighs, his body language calm and easy. "About last night. Did you hear anything out of the norm?"

She looked into his eyes, the sudden seriousness of his expression making her tummy tighten. "Oh, God. Why?"

He didn't answer.

"Not another dead coyote?" *Please, not another one.*

He shook his head and lifted an empty white Styrofoam cup, complete with lid and straw.

"Trash? Where did you find that?"

"On the opposite side of the clearing from where I came in." He paused, his eyes on hers, still calm, but just behind it, she could sense anger. "It wasn't here when I left you."

She let out a low breath. So someone *had* been with her last night, watching her. "Another hiker?"

His silence said he didn't know. "Come on. Let's do your thing, then get the hell out of Dodge."

They sat on the plateau waiting for the sunrise. Harley pulled out her binoculars. "Still too dark to see down to the meadow floor," she murmured.

TJ dug into his backpack and handed her . . .

"Night-vision goggles?" She stared at him, then grinned as she took them. "Okay, I take back all the bad things I ever thought of you."

"But bad good, right?"

"Ha." And *yes*. She slipped on the goggles and hummed in pleasure. "Wow! These are amazing! Think the Forest Service would ever issue these?"

"At nearly four g's a pop, I doubt it."

Holy shit. She turned to him, able to see him perfectly. "Why do you have them?"

"It's a new toy that just came in. Stone brought them to me." Reaching out, he tugged at a strand of hair. "We like to play."

No kidding! Even in the dark she could feel the force of his personality, the heat in his dark gaze. "Too bad playing with you is more dangerous than playing with matches."

He said nothing to that, but the gleam in his eyes suggested her assessment might be true. He turned and looked out into the dark, leaving her to her thoughts.

Suddenly, she had to know. "TJ?"

"Yeah."

"So we're doing this, becoming . . . friends?"

"Yeah."

He sounded a lot more sure than she felt. But if they managed it, she knew she couldn't have a better man for the job. He was intelligent, funny, strong hearted, and steady as a rock.

And yet . . .

And yet she didn't see them being *just* friends. Not with this crazy heat between them. Eventually, he'd wear her down with his sexy innuendos, with the sheer magnitude of his hotness.

He'd ruin her for all other men.

She'd never be the same.

He'd ruin her for Nolan, whom she hadn't thought about all night. With a grimace, she adjusted the goggles and watched for any movement in the meadow below. In the distance she caught sight of three deer, leaping through the bush, bounding gracefully with mind-boggling speed.

Something had startled them.

Probably something that had set sights on them for breakfast. Coyotes?

Or maybe whoever had been drinking from that Styrofoam cup.

She didn't want something ominous there in her favorite place on earth, but it happened. It happened everywhere, and if she was being honest, it especially happened there in the Sierras, in real time. It was called the circle of life.

They'd seen it yesterday in its most vicious form when they'd come across the shot coyote. The irony didn't escape her, that the mountains she loved with all her heart, the place that she needed in order to be happy, could also bring death so swiftly.

But the fact remained. Those mountains *were* deadly, and the rescue last night had almost proven that. Every single season at least one tragedy occurred because someone got stupid, lazy, or lost their concentration while doing something dangerous. Hell, even TJ and his brothers weren't immune. A year and a half ago, Cam had nearly killed himself in a snowboarding accident. Stone had had a couple of close calls on S&R. And TJ had lost Sam.

What would she lose, she wondered.

First you have to actually *have* something to lose, she reminded herself. Her life hadn't lent itself to that, but she was working on changing it. She was getting herself where she wanted to be, and for the first time she could honestly say she was trying to move toward a life she could enjoy.

"Deep thoughts?" TJ asked.

"Did you know how much your work would come to define you?"

He looked at her for a long moment. "Are you looking for definition, Harley?"

"Maybe."

He was quiet a moment. "When we first started Wilder Adventures, it was about getting food in our bellies and keeping a roof over our heads, doing the only thing we knew how to do well. Getting paid to play was a bonus."

"And now?"

"And now . . . now I can't imagine doing anything else." He paused. "Is that how you feel about wildlife biology?"

It was her turn to pause, as she looked at the blazing glory of dawn. She handed him back the night-vision goggles. "Yes. But I don't think I have the job right yet."

He smiled and slung an arm over her shoulders. "You will."

"You sound so sure."

"I am."

The sun continued to slide up the horizon, quietly spectacular. "You must be exhausted," she murmured. "Why aren't you home in bed again?"

He turned his head. The bright rays of the sun slanted over him, lighting his hair, his eyes. She braced for the assault on her senses, especially the sensual ones. If he kept it up, he'd wear her down in no time, and she knew it.

"I wanted to walk you out," he said simply.

The words, softly and genuinely uttered, gave her a flutter a hundred times more devastating than she'd anticipated, and she sighed, softening as she slid a hand around to the back of his neck, her fingers playing with the ends of his unruly, silky hair.

His eyes dipped down to her mouth, then back up again in question.

She lifted her other hand to his chest, and felt the very welcome heat of him, his muscles hard beneath her hand. His heart was steady and strong, like the rest of him. "What's it going to be like for us?" she asked. "In the real world, I mean. Because there's all kinds of . . . friends."

One corner of his mouth slowly curved up. "Like the naked kind?"

A laugh bubbled out of her at his hopeful tone. "Maybe we should go with the kind that doesn't necessarily ignore or bicker."

He let out a breath. "Not as good as Naked Friends."

No, it wasn't. And that thought shimmered between them for the rest of the hike back.

Chapter 16

Back at the lodge the next day, TJ was sitting at his desk, not at all happy. A few kittens were working on his shoelaces as he went through a mountain of paperwork that Stone had deemed his to handle. Normally he got through such a boring task by fantasizing. The fantasies varied in length and levels of sexual explicitness, depending on his mood. Could be a stacked brunette on her knees beneath his desk one day, or a curvy redhead riding his motorcycle in nothing but thigh-high boots the next.

But today his fantasy wasn't make-believe. He had a specific face in his head, a very specific woman.

Harley.

In a sleeping bag—

He hissed out a breath when a gray kitten climbed up his leg. He no sooner extracted her claws out of his skin when her sister did the same thing to his other leg.

"Mew." The soft cry was accompanied by the sweet batting of clear baby blue eyes.

"Try *ouch*." He plopped both kittens to the floor. Where was he? Oh yeah, fantasizing about Harley . . . Doing so was even better since their trip, because thanks to Desolation he knew exactly how her soft skin felt under his fingertips, beneath his tongue. He knew how she squirmed when he kissed the spot beneath her

ear, how her breathing changed when he stroked his fingers between her thighs, and he knew how she sounded when she came,
those sexy-as-hell breathy little whimpers driving him right out
of his mind.

Christ. He shifted in his chair and nearly stepped on a kitten.
Bending, he pulled them both out from beneath his desk, set
them on his chest, and looked at them.

They stared back up at him solemnly. "I'm not fooled," he
said. "You're both menaces to society."

They yawned in innocent tandem. Innocent his ass. They'd destroyed three important files and dumped his trash in the last five
minutes alone. With a sigh, he set them back down and they curled
up in a pile and went to sleep; cute and dangerous.

Like Harley. He'd told her he could fall hard and deep, and
he'd been completely serious.

"TJ? Line two," Katie called from down the hall. "Prospective
hiree."

They'd had the ad in the paper for weeks, and so far they'd
gotten no serious contenders. This guy was no different. Within
two minutes TJ figured out he'd never hiked or climbed above
seven thousand feet and had no winter experience. That wasn't
going to work, not in the Sierras, where most of their climbs were
well over seven thousand feet—try *ten* thousand—and in certain
years, winter could last for six months out of the twelve.

TJ hung up and went back to the Mt. Everest of paperwork in
front of him. It wasn't even noon and already he was bored off
his ass. By evening he'd be in the loony bin.

Stone came in and dropped into the chair in front of TJ's desk.
"Little glitch. In two days, Cam and I each have a trek."

"So?"

"So someone let Annie answer the phone, and she accepted an
unscheduled two-day kayak trip down Snake River."

"And?"

"And you're going to have to take it."

"Why is that a glitch?"

"Because it's the sort of trip that probably we should send Cam on so that Katie could go with him, but he's already inked on a project, and he was specifically requested."

"Still not seeing the problem."

Stone's eyes were laughing, but his mouth didn't so much as twitch. "It's four sorority girls. Cal Berkeley students looking to experience nature on the river. They want to see deer, rabbits, and wildflowers, that sort of thing."

"Disney does Snake River?"

"Not exactly Disney. Sorority sisters. Which means it'll be more like Girls Gone Wild in the Wild."

Ah, hell. They'd been down that road. "You mean they want to be scared shitless while living their version of the Blair Witch project in the big, bad, wild Sierras."

"Yep." Stone stopped trying to hide his smile. "And have a big, bad wild trek guide there to protect them."

"Christ." TJ shook his head. Those trips had been lots of fun several years back, but somewhere along the way they'd lost their entertainment value. "I'm not taking that one alone."

"Agreed," Stone said, opening his phone.

"What are you doing?"

"Booking you a co-guide. A biologist and a photographer. Harley," he said when TJ just stared at him.

TJ opened his mouth to protest, then shut it again. "Just two nights?"

"Surely you can handle four coeds for that long."

"Yeah." Except it wasn't the coeds that worried him.

Harley was once again attempting to balance her bank account when her cell phone vibrated. It'd been buzzing on and off all day. Seemed she and TJ had been seen coming off the mountain together and word had gotten out. Just about everyone she knew had called her to ask if TJ Wilder was as good as women claimed.

Since she happened to know he was even better than good—try amazing—she wasn't in a great mood. So when her cell buzzed for the dozenth time, she picked it up and said "I'm not talking about the time I spent with the Wilder sex god, and you can't make me."

There was a beat of silence, then "Hey, Beautiful."

Oh, God. Perfect. It was Stone. The sex god's brother. She winced and set her head to the table.

"Anything you want to tell me?" he asked.

"No." *Most definitely not.*

"Okay, but for future reference, I'm the sex god in the Wilder family."

"Good to know," she said weakly in tune to his laugh. "Everything okay?"

"No complaints. Got a favor, though."

How many scrapes had Stone, or any of the Wilders for that matter, helped her out of over the years? Too many to count. "Anything."

"Glad to hear that. You still love to kayak?"

"Yes. Why?"

"We have a group of students coming in from Cal Berkeley. They want a two-day kayak down Snake River. They're hoping to experience some wildlife and get pictures of them doing it. Think you can go along as a co-guide and photographer?"

"TJ put you up to this, right?"

"No. Actually, it's Emma. She's afraid the coeds will eat me up for lunch."

She laughed. Stone was one of the most easygoing guys she'd ever met, with an utter will of steel. He loved Emma more than his next breath. He wasn't going to stray, ever. "I don't have any guiding experience, Stone. You know that."

"No, but you're an advanced kayaker and you know the wildlife. Plus, you're a great photographer."

Much as she loved Stone, she didn't really want to spend two days listening to him wax poetic on his love life with Emma. Or that, apparently, he was a sex god, at least in his own mind. Plus, she needed to put some hours in at the garage for the sake of her checkbook.

"We're paying," Stone said. "And trust me, it'll be worth your while. Let me bring over the employment app and papers I'd need to hire you, and you can think about it, okay?"

"Okay." She had to admit, the "we're paying" had been a pretty good argument. "I'd think Emma would want to go with you on this one, and keep you safe from the scary coeds."

"Um, yeah. About that—" He broke off suddenly, and it sounded like he covered the receiver before he came back on. "Sorry, Harley. Bad reception, gotta go. See you in a few."

She hung up, set aside her checkbook, and did some data processing for the internship, frowning when she found that two of her red group coyotes weren't transmitting. She ran some errands, fielded more TJ questions, and came back to find the folder of employment papers stuck in her door. She set them on her table and went back to the new data she was getting from the field camera.

Those two coyotes were still not transmitting.

It was worrisome, but after a while her mind wandered from coyotes to a certain tough, sexy guide who could rev her body with a single glance.

Hell, she was *still* revved. She should have just jumped him in that damn sleeping bag.

Only one thing had stopped her—the fact that she wasn't made for casual sex, and he didn't tend to do anything but. Not to mention that though he'd played and teased and flirted with her, and made her feel like the only woman on earth, he'd also told her to follow her instincts, even though he knew that those instincts were telling her to keep her distance.

One thing she could count on TJ Wilder for—honesty. He said what he meant and meant what he said. No lies, no subterfuge.

Hot and sexy as he was, he was not good for her. She looked at her coveralls lying over the back of her chair. Nolan was good for her. She was yearning for someone in her life, someone with a penis, and she was quite certain he had one.

But TJ had one, too.

Clearly, she was crazy. She pushed her laptop away and looked at the file of employment papers from Stone. She'd told herself she wasn't interested in assisting in guiding a trip, or taking vacation pictures. She had plans. Research biologist plans—which unfortunately wasn't going to earn her a damn penny. She opened the application.

It was a *paying* job, one that didn't require coveralls, grease, or dirty fingernails. Just to see how it would look, she put her name on the application. And then her address. But under qualifications, she hesitated. The story of her life, having to prove herself.

But the real truth was, other than her biology degree, she wasn't sure what her true qualifications were. Somehow she didn't think "loves the great outdoors" was going to matter. She found herself writing two names, Nolan and TJ. Huh. Guess this wasn't about her. Nope, juvenile as it was, she was going to make a list of *their* qualifications.

That should clear things up. Under Nolan's name she wrote:

Pro—gave me a paying job
Pro—nice smile
Pro—nice body
Pro—well liked
Pro—sweet, steady, stable
Con—haven't wanted to kiss him since I kissed TJ

Only one con, and to be fair that con was hers, not his. Under TJ's name she wrote:

Pro—best body in Wishful, maybe the planet
Pro—gave me my first man-made orgasm all year
Pro—offers me his company, his expertise, his friendship, and
    would also give me the shirt off his back if I needed it
Pro—kisses like heaven
Pro—knows me, perhaps more than I'd like
Con—knows me, perhaps more than I'd like
Con—can't stop thinking about him

Con—he'll break my heart if I let him
Con—not sure what his intentions are

There. She stared at the list and chewed on her pencil as she studied the data. The knock at the door startled her out of her analysis. It was Nolan. He smiled warmly and held up an envelope.

"What's that?" she asked, returning his smile. It was easy to smile at him. He was the kind of guy that inspired . . . comfortability. He'd moved here from San Francisco a year ago, though he still hadn't lost the air of being "city." He was slightly under six feet, and his rangy, runner's body always looked good in his clothes. He wore dark jeans that had been professionally distressed, a pale blue button-down, and cool Vibram-soled shoes.

"Your paycheck," he said, waiting patiently for her to step aside and let him in, unlike *some* men she knew who just barged in invited or not. That should probably be a pro for Nolan.

She took the envelope, knowing the number on it would be pathetically low, as she'd only managed to get in twenty hours. "You didn't have to deliver it. I'm working tomorrow, I could have picked it up then."

"I didn't mind." In her living room, he turned to face her, hesitated, then came close, his hands going to her arms. "Sorry about dinner the other night."

"Me too."

"We keep getting postponed."

She nodded, and his body shifted a little closer, his eyes on hers. She realized he was going to kiss her. And she wanted him to.

Or she had, before Desolation.

No. Stop. Erase that. She *still* wanted his kiss. She wanted all of it. Passion. Heat. Love.

Nakedness.

Nolan was the perfect candidate, sweet and loving and kind. He was a long-term candidate as well, a safe one. She let her eyes drift shut and quickly darted her lips with her tongue to moisten them, because there was nothing worse than having lips get stuck together, especially during a first kiss. Briefly she tried to remember which underwear she had on, and if it was cute or sexy. Or God forbid, if it was her laundry day underwear, because—

"Harley? You okay?"

She blinked and found Nolan's face peering into her own, a bemused smile on his lips. "Yes, why?"

"You look like you're thinking way too hard."

"Nope. Not thinking." She closed her eyes. "Mind's empty. Carry on." She sensed his smile. To help him along, she leaned into him, lips puckered as she wondered—*did he kiss good?* With tongue? Without? Or worse, with too much tongue. Her eyes flew open, and she found his lips nearly touching hers. "Oh! Sorry! Um, would you like some water? I'm really dry, I think I need some water."

He opened his eyes. He didn't sigh, but he looked like he was thinking about it. "I'm fine, thanks. Harley—"

"Hang on." She whirled into the kitchen, moved to the cupboard for a glass, and set her forehead against the wood. *What was that?* You can do this, she told herself. You can be attracted to someone other than TJ. You can be attracted to Nolan. You were only a few days ago.

"Harley."

Almost yelping in surprise at the sound of him just behind her, she straightened and filled her glass at the sink. When she turned, Nolan was leaning back against the fridge, once again studying her with that slightly bemused expression.

She realized she caused that expression in men a lot.

"Better?" he asked as she drank.

"Much."

Nodding, he came close again, his intent in his deep blue eyes. *Okay, Harley, this is your chance. A nice man. A good man. A long-term, happily-ever-after man.* She let him take the glass from her, which he set in the sink. See, he's neat, too, she told herself as he shifted closer, his eyes lit with pleasure, and then—

and then the alien within her lifted her hand between them, halting his progress. "I forgot to get my mail today."

He went still for a beat, then blinked. "And . . . you need to get it right now?"

Her heart was suddenly thundering. "Um . . . no. That would be silly." She gripped his shirt and forcibly pulled him in. His hands went to her hips and his gaze dropped to her mouth. "Nolan?"

Again he stopped, his eyes suddenly flashing with both wry humor and resignment. "Are you thirsty again?"

"No," she whispered miserably. "Worse."

His smile faded but he remained gentle as he ran his hands up and down her arms. "It's okay. It's okay, Harley."

"No, it's not." She closed her eyes, then felt the sweet press of his mouth on her forehead. "I'm sorry," she whispered.

"You can't fake chemistry," he said.

"It's not you, it's me."

He let out a soft, regretful laugh at the clichéd line, and she winced. "I mean—"

"I know."

"God, I'm such a jerk."

"No," he said. "You've clearly got your mind on something else. Or someone else." He paused thoughtfully at her grimace. "I heard you had a long two nights out there in Desolation."

"Yes."

"And that TJ Wilder was your guide."

She grimaced again. "Not guide, exactly."

"Ah." He let out another low laugh, this one mirthless, as he nodded, not looking thrilled. "So it *is* a someone."

Dammit. "I don't *want* there to be, trust me." But unfortunately, her head and her heart were two very different beasts, with two very different tastes. "I'm really so very sorry."

He opened his mouth just as Skye bounded in from outside. "Hi honey, I'm home!" she yelled, shutting the door, not yet looking into the kitchen. "I heard you and TJ Wilder had a romp worthy of his last name. It's all over town that—" She turned, and her eyes nearly bugged out of her head at the sight of Nolan.

Smile frozen, she gave him a little finger waggle. "Hi, Cute Stuff. Has Harley ever told you that I have a drinking problem? I'm coming off a three-day bender as we speak."

"Skye," Harley murmured.

Nolan looked like he was thinking about smiling. "It's okay, Skye. I was dumped before you got in the front door."

"Dumped?" Skye looked at Harley and raised a curious brow. "*Interesting.*"

Nolan made to leave, but Harley grabbed his hand. "Nolan—"

"It's okay, Harley. No hard feelings."

Well maybe *he* didn't have hard feelings, but she sure as hell did. This was TJ and his magic fingers' fault. If he hadn't given her that orgasm, she'd have been fine. *Fine.*

Okay, so it wasn't TJ's fault, but she wanted someone to blame. She supposed she should grow up and look in the mirror. "I want you to know, Nolan, that whatever you heard isn't true." Well, unless he heard that she'd crawled into TJ's sleeping bag and let him—*oh*, God. "Most of it anyway."

"Harley," he said with terrifying kindness. "It's okay to stop talking."

Right. Miserable, she nodded. And when the door closed behind him, she turned to Skye, who lifted her hands in surrender.

"Hey, I'm just the messenger," Skye said. "You can't shoot the messenger."

"Wanna bet?"

"So you and TJ . . . ?"

"Ohmigod. Why is everyone talking about this?"

"Because Shelly was with Annie when the two of you came back together. Shelly went to work her shift at Moody's and told someone who told someone—hell, Harl, you know how it works." She shrugged. "This is what happens when you go out with the town's hottie."

"We didn't go out!"

"No, even better, you went directly to the overnight portion of the program. Was it the romance novel I gave you? It was, wasn't it?"

"Oh my God, this is out of control. TJ and I are . . ." What? "Nothing. We're just friends."

"Since when?" Without waiting for an answer, Skye headed straight for the refrigerator. "Jeez, we need food."

"We?"

"Okay, me. I need food. Whadda ya got for dinner?"

Harley sighed, reached into her purse and looked in her wallet.

A ten and two ones.

She handed it over.

There was no fast food in Wishful, so their choices were limited to the café, the grocery store, or the gas station convenience store. They both knew there was only enough money for the latter.

"I'm going to take your truck," Skye said. "I'm low on gas. Hot dogs? Taquitos? Burritos?"

Harley sighed. "All of it. No, wait." All of it would require that she go for a run tomorrow. "Two hot dogs," she decided.

"Chili? Cheese?"

"Sure. But make it *one* hot dog." She sighed. "My jeans are tight."

Skye laughed.

"It's not funny. It means I need to go running." She hated running. "Okay, skip the chili and the cheese, but add pickles. Pickles are low in calories, right?"

"Well yes, when compared to the actual hot dog itself," Skye said, amused.

"You know what, add the cheese. I really need the cheese."

"You're going to hell in a handbasket, Harl."

Harley thought of what she'd let TJ do, what she wanted to do to him, and sighed. "Don't I know it."

CHAPTER 17

TJ sat at his desk and looked at the mess on it. He hated paperwork. He hated filing. He hated sitting.

He hated not having fresh air in his lungs.

Huh. That was sort of fun. What else did he hate about office
work? How about the fact that there were walls all around him
instead of the elements? He hated walls. He hated being en-
closed. He hated the electronic hum of the office equipment.

His phone rang. He hated that, too, but he answered it.
Turned out to be a good call—a last-minute Alaska trip, leaving
in a week. Didn't get better than that.

Well, actually, it could get better than that. He could be back
out at Desolation with Harley.

He looked at the paperwork again and decided it was time for
a field trip. He headed to Cam's office, intending to grab him for
help cataloguing their inventory for month-end, and then they
could go on a hard, fast, mountain bike ride.

Cam's laptop was open on his desk. Next to it lay a cell phone
and keys. Next to that, an iPod, with Radiohead blaring out of the
headphones. There was also an opened soda and bag of chips.

Had there been some sort of emergency? TJ couldn't think of
another reason why his brother would leave so quickly with an
unfinished bag of chips lying out, just begging to be stolen. Cam
didn't leave his food.

Just then, the cell phone rang. The screen ID'd Nick. "Yo," TJ answered.

"TJ? Where the hell's Cam? I'm out back waiting for him."

"I have no idea." Then he heard it. A rustle and a . . . moan? Both came from the closet behind the desk.

And then, a soft, husky female voice that sounded suspiciously like Katie saying, "Oh, God. Cam . . ." Something thunked against the closet door from the inside. And then a soft moan. "*There*, Cam. Right there."

TJ went still. "Jesus."

"What?" Nick asked.

A rough gasp came from the closet.

Fucking almost-newlyweds. TJ rubbed a hand over his face, even as he wished *he* was in a closet causing Harley to make those sounds. "Call it a hunch," he said to Nick. "But I think Cam's indisposed."

"Ah, jeez," Nick said with a sigh. "Again? That's the third time this week."

TJ shut Cam's phone, dropped it back on the desk, and beat it to the door, but didn't get out before hearing Cam's low groan and roughly uttered, "Christ, Katie."

Out in the hallway, TJ stopped to bang his head against the wall a couple times. When he straightened, Annie stood there, brow raised.

"You'll shake something loose," she said.

Yeah. That's what he was hoping. Trying not to be jealous as hell that his brother was getting laid, and quite well from the sounds of it, he brushed past Annie. "I'll be categorizing and inventorying equipment in the garage for month-end."

He'd been at it twenty minutes, going through all the dirt bikes, helmets, and protective gear, when the door opened and quickly closed.

Stone.

Still facing the door, TJ's brother crept backwards, farther into the shed toward him. Clearly Stone was sneaking around, and clearly he didn't want anyone to follow him.

TJ waited until Stone had almost backed into him before he said, "What's up?"

"Jesus-freaking-Christ." Stone whipped around so fast he fell over one of the bikes.

TJ leaned over his prone body with a smirk. "Been walking long?"

"Shut up. And shh!" he whispered when the door opened.

Emma stood in the doorway.

From flat on the floor, and not yet visible to Emma, Stone sliced a finger across his throat in a clear gesture that meant he was not there.

"Hey, Teej," Emma called out, holding her black medical bag. "I'm looking for Stone. He keeps postponing getting his shots for our Belize trip."

There was only one thing in the entire world Stone was afraid of. Well, two.

Emma's wrath.

And needles.

Still on the floor, Stone was giving him the desperate eyes, the please-save-my-ass eyes, and TJ knew that he could probably extract any price for his silence. And while there were times having his brother owe him a favor would work to his advantage, at the moment, he couldn't think of a single one that would be more rewarding than watching Emma stalk and terrorize Stone with a needle.

Stone's hopeful gaze narrowed as he read the intent in TJ's mouth a beat before TJ pointed at him.

Emma gave him an *Are You Kidding?* look, and Stone flipped TJ off. Emma came around the bikes and found Stone, who lifted his head. "Hey, baby."

Crouching at his side, Emma shook her head. "Seriously?"

"I was just taking a nap."

"You're marrying an idiot," TJ said to Emma.

"Yes," Emma said on a shake of her head. "And there seems to be a lot of that going around." She sent TJ a knowing glare.

"What? I'm not getting married."

"You're still an idiot."

"Gee, thanks."

"To be clear," she said, "I mean because of Harley."

"What about her?"

"See," she muttered to herself. "Idiot." She smiled down at Stone still sprawled on the floor, then got down on her knees as he pushed up to a sit. She tossed aside her black bag and crawled into his lap.

He grinned and put his hands on her ass.

In the next second they were kissing as if they had three minutes left to live.

TJ rolled his eyes, grabbed his motorcycle, and rolled it out of there, then nearly ran it right into Cam.

Who was looking pretty damn loose and sated. "What are you, eighteen?"

"Jealous?" Cam asked.

Maybe. Probably. Then he realized that while Cam was looking quite thoroughly tumbled, he wasn't smiling, and his eyes were somber. "What is it?"

Cam shook his head. "The Forest Service had a break-in at station four."

Which was the sole ranger station in Desolation. It was remote and unmanned, and only three miles from where he and Harley had been.

"Nothing was damaged," Cam said, "But it looks like several people camped out there."

"Wonder if that's who I saw."

"Gets worse. Two more coyotes were found shot."

Ah, hell.

"Is Harley going back up there for any reason?" Cam asked.

"I don't know. Probably, when she hears this. She'll want to take a head count on her groups." *Goddammit.* "I'll be back in a bit."

"You going to tell her?"

"Yeah. She needs to take one of us with her if she goes."

Cam arched a brow. "One of us? As in me or Stone?"

"Guess again."

"Nick?" Cam was looking amused. "Or Nolan. Yeah, I bet Nolan would love to go with her and camp all night, alone in the wilderness."

"You're an asshole."

Cam laughed as TJ straddled his bike. "And you are so screwed."

Very true.

"You're not really going to go to Harley's and tell her that she can't go back out there alone."

"What?"

"It's *Harley*, TJ."

"Yeah. So?"

Cam shoved his hands into his pockets and rocked back on his heels. "I'll give you a minute to catch up to me. Go ahead and take your time."

"Okay, so she hates to be told what to do."

"Very good."

TJ started the bike and revved the engine. "I'll figure it out when I see her."

"Good luck with that."

Between Wilder Adventures and Wishful there was nothing but 75,000 acres of wilderness that TJ knew like the back of his hand. With the dirt bike roaring beneath him, he ignored the well-traveled road toward town and took off through the woods, making his own trail.

Back when he was a kid, he and his brothers would ride out there as often as they could, to avoid school, work, or their father's fists. They'd ride until they ran out of gas, then push the bikes back. Sometimes Annie would be with them. Sometimes Harley, who'd been in the same grade as Cam.

Harley.

With the wind at his back and the sun on his face, he thought of her. She was probably working, either the internship or at the garage, or hell, maybe she was out with Nolan.

None of his business.

Except . . . except she felt like his business.

When he finally came into town, he idled at the end of Main and let out a breath. Wishful had been one of the original Old West mining towns, and its sidewalks were lined with nineteenth-century false-front buildings that had—back in the day—been wild saloons and lawless whorehouses. Mining was no longer productive, but the town lived on thanks to its proximity to Lake Tahoe and the endless stream of tourists looking for an outdoor adventure.

He'd made a lot of money off those people doing what he loved, and he *still* felt restless.

So fucking restless.

He supposed he'd go by Nolan's garage first and if Harley's truck wasn't there, he'd check out her place, but before he hit the gas, a jogger came around the corner.

The sun was behind her, highlighting her sweet curves. She wore a tank top and running shorts, and though the sun cast her entire form in shadow, he knew exactly who he was looking at, knew the choppy layered hair falling to just above her shoulders, knew the even stride.

He'd like to say he could remember what that body felt like beneath his, but much as he racked his brain about that long-ago summer night, he couldn't . . . quite . . . get his fingers on the memory. He had flashes of smooth, white skin, images of an intense connection that had seemed out of place at the time, and feelings of being warmed heart and soul in a way that had felt alien to him.

Nothing more.

He knew the exact moment Harley saw him straddling the bike in front of her because she nearly tripped. Her steps slowed. She shoved her sunglasses to the top of her head and put her hands on her hips, her breath coming in short pants. She hated running, hated exercise of any kind, and the sight of her doing it made him smile.

"It's not funny," she said. "My jeans are getting tight."

He liked the way she looked in jeans. It was part of his problem. He liked the way she looked in damn near everything, but he'd especially liked the way she looked in her bra and panties, running like a bat out of hell around the campfire toward him.

"Stop that," she said shakily, pointing at him.

"I didn't do anything."

"You're thinking it."

"Got me there," he said on a smile.

She blew out a breath. Her skin was covered in a fine sheen of perspiration, making her glow. Still huffing and puffing, she bent at the waist and sucked in more air. Her top rode up in the back. Her shorts were low-riding, revealing a strip of smooth skin, and twin dimples right above what was a perfect heart-shaped ass.

"You have a way of seeing me at my worst," she muttered, straightening.

Was she kidding? He wanted to put his tongue to those dimples and work his way down . . .

"Covered in mud," she went on. "Drenched. *Sweaty*."

"You look frighteningly sexy in all of those scenarios," he told her.

"Humph."

Taking another, longer, more careful look at her, he realized there was far more bothering her than her jeans being tight. He wondered if it had anything to do with the rumors swirling around town about the two of them, and then realized he was giving himself far more credit than he was probably due.

She probably hadn't given him another thought.

"I hate running as a calorie burner," she grumbled.

"I can think of a better way to burn calories," he said.

She actually laughed, which he took as a good sign. Whatever was bothering her maybe wasn't his doing then. "Want a ride?"

She eyed his bike with pleasure, but shook her head. "I don't know if the gossip mill has room for any more stories about us."

So she *had* heard.

"Could have been worse, though," she said. "They could have said I was having an alien's baby."

"Well, hey, since it could have been worse . . ." He patted the seat.

"Yeah, but what about that whole calorie-burning thing?"

"How about if I promise to irritate you like I do so well?" he asked. "Irritation burns calories." So did sex . . .

Something came and went in her eyes so fast he couldn't place it. "Yeah, what the hell," she said, surprising him again. "Since we've already entertained everyone, ruined the thing between Nolan and me, and possibly cost me my only paying job, why not?"

He caught her arm before she could get on behind him. "Nolan fired you?"

"Not exactly."

"Then what exactly?"

She sighed.

"Harley."

"Let's just say I'm no longer sure where he stands on the idea of having me as an employee, especially since I won't be getting to a third date. Or third base," she muttered.

"What happened?"

She lifted a shoulder. "I realize it wasn't exactly a *thing* with Nolan, but to be honest, I was really looking forward to one."

She said this so wistfully, he felt himself wanting to smile again. "Define thing. Because I've got a thing."

She crossed her arms over her chest. "You're right. I can feel the irritation torching calories as I stand here."

"Tell me what happened."

She looked down at her running shoes. He waited patiently for her to elaborate, but she managed to hold her silence. Gently he touched her jaw. "Let's try a different angle. What's going on with you and me?"

She lifted her gaze. "Well, that's the big mystery, isn't it?"

Yeah, and he knew the problem. From the moment he'd woken up in his sleeping bag with her, he'd known. She didn't do casual sex. Never had. Even that one time with him hadn't counted as casual, not in her head. He'd not allowed himself to dwell on the implications of that, or even how she'd feel, after what they'd shared in Desolation. He'd only thought of how *he'd* felt, which was easy—he'd felt turned-on as hell.

Still did.

"When Nolan stopped by, he—I tried to—" She swiped the sheen of sweat off her brow with her forearm and sighed. "I ended up giving him the 'it's not you, it's me' speech."

TJ felt a twinge of sympathy for the guy. And relief. And an odd twinge of something else. Unease—which was asinine. He hadn't wanted her with Nolan. And he didn't want her single for yet another reason that he didn't want to think about.

He was fucked up.

She was looking at him, her eyes suddenly sharp. "Look at you, all worried that I'm going to set my sights on you now. Don't worry, TJ. I know better."

He opened his mouth, but when she arched a brow, he shut his mouth again. When it came to women and permanence, he'd never had what it took, and they both knew it.

Hell. He should have left well enough alone, let her have her "thing" with Nolan. She deserved it, and Nolan was a good guy. He'd have taken good care of her.

"Christ, TJ," she said. "Get over yourself."

Good plan. They stared at each other for a moment. "I'm sorry about Nolan," he finally said. "Was it because of what happened between us?"

"No." But she didn't meet his gaze. "Because there was no us at Desolation."

Yeah, that was his story, too. He wondered how long they could go on keeping that delusion. He pulled off his helmet and handed it to her.

"I'm not taking your helmet."

"Yes, you are."

"Look, I realize your head is impossibly hard and probably indestructible, but you still need the protection."

"Okay, I didn't want to go there," he said evenly, doing his best not to smile. It was hard. Even when he was completely baffled by his emotions for her, she made him want to smile. A lot. Something to think about later. "You owe me."

"I owe you?" she asked incredulously.

"Yes. And this is how you can repay me."

"Let me get this straight," she said. "You gave me an orgasm and I give you . . . wearing your helmet?"

"You don't owe me for the orgasm. You owe me for something else." He just smiled and held out the helmet.

Harley blinked at him, feeling off her axis. She told herself it was from what had happened earlier with Nolan, but she knew the truth. It was TJ, straddling his big, bad bike, looking like sin on a stick. He wore another pair of Levi's, soft and faded, torn in one knee and the other thigh, along with a pair of battered boots, a long-sleeved pullover Henley, and mirrored sunglasses. She had to suck in all the air in the entire county to even look at him, and when she did, she ached with that nameless need again.

Oh, who was she kidding. It wasn't nameless. It was *lust*, pure and simple. "What do I owe you for exactly?"

"Well, you were mad at me for a very long time." He pushed his sunglasses to the top of his head. "Years."

His eyes were the color of moss on a rainy spring day, and she lost herself in the warm heat of them for a minute.

"But as it turns out," he said softly, "you didn't really have a right to be mad. You withheld your friendship. I forgive you," he said magnanimously, his eyes lit with good humor. He was teasing her! "But the least you can do is this one little favor."

"I didn't have a right to be mad?" she asked.

"You climbed into my truck. You seduced me. If anything, *I* should be mad at *you*."

She choked out a laugh and slipped on the helmet. "You really are a nut."

He grinned. "Just being your friend."

There was that F-word again. "So which kind of friend today? My funny friend?"

"Again, I'd prefer to be—"

"Naked friend. Yeah, yeah." She laughed instead of admitting that that was sounding pretty damn good. She put a hand on his broad shoulder, feeling the muscles beneath as she used him for balance to swung a leg over the bike. Behind him, she stared at the expanse of his back stretching his shirt and her mouth watered as she tried to hold herself away from him.

"You're going to need to hold on," he said.

"I'm all sweaty."

"As we've already established, I like you that way."

She sighed and pulled herself closer, her chest, belly, and hips tight against him, not to mention her thighs straddling his so that it affected her breathing in a way she couldn't blame on the running. Her arms encircled his lean waist, her fingers brushing up against his ridged, *perfect* abs.

"You know, Mariposa Canyon is a virtual biological wonder this time of year," he said casually.

Mariposa Canyon was a hidden meadow about two miles from there, hidden because the only way to get there was by four-wheeling in, over natural hills and through crevices, making it a perfect balls-to-the-walls quad course. The canyon wasn't a "biological wonder," it was a four-wheeling gift from heaven.

He flashed her one of his wicked grins over his shoulder. "As a biologist," he said solemnly, "you'd probably want to take the long way to your place, maybe take just a quick drive-by through the canyon to make sure you aren't missing anything good."

She couldn't think of a single thing that could improve a shitty day more than being beneath the wide, expansive sky, surrounded by the majestic, glorious peaks, with 686 cc's between her legs and the hottest guy in the universe to hold on to . . . "Well, if it's not too much trouble," she said demurely, making him burst into laughter.

God, she loved his laugh. It made her laugh, too, and she felt it bubble out of her with sheer joy, which backed deliciously up in her throat when he hit the gas. In three minutes they were off road and heading toward Mariposa Canyon, and then they were at the top of the basin, looking down at it.

"Hold on," he said, and they leapt forward, for a minute completely airborne as they flew down the hill.

Her heart landed in her throat, in a very good way, in the best roller-coaster kind of way. Manzanita bush and wild growth whipped past in a blur as TJ followed the line of the trees straight down. She found herself screaming in delight, probably making him deaf, and she didn't care. She leaned with him into the turns, her hands gripping him for all she was worth. Beneath her palms she felt the tight, hard muscles in his abs work as he maneuvered them up and across the steep, spine-tingling moguls.

"Crash, and I'll kill you," she yelled in his ear.

"You're safe with me."

"You're the one without a helmet. It's *your* thick skull that I'm worried about—"

She broke off with another little scream as he took them off a sharp cliff, then up and over the dirt moguls, through the brush and mud. She was still grinning an hour later when he pulled up to her place.

She slid off, pulled off the helmet, and eyed the bike. "Your bike's all muddy now."

"It'll wash."

"I guess since I enjoyed the ride so much, and we're making such a concerted effort to be friends and all, I could offer to help."

His eyes went all smoky. "What would you be wearing for this bike-washing event?"

"Oh my God. Are you going to turn *everything* back to Naked Friend?"

"Yes. But I'll settle for a bikini top and short shorts friend."

She couldn't help it; she laughed again and turned to head inside, then found herself being slowly pulled back into him. "I don't have any short shorts at the moment."

He turned her around to face him. "You can owe me. Listen, I was actually hoping we could talk."

Uh oh. His solemn expression sank in and her smile faded. "Just what I need. More talk, more trouble."

"I'm sorry about causing you trouble," he said quietly, all

humor gone. "But I'm not sorry I went with you to Desolation, or that I learned what the problem was between us."

She closed her eyes. "TJ."

"In fact, we should work on that problem. I could fix it, if you'd let me."

"Really?" she asked curiously. "How?"

He was quiet a moment. Lifting his head, he ran a finger over her shoulder. "By making a better memory."

"Is this because I told you it was fine?"

He grimaced. "I'd like to think I'm not quite *that* Neanderthal." He paused, then gave her a small smile. "But fine sucks, Harley."

"We were teenagers."

"Sort of my point. I do better now."

She laughed softly and shook her head. "The Wilder ego," she murmured. "Needing to be the biggest, the baddest, and the best in everything, especially bed. Nothing personal, TJ, but I'd rather have sweet, steady, and stable."

"Like Nolan."

"Like Nolan."

"Then why did you cut him loose?"

"I told you, he—"

He just looked at her, and she let out a breath. Right. She could have turned that around—if she'd tried hard enough.

"But that's not what I wanted to talk about," TJ said quietly. "Can I come in?"

Had she ever been able to refuse him anything? "Yeah."

CHAPTER 18

Harley unlocked her door, went directly to the kitchen, opened her refrigerator, and frowned in disappointment.

TJ stopped at her table and looked at the maps she had spread out there. "So you're going to fill this out?"

She went utterly still for a beat, suddenly realizing what was with the maps—the employment application. And her pro/con list of his and Nolan's qualifications. Embarrassment and horror filled her as she whipped around and leapt toward him. "Give me that."

Not yet having caught sight of the list, he smiled. "It's okay. The form's just a formality for our pesky attorney." He stopped short and blinked as he got a good look at what he was holding. "What's this?"

She launched herself at him. "TJ, dammit, that's personal—"

"Qualifications. Nolan." He paused. "Gave you a job, nice body, nice smile."

She was practically crawling up his body, trying to grab the paper. "Give it back."

"You're right," he said, nodding his head. "Nolan does have a very nice smile." He perused some more. "'Haven't wanted to kiss him since I kissed TJ.'" He cut his eyes to hers. "We'll definitely be circling back to that."

With a miserable groan, she gave up trying to reach the list and plopped her head to his chest. Beneath the hard muscle she could feel his heartbeat, steady and sure.

Hers, on the other hand, was racing.

He stroked a hand down her hair. "My pros. Best body in Wishful, maybe the planet. Nice to know." He shot her a look so hot it singed her every nerve ending. "Right back at you, Harley."

She smacked him in the chest. She didn't put a lot of heat into it because she really wanted him to lower his arm so she could grab the paper before he got any further.

"Gave you your first man-made orgasm all year," he read. He went silent at that. She could feel him watching her but she didn't lift her head. Instead she smacked him again.

He cuffed both her wrists in one hand and backed her into the counter, effortlessly holding her there with his body. "So what exactly is it you don't want me to see, Harley? That I know you? More than you'd like?" She could hear the smile in his voice. And that wasn't all. She was plastered to him and he was hard.

She thunked her head against the rock-solid muscles of his chest. "You are such an ass."

He laughed softly as he nuzzled her neck. "What if I told you same goes, that I can't stop thinking about you either? And that if anyone's heart is in danger here, it's mine." He said this in a low, rough whisper. "As for intentions . . ." He tossed the list aside and pressed into her, allowing her to feel exactly what his intentions were.

Suddenly it felt as if there was a whole heck of a lot less oxygen in the room than there'd been only a moment before, which had to explain why she'd melted into him when she hadn't meant to. She tossed back her head to say something defensive, but the look on his face stopped her.

His smile was warm, affectionate even. His eyes . . . smoking hot. Bending his head, he pressed his jaw to hers, then kissed her temple, her jaw, that spot beneath her ear. "You have no idea what you do to me," he murmured, running his hands over her.

"Because if you did, you'd shove me out and bolt the door."
Then he kissed her mouth, long and hard and deep, and just when
she was panting for air, desperate for more, he let her go.

Legs weak, she walked into the living room and plopped onto
the couch.

Silently, TJ joined her. He looked at the spot where her TV
had been before she'd sold it to cover her mom's mortgage.

"Don't," she said softly.

"Work for us this weekend, Harley."

"What's the catch?"

"No catch. We get the help we need. You get a sizeable chunk
of cash."

Ah, there it was. "So it's a pity job."

"Harley, there are pity dates and pity fucks, but there are no
pity jobs. You're going to work your ass off, trust me. Not to
mention get some of that great escape we both find out there on
the mountain that we can't seem to find anywhere else."

She turned her head toward him and had to admit he was
right on that score. "Okay."

"Okay," he repeated, relieved.

She leaned back and rested her head. "So what did you want
to talk to me about?"

"How's your research going?" he asked instead of answering.

"Good. Except the second battery pack on that third camera
failed, too. I knew I should have replaced it while I was out
there. Also, two of the coyotes are no longer transmitting. I need
to get back out there."

"Yeah." He scrubbed a hand down his face. "That's why I
came looking for you. We got a call from the forest station out
there." Regret and unease flashed across his face and she braced
herself. "They found two coyotes, shot and deserted."

She stood back up and walked to her table. She shoved aside
the bills and the stupid list and spread out the map of the entire
Desolation Wilderness. Staring down at it, vision burring, legs
quaking, heart aching, she drew a breath. "Where exactly?"

"Harley—"

"Show me."

He looked at her for a long beat, then moved close, leaning across her, his long finger going to a spot on the map where two of her red data group had stopped transmitting.

Nodding, she put her finger on the spot where she and TJ had camped, then looked at the proximity of their fingers.

"Waaaay too close," he murmured softly, and set a warm hand low on her spine. "They were yours?"

She swallowed convulsively. "I think so, yes." She felt the intensity of his eyes on her, but she didn't look at him. She was too busy locking her knees at the wave of pain.

"They're not issuing any more permits for Desolation until they catch whoever's out there with a shotgun," he said.

There was that, at least.

"Harley? You okay?"

She nodded, then slowly shook her head. She'd been holding her breath, but the grief was catching up with her. "I don't get the hunting thing. I mean if it's for food, that's one thing, but this isn't. It's not to protect a farm or ranch, either. It's for sport, for cruel sport—" Her voice caught, and she stopped talking to breathe instead.

His hand was still on her back, rubbing soft, soothing circles, and it felt like the most natural thing in the world when he pulled her into his arms. Just like that she slid into his comforting embrace, and though she told herself she was strong and tough, that she didn't cry, she felt the scalding rush of tears.

Murmuring to her softly, he tightened his arms around her and was nice enough to not mention the fact that she was making his shirt wet. They stood like that, her pretending not to cry, him letting her have the pretense, until the pain in her chest eased. She could feel the steady, calm beat of his heart beneath her ear. Her hand was over a pec, gripping his shirt, and without thinking, she smoothed the material, then let her fingers trail down, over his stomach.

His muscles leapt beneath her touch.

She looked up at him. Lifting a hand, he rubbed his thumb over her cheek, catching a stray tear.

She took a step back, and his hands fell from her.

"I can't help but think this is somehow because of the study," she said.

"I think it's more likely that you've stumbled by accident into an area where a group of hunters have sort of staked their claim."

"But it's illegal to hunt in Desolation Wilderness."

"It's also illegal to leave your kill. Or to be out there without a permit. I doubt they're concerned about any of it. It's not called Desolation for nothing. The place is a graveyard this time of year."

"What if someone went out there and scared them off?"

He stared at her. "Someone?"

"Yeah. Maybe if I made more of a presence out there—"

"No," he said, watching her face. "Hell, no."

"I'm going t—"

"Stay the hell away from those hunters," he finished for her.

"Well, of course. But since I have to go back out there anyway—"

"Jesus." He pressed the heels of his hands against his eyes. "I'm already hating this conversation."

"I'm not going to do anything stupid, but those coyotes are vulnerable."

He blew out a breath and nodded. He knew that.

"I'll help you guys this weekend," she said. "Then I'll go back to Desolation."

"By that time, I'll be in Alaska. Yeah," he said at her start of surprise. "I caught a trip. Harley, tell me you won't go alone."

"Don't worry," she said, distracted by the fact that he'd be leaving again, and so soon. "I won't be the stupid girl in the horror flick."

"Promise me, Harley."

"An easy promise to make," she said softly, meeting his gaze, letting him see she meant it. "I promise I won't go alone." She opened her freezer and reached for her long-lost lover, a quart of double fudge ice cream.

"Is that dinner?"

"It's called comfort food. After losing a boyfriend, two coyotes, and probably my job all in one fell swoop, I think I'm entitled."

He took the carton out of her hands and stuffed it back into the freezer. "You'll just torture yourself with another run tomorrow if you eat this."

If she wasn't having sex, she was damn well having ice cream. "Don't get between me and my sugar, TJ. It won't end well for you."

A corner of his mouth tipped up. "I have a better way to comfort you."

"Alcohol?"

He smiled and stepped into her again. "Something better."

And, she had a feeling, something far more devastatingly hard to resist.

He trailed his fingers lightly up her spine, no longer comforting or sweet—which worked for her.

Without taking the time to think it through, she tugged his head down. When he was only a breath away, she paused, their breath commingling, eyes connected in a beat so charged she shivered. And then, with the anticipation humming through them, she closed the gap and kissed him. With a low groan, he took over, sweeping his tongue against hers, entangling a hand in her hair to hold her in place. His other hand curled around her hip and yanked her into him so that their bodies were touching from chest to knee, like the last two pieces of a puzzle.

A perfect fit.

Arrows of heat bolted through Harley, bouncing off all her erogenous zones, and only when she needed air did TJ gentle the kiss, then slowly pull back, dropping his forehead to hers.

"Every time," he said in a raw voice.

Yeah. She'd have thought the one orgasm he'd given her on the mountain would hold her over for awhile, but it'd been the opposite. Her motor was going. She closed her eyes and gulped in air. After a long moment, she forced herself to take a step back and turned to brace herself on the sink.

"What are you doing?" he asked.

"Considering a very cold shower."

He let out a low, ironic laugh. She heard his footsteps behind her, could feel the body heat radiate off him a beat before she felt him brush against her. The urge to press her bottom into his crotch was so strong she had to suck in a breath and grip the edge of the counter. But in the end, she couldn't control herself. She wriggled, feeling his hard, hot length nestle against her.

He let out a rough, ragged breath, then leaned down and pressed his mouth to the nape of her neck. Her entire body erupted in goose bumps. She heard a shockingly needy moan and realized it was hers.

His hands slid up her arms to her shoulders, his thumbs rubbing the tense muscles there. "So tense." He dug in a little and it was so good she moaned again.

His soft laugh huffed against the side of her throat, just beneath her jaw.

"You're laughing at me." Her eyes fluttered closed. "I'm melting into a puddle of goo right here and you're laughing at me."

"Not at you." His tongue flicked on the shell of her ear, then danced along her skin in a tantalizingly slow motion that matched the rocking of his hips. "*With* you. You're not the only one who's . . . tense."

His fingers were currently killing brain cells at an alarming rate, not to mention what that very large erection was doing to her. She opened her mouth to say something, but he had his thumbs on the nape of her neck, running them up and down her tense muscles. All she managed was a garbled moan.

When he slid those talented fingers down the entire length of her spine, she shuddered. He stopped just short of her ass, digging into the knot of muscles low on her spine. "TJ . . ."

"Yeah." His mouth worked its way to that sweet spot just beneath her ear.

She could feel the stubble on his jaw, could feel his warm lips, the heat of his exhale while his hands continued to work their magic on her body. "TJ . . ." His fingers were beneath her shirt now, skin to skin. Her eyes actually rolled back in her head. "TJ . . ."

"You said that part already."

"Yes, but your hands—I keep forgetting what I want to say."

Then those hands slid around to her belly, and just as she had that night in Desolation, she ached, *ached* to feel him wrapped around her.

"Oh, God," she whispered as his fingers slid up . . . and her head fell back to his chest. "I need—"

"Tell me."

"I need—"

"This?" He cupped her breasts, his thumbs slowly rubbing over her nipples, sparking a flash fire inside her that was nearly an orgasm.

At the sound she made, he whipped her around to face him and backed her to the counter. "I'm going to ask you again," he said, his mouth busy on her throat, his fingers on her breasts. "What's going on with you and me?"

"Um . . ." God. He was hard. And she was getting wet. *So* wet. She and Nolan had spent plenty of time together, if not on dates, then at his shop. This overwhelming need and raw, desperate lust had never happened.

"Harley."

"Wh-what do *you* think is going on?"

"Oh, no." His breath was hot on her skin, his voice pure sex. "We both know what *I* want to be going on. We're waiting on you to decide."

CHAPTER 19

Harley knew TJ was braced for her answer. How to tell him that making the decision wasn't the problem? Facing it was. Because if she did as she should and sent him home, she'd always wonder. And if she did what she wanted and ate him up for lunch, she was going to get good and hurt.

Yet that seemed intangible at the moment, with his hands on her, his eyes dark and sexy as he waited.

He wanted a sign.

Lifting his head, his eyes met hers, silently waiting on her to take the next step. Just one little step, that was all she had to do, and he'd get her to where she wanted to go, she knew him that much. Trusted him that much.

Through the last of her resistance came one thought—he brought what she'd been yearning for.

Passion.

He brought it without strings, and she was hungry enough for him that the promise of it overrode common sense.

"Harley?"

Into show and tell instead of words, she sank her fingers into his hair and dragged his mouth to hers, kissing him long and deep.

Apparently he got the message. His fingers tugged the cups of her bra down and stroked her bare nipples. When her legs threatened to give, TJ solved that problem by sliding a rock-hard thigh between hers.

She slipped her hands beneath his shirt and felt warm skin, hard sinew, and the beat of his heart, faster now, not as steady. Keeping her eyes locked on his, she shoved up his shirt.

Reaching up, he tore it off over his head.

Oh good Lord. If he hadn't been holding her up, she might have slid to the floor. He was so beautifully made she leaned in and took a lick. Buoyed by the shuddery breath that escaped him, she did it again, her tongue catching on one of his nipples.

Swearing softly, he tightened a hand in her hair and lifted her head for a plunging, deep kiss as he pulled off her tank top. Lifting his head, eyes still dark and heated, he watched as his fingers trailed up her arms, then slid her bra straps from her shoulder.

She let out a shuddery breath when his lips and teeth gently nipped the skin he'd exposed. "Bedroom," she said.

He took her hand and led her there without hesitation. Nudging her inside the room, he shut and locked the door behind him, leaning back on it to look at her from beneath sleepy, sexy eyes. "You sure?"

In answer, she let her bra fall to the carpet.

"Okay, you're sure," he said on a shaky breath. Pushing away from the door, he headed toward her, then nudged her onto the bed. With a knee to the mattress, he followed her down until he was over her, his forearms flat on either side of her head, his big hands on her jaw, the tips of his fingers in her hair. His hair was a sexy mess from her fingers. She took a deep breath and inhaled the scent that was TJ, all warm, heated male.

He smiled and kissed her, soft and slow at first, giving her time.

She didn't need it.

Running her hands down his gorgeous back, she cupped his most excellent ass and pulled him in, hoping to get him hot and heavy again.

He lifted his head and raised a brow. "In a hurry?"

"As a matter of fact."

He was smiling when he skimmed a hand down her belly, heading for her shorts, and suddenly she realized—it was broad daylight. What the hell had she been thinking? It was bright in the room. He'd be able to see every single fault on her body. "You know, I'm thinking maybe—"

He shook his head. "No thinking."

"Yes, but it's so light, and—"

"I want to see you." His voice was low and husky, and as if it possessed the magic to both calm and seduce her, her body arched up into him.

His mouth was still curved in a smile as he looked deep into her eyes, a warm, sexy smile that held lots of promise as his hands came up, his thumbs caressing her jaw. "It's going to be okay, Harley."

"Yeah, well, you know I can't turn my brain off. It's a problem—"

He kissed her. Long and wet and deep, and just like that, her brain obeyed his silent but effective demand and turned right off. He kissed her for long moments, revving her up again as he held himself braced on his elbows, careful to keep his weight from crushing her.

As for her, careful had flown the coop. In fact, she was feeling as far from careful as she could get, practically writhing with need beneath his long, hard body.

Unconcerned with the state she was in, he ran a large warm hand over her throat, her collarbone . . . her breast, where he paused to play with the pebbled tip. "I love your skin." He bent to suck on her neck. "So soft . . ."

His skin wasn't bad either, all sleek and smooth and hard, and suddenly she blessed the bright daylight. She couldn't stop touching him, running her hands over him, moaning when he slid a thigh between hers, spreading her, making room for him to lie between her parted legs so that his hard sex cradled against her core.

God, she wanted him.

His mouth between her breasts, he turned his head and slid

his tongue over a nipple. With a gasp, she arched up into him, gliding her hands beneath the loose waistband of his jeans, squeezing his ass again, pressing him into her.

Obliging, he rocked into her, and she shivered. "Off," she said, slipping her hands around to try to pop open his jeans so that she could get her hands on something else. He kneeled up, giving her access, and she hummed in pleasure as her fingers wrapped around him.

He was big and hot and velvety smooth. When she stroked him, he let out a sound that reminded her of a huge wild cat, like he was both growling and purring at the same time as he thrust up in her hands.

He tugged open her shorts, then pulled them and her panties off, tossing both over his shoulder. Pushing her legs apart, his hands slid from her knees to her inner thighs, caressing as he went, teasing her into a writhing mass of desperation.

"Easy," he whispered, and then slowly, with devastating precision, outlined her with the pad of a single finger, back and forth until she was so wet and ready that she was crying out for him, begging. No easy way about it.

"Please," she gasped, thrusting her hips up mindlessly. "Oh, please."

He slid two fingers deep, and on his second long, slow, sure stroke, she exploded.

While she struggled to return to her senses, a couple of things hit her at once. Not only had she done it again, come without warning, she actually had a death grip on him, and her teeth were clamped on his throat. She was panting for breath, her hand still wrapped around his hot and pulsing length, mindlessly stroking him.

"Harley," he whispered in a raw voice, and thrust into her hands, clearly close.

And then—her front door slammed—the worst possible sound that she could have heard in that moment.

"Christ," TJ groaned, his face tight. His whole body tight.

Harley struggled to catch her breath. "You locked my door."

"Yeah." He rubbed his jaw to hers, his thumb brushing over her center again, making her jerk. "Maybe they'll go away."

"Harley!" Skye yelled from the living room. "I need you!"

With a low breath, TJ rolled off her to his back, flinging an arm over his eyes. "Fuck."

Yeah. Just what Harley had hoped to be doing. She sat up to apologize, pulling TJ's arm away from his face. His eyes were closed and he was chewing on his bottom lip, breathing hard. She ran a hand down his tight abs, but he groaned and caught her hand, stopping her. "I'm going to need a minute."

"Are you okay?"

"Yes. I might cry, but I'm okay."

"I owe you," she said softly.

"I've heard that one before."

"Harley!" Skye yelled again. "Who's the guy?"

Harley held her breath. "What guy?"

"The one with you."

"There's no—"

"He left his shirt on the floor, inside out. Which indicates he was in a hurry, or otherwise occupied. Am I interrupting something good? 'Cause I can come back. How close to done are you?"

"Shoot me," TJ muttered.

Harley's gaze ran down his gorgeous, sinewy, tightly wound body, stopping where his jeans were completely undone, leaving little to the imagination. Her mouth watered. "I'll do you one better," she whispered. "I'll shoot *her*."

TJ rode home, a spectacularly uncomfortable thing to do since he was hard enough to pound nails. He entered his cabin fifteen minutes later and found Cam and Stone sitting on his couch, a game on his flat screen, *his* six-pack between them. "Girls' night out?" he asked sarcastically.

"It's called Wedding Evasion," Cam said. "Katie and Emma are working on the shower."

TJ raised a brow. "Katie and Emma together in the shower? And you're here?"

"The *wedding* shower." Cam narrowed his eyes. "Are you picturing Katie naked?"

"Yes," TJ said. "With Emma. They're good in the hot water together. Thanks for the visual."

Now he had *both* Stone and Cam snarling at him. Good. Their moods all matched perfectly. TJ kicked Stone's feet off the coffee table so he could get to his own damn couch, and plopped between them, grabbing a beer.

They watched the game in silence.

"That second Alaska trip is a go," Stone said at the commercial. "Six more weeks gone. If you want it."

"I want it."

Stone lifted a brow.

"*What?*" TJ asked him.

"I thought maybe you'd want to stick around, seeing as you're doing something with Harley."

"I'm doing what with Harley?"

"I don't know. You tell me."

Keeping his gaze on the TV, TJ took a pull of his beer and said nothing. Yeah. He was doing something with Harley. He just wasn't sure what exactly.

He knew what he wanted. He wanted her. In a bed, for longer than a single orgasm.

But he also wanted more.

Since that "more" happened to fall in a pretty big gray area, he hadn't been able to define it. "The game's back on."

They were silent until the next commercial. Cam spoke first. "Heard you gave the Harley quite a ride."

TJ snapped threatening eyes in his brother's direction, and Cam let out a sly grin. "Oh wait, you were on your Honda and *with* a Harley. Sorry, man. My mistake."

"You're a dick."

Stone put a hand to TJ's chest to hold him back and shook his head at Cam like he was shocked at his stupidity. "You've been sitting on that one, haven't you? Bet you practiced that one in the mirror."

Cam grinned. "Too good to pass up." He looked at TJ. "You and Harley stop sniffing around each other and do the deed?"

"I'm going to kill him," TJ said conversationally to Stone.

"Can't. We're triple booked this week, remember? We'll lose clients."

"It'd be worth it."

"Let him earn his keep first," Stone said, and when Cam opened his mouth, Stone simply covered Cam's entire face with his hand and shoved while keeping up the conversation with TJ. "If you still want to kill him after he brings in the dough this weekend, I'll help you."

CHAPTER 20

Harley and Skye shared the last of the ice cream on Harley's porch as the sun sank below the horizon.

"So," Skye said. "You and TJ."

"I don't want to talk about it."

"He looked hot without his shirt."

"Yeah." Even more so with his low-slung Levi's unbuttoned, revealing his—

"Is he as good in bed as he looks?"

Yes. "Not talking about it, Skye."

"Okay but tell me you nibbled on those abs 'cause *I* want to nibble those abs. Our dead aunt Trudy would want to nibble on those abs."

"Skye!"

"Right. Not talking about it." She pouted. "But if I had a guy that hot, I'd let you drool over those abs."

"Can we talk about something else? *Anything?*"

"Oh, come on. It's not fair. You have all this . . . excitement in your life. I'm just trying to live vicariously through you."

Harley turned and stared at her sister in utter shock. "Excitement? *My* life?"

"Hey, I'm not the one becoming a fancy biologist marching through Desolation, harboring the sexiest single guy in all of Wilder in my bedroom, naked to boot."

"*Half* naked," Harley corrected, but suddenly she realized Skye was right. Her life didn't suck nearly as badly as she'd thought.

"So are you really going to co-guide that kayaking trip for Stone?"

Harley licked her spoon as she tried to find resentment over having to take the trip, but the truth was, she couldn't wait to get back out there. "Yeah. I'm going."

Skye fell asleep on the couch, hugging the pillows, looking young and vulnerable. Harley covered her up with a blanket and went to bed—where she dreamed about a certain gorgeous Wilder with magic fingers and mouth.

She woke up before dawn and put in several hours at her laptop processing data and getting caught up so she could head out the next morning on the two-day trip for Wilder Adventures. Then she eyed the pile of unpaid bills still stacked there, waiting to be paid. She wasn't the only one who needed this trip. Her bills needed it, too.

If she still had a job with Nolan, she was due to work two half shifts on the weekend, so she needed to ask him if she could postpone those. He hadn't returned her call yet. It was too early to try him again, plus she didn't know what to say, so she called the lodge to deal with her other problem. Katie answered with a crisp, sweet "Good morning, Wilder Adventures."

"Katie, it's me. I sort of need a new employment application, I got . . . something on the back page and—"

"Yes! You're going to forget Colorado and stay here."

"Actually, I won't know if I even got the Colorado job until spring."

"But TJ said you're a shoo-in for it."

"Well, I hope that's true. But in the meantime, I'm filling in with you guys as needed."

"Oh, you're needed. I'll have another application out and ready for you."

"Thanks." Harley drew a breath. "Listen, about the kayaking trip . . ."

"Not much to tell yet. The departure date's only tentatively set for next week. TJ's waiting on the client, and on some sort of special permit he needs to get on to a parcel of private land because this time they're going to be climbing some peak that—"

"Whoa." Harley shook her head. "I meant tomorrow's trip. What are you talking about?"

"We just took on two big Alaska trips. TJ's going to take both. One is a partial kayaking thing. I thought that's what you were talking about."

Okay, so TJ was usually gone more than he stuck around. She knew that. Everyone knew that.

And yet she'd allowed herself to forget. "He mentioned he might be leaving."

"Yes." Some of the smile went out of Katie's voice. "But then again, eventually so are you."

Right. Yes. Yes, she was.

Katie was quiet a minute. "Harley, I know you two have been . . . different lately. Closer."

Harley found she couldn't get her throat to work, so she nodded, which was ridiculous, as Katie couldn't see her.

"You know," Katie said very quietly. "I'm going to step out on a limb here and give you some advice on the Wilder men."

"Not necessary."

"They're big and bad and strong," Katie said anyway. "Mind *and* body. You know that. They're tough, capable, and . . . well, sexy as hell. You know that, too."

"Katie—"

"But they're also a little slow on the uptake. It's not their fault really. They barely had a childhood, and certainly had no softness in their lives. I mean they had Annie, but hell, she's as tough as they are."

"You don't have to tell me," Harley said. "I grew up with them. I know—"

"Do you? Do you know that if you want him, all you have to do is tell him? Because he grew up where there was no unconditional love, where being cared about was rare. You're going to literally have to hit him over the head with love, Harley. And to do that, you're going to have to put yourself out there."

"I—"

"I mean you have to step on the edge of the cliff, toes hanging off, and take the plunge. It's the only thing he'll understand." Katie's voice gentled. "I know it seems terrifying, especially for you. You've been through a lot, too, and you're careful. You like to think things out. Hello, you're a research specialist, it's what you do. But in this case, all you need is faith. If you make the jump, he will catch you."

Harley swallowed the huge lump in her throat. "That seems like a huge leap of faith."

"Trust me, it's worth it."

Harley closed her eyes and let herself pretend for a minute that it could be that easy. "Fact is, we're soon to be geographically incompatible, so really, there's no leap to make."

"Honey, there's *always* a leap to make. Just think about it."

After promising to do just that, Harley disconnected and cleaned up her table. Not wanting to wake Skye, but feeling restless, she opened her front door, planning to sit on the front porch with a mug of tea.

Instead, she stared down at the large plastic bag with a big green bow on it.

"Is it Christmas?"

Harley turned and faced a groggy-looking Skye, who smiled sleepily and took the mug to sip for herself. "Yum. Who left you the present?"

"Don't know." Harley sat next to it and pulled off the small folded piece of paper taped to it. The paper was notepad sized and imprinted with WILDER ADVENTURES across the top. In pen was TJ's unmistakable scrawl. He'd written:

Your own magic bag of goodies.

"Bag of goodies?" Skye took another sip of Harley's tea. "Think it's full of sex toys?"

Harley choked out a laugh.

"Because if it is, wow. And I bet he knows how to use all the good stuff, too."

"Skye!"

"What, you think the guy doesn't know his way around a sex toy? Please. He's a walking orgasm."

Harley felt her face heat. Yes. Yes, he was.

Skye arched a brow. "Something you want to share with the class?"

What could Harley possibly say? That every single time he'd gotten his hands on her she'd gone up in flames with embarrassing, horrifying, shocking ease?

Skye pulled her lips inward as if greatly amused. "You're blushing."

"I am not."

"You told me nothing happened. I'm no longer buying it, Harl." She continued to eye her sister speculatively. "So you *did* do it with the sexiest Wilder of them all? Holy smokes, and to think I believed you when you said I interrupted you guys before anything happened because you're such a prude, but—"

"Excuse me? A prude?"

Skye smiled with affection and fondness. "Do you want to admit how long it's been since you got naked in a social setting, at least before TJ?"

No. No, she did not.

"Let me get this straight," Skye said before Harley could open the bag. "So you and TJ did the deed?"

"Depends on the 'deed' you're referring to," Harley muttered.

Skye burst out with a joyous laugh. "Ohmigod, it's working! He's lightening you up already! I love it. Okay, obviously it wasn't *the* Deed. But there are plenty of smaller deeds leading up to it. Kind of begs the question though—which one did you do?" She tapped her lower lip with a finger as she studied Harley's face.

"Let's do this. You tell me how many deeds you know about and I'll guess which one you did."

Harley rolled her eyes. "I am *not* playing that game."

Skye grinned. "You can't even think of more than one, can you?"

"I'm older than you, of course I can think of more than one."

Skye sat down next to her, a wide smile on her face. "Name three sexual acts, Harl. Hell, name two."

"I'm trying to open a gift here."

"I'll go first. A blow job."

Harley choked. "Skye—"

"Now you. Name *one*."

Harley closed her eyes.

"How about the opposite of a blow job," Skye said helpfully. "You know, when he uses *his* mouth on you to—"

"Okay, we are so not talking about this."

Skye was still grinning. "Is that what he did? 'Cause, baby, if that's what happened, let me just say *lucky you*. And also, you're going to owe him."

Harley stared down at the bow in her hands. She did. She owed him big-time . . . Worse, she'd started dreaming, both night *and* day, about ways to repay him.

"And since he's a Wilder, maybe he'll want something kinky. Like a threesome. Or some butt—"

Harley covered Skye's mouth. She could feel the huff of her sister's laugh, so she narrowed her eyes and tightened her grip on Skye's mouth. "When I take my hand away, you are going to be silent. You are not going to talk about blow jobs or threesomes or butt—*stuff*," she finished. "Understood?"

Skye smiled.

Harley pulled her hand away.

Skye opened her mouth.

Harley pointed at her. "Not a word. Not a single word. And give me my tea back."

Skye handed her the empty mug.

"Go make more," Harley demanded as she opened the bag.

Inside sat a brand-new backpack, and she stared at it in surprise.

"Maybe the sex toys are on the inside. You know, like a sex toy adventure pack."

Harley glared at Skye, who laughed and held up her hands. "Sorry. Not another word."

The backpack was full of everything Harley could ever need on any trek, and more importantly, it was completely organized. She went through it in marvel, smiling warmly at the can of soup he'd replaced, at the brand-new utility knife. "What do you think?" she asked Skye.

"I think it's badass. I think he's badass. And you? You're a stupid ass if you don't go for the Main Event with him. Not to be confused with the Deed, mind you. The Deed is sex. The Main Event is bigger."

"What's bigger than sex?"

"Love."

"Oh my God. Why do people keep flinging the L-word around? We're not—I'm not—" She broke off and found Skye watching her with a warm, little smile on her face.

"Ah, Harley," her sister said very softly as she dropped to her knees and hugged her tight. "All this time I thought you were just having fun driving him freaking nuts. I mean, you're so good at it. I also thought you might be in lust. I didn't know it was love. I'm sorry I gave you such a hard time."

"You don't know what you're talking about."

Skye just smiled. "Does he know? What am I saying? Of course he doesn't know. You're not exactly forthcoming with your feelings."

Harley ignored that. One, because while it might be true, she was not in love, and two, because she'd just found the small bag of "magic tricks" that TJ had put together in a side pocket.

"Sweet of him," Skye murmured.

"Yeah." Dental floss and Fritos. At the sight of the chips, Harley's throat tightened. Feeling a little wobbly in the heart region, she sat hard on her butt right there on the step. Without even knowing if she was going to help out Wilder or not, he'd put this together for her, just for her. She looked out into the still dark dawn and wondered when he'd brought it.

And what it meant exactly.

It meant he cared, she decided. It meant she was on his mind.

She decided she could live with that, quite nicely.

But it wasn't love. It wasn't.

At least not if she could help it.

CHAPTER 21

The next morning TJ stood in front of the lodge doing a last-minute equipment check with Nick.

Stone had already left for his trip to Eagle Falls at the crack of dawn, and Cam had just driven off for his trek to Squaw Peak.

TJ looked at his watch. In half an hour he'd be gone, too. And yet all he could think about was *not* the trip, *not* the clients, *not* the shitload of work this was going to entail without help, but Harley.

"She coming?" Nick asked.

"Who?"

Nick gave him a don't-be-stupid look. "The woman who left that bite mark on your neck who."

TJ put his fingers to the base of his throat, vividly remembering lying on Harley's bed with her hot little bod squirming all over his as she'd sucked on his skin.

"Annie see that?" Nick asked.

"No. Why?"

"'Cause if she finds out you're just playing with Harley, she's going to kick your ass. She loves that girl."

"Harley's a grown woman, not a girl, and *she* bit *me*. How do you know she's not just playing with me?"

Nick laughed. "Play is your middle name, man." He studied

TJ a moment, and slowly his smile faded. "Huh. That's interesting."

"No, there's nothing interesting."

Nick was still looking at him, as if maybe he could read right through the bullshit and into his soul. "Are you, TJ? Playing?"

Yeah.

Fuck.

No. No, he wasn't playing.

And he had no clue what that meant. All he knew was that for two nights running, he'd gone to bed with a bad case of DSB.

Deadly sperm buildup.

He thought he'd taken care of that problem in the shower this morning, but apparently not.

"So." Nick was still looking at him oddly. "Is she coming or what?"

"I don't know. She told Katie she would, but—"

"Look at that, the mighty TJ Wilder actually not knowing something. Even more interesting." He smiled and clasped TJ's shoulder. "She's good for you."

"How the hell did you get to *that* conclusion?"

Nick shrugged. "She keeps you guessing. Takes away your careful plans and control."

Well, Nick had him there. Harley absolutely played havoc on his plans and shot his control all to hell. He heard her truck on the road before it came around the turn and exchanged a look with Nick. "She's coming," TJ said to Nick's smirk.

Harley pulled into the driveway, turned off the engine, and hopped out. The early sun played with her shiny hair and fair skin as she stood there, hands on hips, eyes covered by dark sunglasses. She wore a pair of hip-hugging cargoes and a snug, long-sleeved Henley, both of which were normal clothes for that type of life, but nothing about his heart rate felt normal. He slapped his clipboard against Nick's chest and headed for her.

Her glasses hid her from him but he knew by her stillness she was watching him. As usual, she wasn't showing much, but he knew her, knew to look past the exterior. She wasn't quite sure why she was there, and was even less sure if she wanted to be. "You came," he said softly when he was near enough that no one could hear them.

A small, slightly embarrassed smile curved her mouth. "Twice now, actually."

He let out a low laugh even as his brain bombarded him with the memory of how she'd looked when she let go for him, how she'd clutched him close, as if she needed to assure herself that he was right there. And he remembered her eyes when she burst, those usually sharp brown eyes losing focus, practically rolling up in her head as she'd come hard.

And great. Now *he* was hard. He needed another shower.

"So where's Stone?" she asked, looking around.

"He already left."

She blinked. "I thought he needed a co-guide."

"That would be me." He paused, studying her face. "I thought you knew."

"No."

"Still interested?"

She didn't answer for the longest sixty seconds of his life.

"I guess it's fitting," she finally said. "After all, I do owe you."

"I like the sound of that, but it'll have to wait, since we have an audience."

She both blushed and laughed, and then met his gaze. "I meant about the backpack. And thank you, by the way, it's perfect."

He reached for her hand, ran his thumb over her knuckles. "Glad you like it."

"You knew I would, but it wasn't necessary. You've already done so much—"

"No tab."

"So you've said," she murmured. "But . . ."

"But what?"

"But you're the one who keeps giving. Your time, your expertise, your resources . . ."

"Anything. Anything you need."

"Now, see, *that*," she said softly. Looking confused and a little anxious to boot. "I don't get it. Because in return, I don't give you anything. I mean I drive you crazy, I'm sure, but that doesn't count."

He shook his head. Then let out a low laugh and nodded. "Okay, yeah, you drive me crazy," he admitted. Hell, he'd told her as much. "But you also make me laugh. You make me feel good. And sometimes, Harley, when you think I'm not paying attention, you look at me like . . ."

"Like what?" she whispered.

"Like I'm worth something to you."

"TJ." She stared at him, her eyes two fathomless pools he could have drowned in. "You always have been."

Simple words. Simple sentiment. Both went straight through him and warmed him in a way he hadn't realized he needed warming. "And you wonder what you give me," he murmured, reaching for her. But the front door on the lodge opened, and his clients came out to sit on the porch.

"Is that them?" Harley asked incredulously.

"Yeah." They were trust-funders and sorority sisters. Ranging in age from nineteen to twenty-one, all some form of bottle blond, and in spite of his firm and absolute instructions to wear comfortable outdoor weather gear, they wore string bikinis, short shorts, and enough coconut oil to grease the entire WWE.

He'd read their files. They were skating through Cal Berkeley on their daddies' dimes. They claimed that this trip was a "back to nature" trek, and that they were matching the price of Wilder Adventure's fee toward a suitable "outdoor" charity to be named later.

He hoped that was true.

Annie was serving each of them a mimosa, per their request. She looked like she was battling either morning sickness or an aversion to their discussion, which was currently stuck on the party they'd all been to the night before last, where three out of the four of them had "scored."

Jesus. He was getting old. He and Harley headed toward Nick, and the three of them moved to the porch together. TJ introduced Harley as his co-guide and photographer.

The girls—Shelly, Tandy, Lani, and no shit, Kitty—eyed Harley with varying degrees of disinterest.

"We're not *that* much trouble, TJ," Kitty murmured. "You could handle us on your own."

Harley turned to TJ and gave him a look that he wasn't sure he wanted to interpret. "How about it, TJ? Want to . . . 'handle' them on your own?"

Shelly—or was it Tandy—smiled. "We'll be good, *very* good."

Harley was still looking at TJ as she deadpanned, "Yeah, TJ, they'll be good."

"Excuse us a moment," he said to the girls. "While I confer with my co-guide." He grabbed Harley's wrist just as she started to back off the porch.

No way in hell was she getting away.

"Nick will get you loaded," he said over his shoulder. "Harley and I need a quick meeting." He tugged her into the lodge and shut the door.

"Aw, they're sweet," Harley said as he tugged her through the main reception area and down the hall, walking fast enough that she had to run to keep up with him. "You can save all that money you were going to pay me and—"

"I'll be saving nothing. I need the bodyguard."

Her eyes went to his body. "A bodyguard," she said doubtfully.

"You have no idea. They tend to think the guide comes as part of the trip. It's awkward to fight 'em off."

"Yeah, right. Are we really having a meeting?"

"Yes." Right past the kitchen was a small pantry/storage area. He opened the door and pushed Harley in ahead of him.

Harley turned in the small closet area to face TJ. "You always have meetings in here?"

He shut them in, gripped her hips, and backed her up against the door, pressing his lower body to hers, hard.

Apparently he was done talking.

And she promptly lost her ability to think clearly. Hell, she'd given up thinking clearly when she'd first parked and saw him. His look was your basic Gorgeous Alpha Outdoor Guy. Sturdy boots, cargo pants that fit across his butt perfectly, lightweight tech jersey—which looked and fit like a standard tee but was a quick drying, thin, webbed material that clung to his broad-as-a-mountain shoulders—and dark shades. He'd shoved those to the top of his head, revealing a slight sunglasses tan line on his temples and sharp green eyes, which softened whenever he looked at her.

He was drop-dead sexy.

He made her lose control, every single time. She couldn't even think about it without feeling a rush of heat to her very core. It shocked her, what he could do to her with a simple kiss or touch. If they ever actually got completely naked together, she'd probably go up in flames.

Hell, she might go up in flames right there, the way he had her up against the door. "I take it the meeting is called to order?"

"Yeah. Take notes." He slid a hand down her back, her thighs, then back up again, pausing to squeeze her bottom with a rough groan before settling a hand at the small of her back to hold her close.

She wanted to wrap her legs around his waist.

"God, Harley. I've been on the edge for some time now, and nothing's worked. Don't ask me why or how, but being with you works."

Yeah. Her, too. At least when their tongues were tangling.

"You have a way of getting beneath my skin," he said softly, spreading his fingers wide on her lower back so that the very tips of them slid beneath the waistband of her pants.

"Something else we agree on," she said a little breathlessly, extremely distracted by those fingers. "But you're leaving next week," she whispered, more to herself than him. "For Alaska. Two jobs in a row. That's like three months."

He put a finger under her chin and nudged it up to look into her eyes. "Maybe. And eventually you're leaving, too. Colorado, remember?"

He was a wanderer at heart, and she was hoping to become one. "I remember." When he nuzzled his face into her hair, she closed her eyes. "So what are we doing?"

"Not sure, but it feels damn good."

"Temporarily."

His mouth worked its way over her jaw. "Sometimes temporarily is all there is," he murmured against her lips.

It wasn't a question, but he *was* asking her something, and she knew what. "You think we could do that?" she asked. "Get involved, then walk?"

"We're not asking me. We're asking you."

Right. He'd made a living out of temporary. But she never had. And yet with him, this . . . thing, this desperate needy thing, she didn't want to walk away from, not yet. "I *have* been wanting to expand my horizons," she finally said.

A heated smile was her reward, then a gentle bite on her lower lip, which made her gasp. Taking full advantage, he slid his tongue to hers.

The shuddery moan that drifted to her ears was her own, she realized, dazed, as he pulled her shirt from her pants so that he could get beneath to bare skin, both of them sighing with pleasure when he did. He hooked his fingers in her bra and gently tugged the cups down, rasping his thumbs over her nipples, groaning into her mouth when they hardened for him.

She would have collapsed to the floor, but he had a hard thigh between hers holding her up, which was a good thing, because then he shoved up her shirt, bent his head, and took her into his mouth.

Her head fell back and smacked the door. One of his hands slid up her back and cupped her head, protecting it as he worked her breast, teasing her nipple with his teeth, then sucking it between the roof of his mouth and his tongue, hard.

Plastered between his body and the door, she cried out his

name, and her mind and body began a countdown to implosion. Her hands were all over him, reaching whatever she could, beneath his shirt, his pecs, his shoulders, his biceps, digging in when he nibbled his way to her other breast.

"God, Harley," he whispered hoarsely against her skin. "You're so beautiful. You taste so good. I want—I need—to taste the rest of you."

He already had her writhing against him, so she was pretty much putty in his hands as he kissed her neck and reached for the button on her pants.

She needed her mouth on him, too. Now. Hell, at that moment, with him sliding a hand inside her underwear to squeeze a bare butt cheek, she'd have happily said yes to anything he wanted.

To everything he wanted.

Someone banged on the door right behind her head, and she nearly went into heart failure.

"TJ." It was Nick. "The natives are getting restless."

TJ took his mouth off Harley's throat but left one hand on her breast, the other in her pants. "Give them another mimosa."

"Another mimosa and you'll be carrying them to their kayaks."

His thumb brushed over her nipple, and she had to bite her lip hard to keep from making a sound. "Five minutes," TJ told Nick, watching Harley's face.

They heard Nick's sigh, and then silence.

Harley hadn't moved. She'd held herself still as need and panic pulsed through her veins instead of blood.

"Breathe," TJ murmured, smoothing back her hair to press his mouth to the sensitive skin beneath her ear when she gulped in a breath.

He nibbled at her earlobe, his arms tightening on her as he continued assaulting her senses, one hand sliding farther into her panties. He had long arms, and she understood that was a bonus as he reached even farther, and then farther still. And when he found her wet and ready, he groaned deep in his throat.

"TJ," she gasped when he slid one of those long fingers inside her. "We can't—"

He added another finger, gliding them in and out of her, using the wet pads of those fingers to graze over ground zero.

As unbelievable as it was, she felt her toes curl. She was going to go over for him. "TJ," she choked out, trying to squeeze her legs together to prevent it, but he had a thigh between hers, holding her open as he stroked her. *God.* "It's your turn—I can't—*TJ!*"

"Christ, I love the sound of my name on your lips," he murmured, kissing said lips, taking her lower one between his teeth and tugging just enough to have her hiss out a breath. "Say it again," he demanded softly as he gently but firmly stroked her, and when she helplessly complied, moaning his name, he smiled roughly against her. "Yeah, like that." He grazed her nipple again, watching from beneath hooded eyes as hers drifted shut in pleasure.

They flew open again when he dropped to his knees.

"Wait! What are you—"

"Just relax. This will only take a few minutes." When his hands tugged her pants to her thighs, her hands went to his hair. She meant to tug him up, even tightened her fingers in the silky strands to do so, but then he pushed her thighs open as much as he could with her pants at half mast. "You're so wet," he whispered, and glided a thumb over her, opening her up for him.

"TJ," she managed, but then he leaned in and kissed her, *there*, using his tongue in the exact right rhythm her body needed.

He knew her body better than she did.

It should have shocked her, but she couldn't obsess over that at the moment because he was making slow stroking motions, holding her hips still for his ministrations, his mouth hot as he sucked and bit, feeding her into a desperate frenzy, and she felt her body tighten, felt every single muscle clenching in sweet agony.

His hair was falling over his forehead as he gave her his fierce, full attention, and unbelievably, as she watched him, she felt the first shudder hit her. "TJ," she cried out, shocked, overwhelmed that he'd been able to get her there again, right there on the edge.

"You taste as good as I thought you would." Then he sucked her into his mouth, nudging her right over that edge, and she exploded.

She was halfway back to earth when the knock came again.

"Goddammit, TJ!" came Nick's hushed voice. "Annie's going to kill one of those silly girls if you don't hurry! She's blaming Not-Abigail."

"Coming." TJ cocked his head up at Harley, grinning at the double meaning.

Harley was still leaning against the door, unable to move. TJ righted her clothes for her while she just stood there breathing like a lunatic, shaky as hell. When he'd finished, he leaned into her again, forearms flat on the door on either side of her head, and with his mouth against hers, smiled, eyes warm. "Hi."

Her lids felt heavy but she managed to look at him. "Hi."

His hips were pinned to hers, pushing against her so that she could feel every solid inch of what was waiting for her, if they ever got that far. "I can't believe you—that I—" She closed her eyes again and shook her head, desperately trying to slow her racing heart and put a thought together. "I've never been like this, you know. Never have been able to—"

"You've never come with a man before?"

Her eyes flew open and she met his steady, patient gaze. "No, I have. Of course I have, I just . . . not this easily." She squeezed her eyes shut again. "It's a problem."

He frowned as he ran his thumb along her jaw. "Problem?"

"Every time you touch me, I . . ." She grimaced.

He smiled. "Come?"

"Yes!" She took a drag of air. "You have to stop that."

"I don't think I can."

"You have to! It's *your* turn!"

His eyes darkened. "Ever since you told me about that night at Long Lake, I've racked my brain trying to remember it, trying to make sure I didn't hurt you, that your first time was memorable, and I can't." He shoved his fingers into his hair, standing there, arms up, taut and strained. "It's been killing me."

She gaped at him. "So is that what this has been? You trying to make it up to me?"

He didn't answer but she saw the truth in his gaze, the soft regret, the heat and desire, and even more devastating, the affection, and it did the unexpected.

It softened her.

For once he seemed unable to read her. He was quietly watching her, and when she didn't speak, he rubbed his bristly jaw to hers. "Are you okay?"

Funny, but she was. Maybe even better than okay. Sure, this probably was going to end in heartbreak, but that was for the future. She'd always lived for the damn future and she was tired of that. For once she was going to live in the moment.

And enjoy every single second of it.

At least for the next week anyway. Putting her hands to his biceps, she turned them, pressed *him* to the door, cupping his face to brush her mouth over his jaw. She was trying to find the words to tell him how okay she was, that he had nothing to make up for, but found herself distracted by how his body felt held between the door and hers, how deliciously hard he was.

Everywhere.

Her hands slid down his chest and he groaned. She kept moving, over his belly, heading for gold.

"Goddammit, TJ!" came Nick's voice through the door. "I've been out there alone for fifteen minutes. Those girls have grabbed me at least twice, and I think Annie went looking for her gun."

"Fuck." TJ let out a long, shuddery breath and straightened, jaw tight. "Ready?" he asked Harley.

"I am." She glanced down at the huge bulge in front of his cargoes. "But I don't know about you."

"Baby, if I was any more ready, I'd bust out of my skin." He closed his eyes. "Now don't talk to me for a minute. I've got to picture somebody's grandma naked."

She heard the laugh burst out of her as his words bathed over her, infusing her with a power she'd never felt before. She'd never been sexually aggressive, so when she found herself reaching out and running a finger over his zipper, and the hot length beneath it, she shocked herself.

A sound of raw desire tore from deep in his throat. "Harley."

She did it again.

With another one of those sexy growls, he grabbed her wrist and gulped some air in. "*Not* helping." He opened the door and gently shoved her out in front of him. "Go."

She looked at him over her shoulder, and he groaned again, squeezing his eyes shut.

She felt another surge of that power and confidence, and unable to hold it back, she smiled.

He took it in and helplessly matched it. "Killing me here, Harley. Killing me."

CHAPTER 22

Outside, TJ and Harley helped Nick load up the coeds and all the gear.

"About fuckin' time," Nick whispered over the top of the truck as they tied on the kayaks. "Jesus, what the hell were you two doing in there?"

"Do we need to have the birds and bees talk again?"

Nick rolled his eyes. "But the closet? With Harley? Seriously, what is it with you guys?"

"Hey, I seem to remember you and Annie just last week in the snowcat."

"That's different."

"Really? How?"

"Well . . ." Nick scratched his head. "We're old married farts."

"You just turned forty. Not exactly ready for the senior home."

"Just trying to keep it interesting. Besides, Annie attacked me. It's the pregnancy hormones or something. I can't keep up with her. She's like a cat in heat. She wakes me up in the middle of the night to—"

"Stop!" TJ covered his ears. "Christ. I do not want to hear this."

Nick grinned, apparently over his mad. "What happened to the no nookie-on-the-job rule?"

TJ and his brothers had come up with that rule a long time ago, when they'd first started the business. No fucking around on the job.

Literally.

There'd been slip-ups, most notably Cam's thing with Katie last year, but for the most part, the rule had kept them from being stupid. "Harley isn't a client."

At that moment, she came up beside them to help tie the kayaks down. Her cheeks were flushed, her hair a little tousled. Her shirt was still untucked.

Nick pulled her in for an easy, affectionate hug and sent TJ a long, level look of warning over her head.

Yeah, yeah. She was like Nick's baby sister, and if TJ hurt her, he was dead. Got it. As for Harley, she was looking adorably flustered, and to TJ, sexy as hell. Just watching her fingers work the ropes reminded him of how they'd felt outlining his—

"I don't understand why you need my help with this trip," she said softly, gesturing to the coeds. "Looks like any guy's idea of a wet dream to me, having those four Mountain Barbies all to yourself." She met TJ's gaze. "Explain it to me again?"

"I need you to protect me."

Nick smirked, then smoothed it into a smile when Harley glanced over at him. As far as "protecting" went, Nick would go to great lengths to do exactly that for Harley. Hell, they all would, which reminded TJ that if he screwed this up and hurt her, there'd be a lot of people looking to strangle him. Specifically Cam, Stone, and Nick. And while he could take any one of them, he was pretty sure that against all three he'd get his ass kicked.

Nick drove them out to the trailhead at the start of the Snake River. The plan was for him to make a food drop at the halfway mark the next day, then pick them all up at the ending point in two days.

Katie had given Harley the trip details to read on the ride, though it was hard to absorb details when she was still quivering from what TJ had done to her up against the door in the closet—which she was absolutely not going to think about.

She forced herself to concentrate on the file. The trip was relatively simple. Kayaking. Two nights of camping. She was to record the trip with her camera, and maybe give out some wildlife facts while she was at it.

No problem. She was experienced enough for that. She could kayak to Mexico if she had to. Cooking might be a little bit of a problem, but hey, TJ knew going into it what her skills were. *He* could cook. She'd happily serve and clean up.

Simple.

TJ rode shotgun in the front seat next to Nick. He was slouched back, looking deceptively lazy and at ease as the girls chattered incessantly amongst themselves. He looked like he was breathing once every other minute or so, and maybe that's what he had to do in order to survive the silliness coming from the back, lower his heart rate to hibernation level.

Lani and Tandy asked about the landscape and the river, and TJ opened a map and showed them the proposed route, passively pleasant and professional. But when Shelly and Kitty asked about him personally, like was he single, did he date college-age sorority girls, and what was his favorite drink, he didn't respond.

Nick shot Harley a glance in the rearview mirror, and Harley bit her lower lip to hold back her smile.

At the staging area, the girls pulled off their shorts and T-shirts, once again revealing their teeny tiny bikinis as they put on the protective gear that TJ and Nick handed out and insisted on everyone wearing. TJ spoke to the girls in detail before letting them into the water, outlining exactly what he expected, and how they needed to listen and respond to him if he asked them to do something.

"Do you think he's this alpha and dominating in bed?" Shelly whispered to Kitty, shivering with excitement.

Again Harley had to bite her lip to keep a straight face.

TJ shot her a look as he checked and rechecked the gear, then got everyone into the water, managing to avoid helping Kitty spread suntan oil on her limbs or helping Shelly tighten her vest across her enhanced and expensive breasts. Much to their disappointment, he let Harley do both.

That part of the river was wide, calm, and flat—which was why they were on it. Harley had her camera out, able to both steer and shoot pictures. The water was so clear and deep that they could see fish gliding through the currents beneath them in the sunny spots. It was like a whole other universe existed down there, and the coeds actually fell silent, soaking it all in, absorbing the beauty.

Until one of the fish broke the surface with a splash.

Startled screams abounded, and Tandy accidentally rolled her kayak. Her friends sat watching her attempt to right herself, tears of laughter streaming down their faces.

Harley got it all on digital.

TJ righted Tandy with ease, making the others sigh and look at each other, clearly wishing they'd thought to roll. Tandy was none the worse for wear, though she did have a brief hair crisis.

A coyote appeared on the shore, visible through the bush. "Wolf!" Kitty cried out. "What if it eats us?"

TJ looked at Harley across the water. Obviously, she was to field this one. "Actually, it's a coyote," Harley told her. "And he's not going to eat you."

"How do you know?"

"There's been only one fatal coyote attack on record, and that was back in 1981, in Southern California. But to be safe, don't ever feed one."

"What if it comes up to us while we're eating?" Tandy asked.

"It won't."

"But what if it does?"

"Then make a lot of noise to scare it off. Wave your hands, yell, throw a rock at it, whatever you have to do."

The coyote bounded off out of view.

"Holy shit," Lani said. "That thing's moving."

"They can run up to forty-three miles per hour," Harley told her.

"Shh," Shelly breathed. "It'll hear us."

"It's already heard us," Harley said. "They have better hearing than dogs."

"It's all alone," Shelly said. "She needs a sorority."

The others laughed. "He or she isn't alone," Harley said. "They travel in packs and hunt in pairs. You just didn't see the others, but they're there."

"How do you know all this?" Lani asked, looking sincerely interested.

"I study them for my other job as a wildlife researcher."

"Cool." Lani smiled at Harley. "I'm a biology major."

They spent a few minutes talking about that, after which the others seemed to accept Harley slightly better. She snapped more pictures and found herself enjoying it. Probably most of that came from their fearless guide, who happened to look damn fine in the lead kayak, wielding a paddle, his biceps flexing as he steered, the rest of his body relaxed and completely in control.

An hour in, Kitty needed—demanded—a potty break. The girls got out of their kayaks, accepted drinks from Harley, then stripped out of their wet protective gear down to their bikinis and plopped on the rocky sand at the water's edge. Harley was wet, too, but left her shorts and tank top on over her bathing suit. TJ's board shorts and performance tee were also wet, but they didn't seem to bother him any. He once again checked the gear—while the girls checked him, whispering amongst themselves.

TJ's shorts came to his knees, his shirt loose. While he looked damn good, his clothes were definitely hiding the true extent of how in shape he really was. After checking and rechecking everything, he peeled off his wet shirt and, in just the shorts, bent to his pack, probably looking for a dry shirt.

Kitty dropped her drink. "Sweet baby Jesus," she whispered.

He wasn't bulky. His body had been hardened and trained over the years the old-fashioned way, from lots of hard work.

"He's even *hotter* than I thought," Lani whispered.

"I don't know what I'd do to him first," Kitty whispered back.

Harley knew. She knew exactly. She'd lick that stomach, then drop to her knees and slowly ease those shorts down over his hips so that she could lean in and—

"Think he's taken?" Tandy whispered.

"Yes," Harley said without thinking.

They all turned and stared at her. "By *you*?" Tandy asked incredulously.

Okay, she was pretty sure that was not a compliment.

Shelly's eyes were narrowed. Clearly they weren't willing to believe Harley could catch a man like TJ—which led to a problem.

Harley was a horrible liar, always had been. The fact was, TJ *wasn't* taken, not by her, not by anyone. TJ belonged to no one, except maybe the mountain.

"Is he with someone?" Tandy asked again.

"Can't really say," Harley whispered. There. How was that for the truth? She couldn't say because she didn't know exactly how "taken" he considered himself.

As if knowing that they were discussing him, TJ looked over, eyes unerringly locking in on Harley.

She forced a smile. He paused, then returned it before turning back to the gear.

Shelly was still staring at Harley. "Why can't you say?"

"Yes, Harley, why can't you say? It wouldn't be right."

Tandy and Shelly exchanged a look. "Why?" Tandy asked. "Are you insinuating that he's . . . gay?"

Harley had to bite her lip to keep from letting the gust of nervous laughter escape. She hadn't thought of that. But maybe if they thought he was gay, they'd leave him alone. "Can't say," she repeated firmly.

Lani sighed in disappointment.

Good Lord, they would actually believe that the big, edgy, obviously testosterone-ridden TJ was gay rather than believe that he'd be in a relationship with *her*.

Finally Kitty shook her head. "No. There's no way he's gay." She narrowed her eyes at Harley. "If you wanted him for yourself, all you had to do was say so. But honestly, I don't see him reciprocating. You're not his type."

The other three looked at Harley in grave disappointment, as if she'd broken some sacred sorority trust. She didn't care, as long as she did her job, which, as TJ had pointed out with utter seriousness, was to protect him.

What can she say? She'd tried.

They all got back on the river, and an hour later came to a sharp turn where suddenly the water moved faster than half a mile an hour. Like one mile an hour.

Still, the coeds shrieked and screamed as if they'd come to the edge of the world. TJ called out directions, his voice filled with quiet but unequivocal command, which in turn forced the girls to shut up if they wanted to hear how to save themselves. He was calm and utterly authoritative, and they leapt to do his bidding, as if pleasing him was all that mattered.

When Harley found herself doing the same, she had to laugh at herself, then let out a surprised squeak when TJ let the girls pass them and snagged her by the back of her life vest, holding her and her kayak next to his. "You're grinning like a Cheshire cat," he murmured, pushing his sunglasses to the top of his head to study her. "Explain."

She looked into his face, then snapped a picture of him, glancing down at her LED screen as the picture flashed there. His eyes readily revealed his intelligence, a sharp wit, and also an inner strength that never failed to give her a flutter. He had a strong face, a beautiful face, though he'd hate that assessment. Did she care to share that he turned her on like no other man ever had? Hell, no. "Inside joke," she murmured.

He eyed the girls' retreating backs, then Harley again. "You know sound carries over water, right?"

Oh, God. What part had he heard, that he was gay, or that she wanted him for herself? She looked into his eyes, but couldn't see anything but the gleam of promised retribution.

Definitely the gay part. "One of us has to catch up with them."

"Yes." He let go of her. "I'll do it. And I'll catch up with *you* later."

Oh boy.

CHAPTER 23

When they stopped for lunch, TJ handled the kayaks and Harley dealt out lunch, serving the girls Annie's pre-made sandwiches beneath the shade of a grove of two-hundred-year-old, towering pines.

Harley took herself off to the side, giving the coeds their privacy. Or, more accurately, giving Harley *her* privacy. TJ ambled over when he was done. "Well, that went well," she said, handing him a big, thick turkey and cheese sandwich.

With an answer that was more of a grunt than affirmation, he plopped down next to her and dug in.

"Hungry?" she asked, amused at his single-minded purpose of devouring the sandwich.

"Even gay men get hungry."

Oh, yeah. She'd almost forgotten. "If it helps, they didn't believe me."

"I wish they had. I'd rather be gay than the boy toy of the month. You should have just told them that we were together. That would have worked."

She opened her mouth and then closed it. And then went on the defensive rather than figure out why his easy solution irritated her. "Must be exhausting to fend off four beautiful young women's advances."

Fend them off he had, with more calm, impassive pleasantry

than she could have managed. "I mean sure, they want to eat you up," she said. "You might have gotten groped a few times getting in and out of the water, but overall, it's been easy enough to handle, right?"

He just looked at her as he swallowed the last of his sandwich.

She grinned. "How many times did you get groped, anyway?"

"I don't know, but I'm bruised. You're supposed to be watching my back."

Yes, but she'd been very busy watching his ass. "You really don't feel anything when they come on to you like that?"

He eyed the uneaten portion of her sandwich. "I feel the urge to wrap my fingers around Cam's and Stone's neck."

She laughed again and handed him the rest of her sandwich.

His eyes warmed. His lips curved as he took her in. "I love it when you laugh," he said simply.

Damn if that didn't make her go all soft and mushy. "You do know they think you're God's gift, that they each hope you'll go alpha and domineering on them in their sleeping bags tonight?"

"How about you? Do you want me to go alpha and domineering in *your* sleeping bag tonight?" he asked, his voice low and husky.

Heat slashed through her, and her gaze ran over his body, all sprawled out and gorgeous. He hadn't put on another shirt. All he wore were those board shorts and a smile. The smile revealed a wicked intent. The board shorts, low and loose on his lean hips, revealed the fact that he could absolutely follow through with that wicked intent.

"See anything you want?" he murmured.

"No. Absolutely not." She turned her back to him and hugged her knees to her chest, watching the river, letting out a low, shaky breath when she knew he could no longer see her face.

"Okay, let's recap." He ran a finger over her shoulder. "You don't want me—"

"As a boyfriend," she clarified. Because she *did* want him. She wanted him bad. She just didn't want to *keep* him. She couldn't.

He was a walking, talking, breathing heartbreak. "I don't want you as a boyfriend."

"Because . . . ?"

"Because you don't want to *be* a boyfriend. Plus, you read my list, you saw—"

"Right. I'm not . . . what did you call Nolan? Sweet, steady, and stable."

She closed her eyes. "Yeah." But the truth was, in spite of the rough-and-tumble readiness, the jagged edges to him, he was those things. Sweet. Steady. Stable.

Which meant that she was another *S* altogether—screwed.

After lunch, they headed down a relatively easy section of the river, floating so slowly Harley could have gotten out and pushed faster. There were no waves, no tumbling rapids, nothing. The water was so flat that the tip of the kayak didn't even rise and fall.

TJ was out in front, his kayak gliding sure and smooth. Behind him, the four girls laughed and giggled and talked about whatever flitted through their heads. Taking up the rear, Harley could see and hear all, not that the girls were trying to keep their voices down.

"Look at his arms," Kitty whispered across the water with a dreamy sigh.

No doubt. TJ had the best arms Harley had ever seen. She'd been taking some pictures and found her lens focused in on them, taut, tanned, and glistening.

"I know!" Kitty said. "Someone rip my top off. That'll get his attention."

"No!" Harley said quickly, and all four girls craned around to look at her. "No nudity on the river," she said. *No nudity on the river?* Jesus, she needed to think faster on her feet.

From ahead, TJ glanced around and gave them a long look, probably trying to figure out if he needed to be in on the conversation or if he should be thinking about running for the border. Harley gave him a little finger wave. She could handle it.

Probably.

"I've got a better idea," Shelly murmured. "Watch this. Help!" she suddenly shrieked, and flailed in her kayak until she managed to tip it over. "TJ, help me!" she screamed.

TJ was already maneuvering his kayak around. Harley knew it would take him no time at all to get to Shelly and haul her out of the water, where she'd probably crawl over him with her wet, warm, curvy body.

As far as tactics went, it was a good one, Harley conceded. And it might be a lot of fun to watch, except for two things.

One, TJ was paying her to avoid exactly this.

And two, she didn't want any half-naked wet woman crawling all over him.

Well, unless *she* was the half-naked wet woman. "Shelly," she said calmly while holding up a hand to TJ to let him know she had it handled. "Put your feet down and stand up. The water's only up to your belly button."

Shelly abruptly stopped screaming and flailing and stood up, sending Harley a pout. "You're no fun." She flounced through the water to her kayak. "You just blew my chance for some mouth-to-mouth."

TJ was wearing his dark sunglasses and his baseball cap, which shaded his face, so it was hard to tell his expression across the fifty feet of water that separated them, but Harley was pretty sure he was amused.

And relieved.

He could thank her later. Maybe with some mouth-to-mouth of their own variety.

They went back to kayaking with no more close encounters of the made-up kind. After awhile, Lani floated up next to Harley and smiled. Harley returned it. "You doing okay?" she asked the coed.

"Yes," Lani said. "It's gorgeous out here."

"It is."

"You're so lucky that this is your job. I think this would be the coolest job ever."

"What are you going to do with your biology degree?"

"I was thinking about teaching, but I know now I want to do something different. I want to do something to help preserve the wildlife."

Shelly turned back and smiled warmly at her friend. "You can do it, Lani."

Kitty nodded agreeably. "You can do whatever you want."

"Easy for you to say," Lani said quietly. "You've both got your daddies' trust funds."

"So do you," Tandy said.

"No." Lani shook her head. "It was all stock options, which are gone."

The others looked at each other, horrified. "You're . . . broke?"

"Just about," Lani said quietly.

There was silence for a few minutes as they absorbed this while floating down the river.

"I'll help you, Lani," Shelly said softly. "I have plenty of extra—"

"Me too," Kitty said.

But Lani shook her head. "No. I mean thank you, but I couldn't take your money."

"It's not mine," Shelly said. "It's my parents', and they don't give a rat's ass how I spend it. It's up to me what I do with it. And I give it to you."

At that exact moment Harley warmed up to the Mountain Barbies.

A few minutes later, they rounded a corner and the water picked up speed. Simultaneously all four girls got into trouble. Lani and Tandy collided and knocked each other into the water, screaming as they went, naturally. TJ went after Tandy, and Harley went after Lani. Just as they got both of them straightened out, the other two girls steered directly into an outcrop of trees sticking out of the water.

And capsized.

There was more screaming, and lots of hair trauma. Then two otters swam right by Shelly, who got her earlier wish about being closer to TJ when she literally crawled up his body to get out of the water and away from the otters. Only she was too terrified to enjoy the experience. Harley explained that the otters were harmless to them, that they were just out looking for beaver dams to adopt, but it still took awhile for everyone to calm down.

When they stopped for the day, the girls sprawled out on the shore in the last of the sun's warmth while TJ and Harley set up camp. Harley pulled the gear out of the kayaks, noting that the coeds had once again stripped out of their protective gear, down to their skimpy bikinis. She had ten years and ten pounds on them, and it was hard not to feel at least a little inferior.

That's when she felt a lean hard body press up against her.

TJ's hand settled on the nape of her neck, causing her entire body to shiver. He'd warned her that his kind of love was temporary. She'd agreed to temporary. So what was she supposed to do with the fact that it seemed like so much more? She was kayaking down Heart Break River without a paddle, but even knowing it, she had no idea how to protect herself. Even worse, she didn't want to. She kept her gaze on the coeds, as gorgeous as the man behind her, and sighed.

"You're beautiful, Harley."

She let out a genuine laugh at that. She was wearing men's board shorts, a loose T-shirt, a life vest, and completing the picture of loveliness, water booties to protect her feet, which had given her a ridiculous tan line. Her hair was undoubtedly a frizzball and she'd forgone her usual mascara and lip gloss in favor of full-protection sunscreen and ChapStick.

He turned her to face him. "Beautiful," he repeated in a low tone, in his authoritative voice, the one that could make coeds jump to attention, and women the world over want to please him.

"You're not so bad yourself," she said, and smiled to lighten the moment.

He didn't return the smile.

Suddenly she wanted to see his eyes. She reached up, tugged off his reflective sunglasses, and caught her breath. He was being serious. Dead serious. Lifting her hand, she ran a finger over his unsmiling mouth until he took her hand and kissed her palm.

Her belly quivered, and again, she ran a finger over his lips.

He bit the pad of it, and even as she gasped, he soothed the ache by slowly sucking it into his mouth.

Her knees liquefied.

He sucked again, a strong sip, the muscles of his jaw working, and she felt every single bone melt right out of her body. "TJ."

He let her finger slowly pull from his mouth with a soft suction sound. "Yeah?" he said, gravel in his voice.

She stared up into his eyes and ended up shaking her head. "I can't remember."

With a soft chuckle, he moved away to strip out of everything but his board shorts so it could all dry while he worked to get camp set up. Harley moved to help him with the girls' tent, but he was so efficient, she ended up just watching him.

She couldn't help it.

No red-blooded woman could have.

"Problem?" he asked, shoving his damp hair back and glancing over at her.

"No." Her eyes roamed over his body. The wet board shorts were molded to him, leaving little to the imagination, and her mouth actually watered.

He looked at her curiously, then down at himself. "What?"

Oh good Lord. To be half that utterly clueless and easy in her own skin . . . "Nothing!" She gathered wood for a fire, thinking she could probably start one off her own body heat alone, but that didn't happen. It took three Frito chips, but she was feeling quite proud of herself, a feeling that turned into something else entirely when she found TJ watching her.

"Nice job," he said as the fire flickered and crackled warmly, bathing his face in the soft glow, revealing the intensity of his eyes, his expression one that she'd never seen before.

"Only required three chips," she told him a little breathlessly, and held up the bag. "More to eat."

He smiled at her, the kind that tended to melt her bones.

Bad bones.

As the sun set, everyone pulled on dry clothes and cleaned themselves up. TJ stood at the fire, barbequing in a white long-sleeved Henley, faded Levi's, and bare feet, looking more appetizing than the salmon Nick had dropped for them.

Everyone ate as if they'd never eaten before, then the girls spent a few minutes complaining about sore muscles and how exhausted they were before disappearing into their tent, leaving Harley and TJ alone by the fire.

"You saved my ass today," he told her. "Thanks for coming."

"You'd have been fine."

"I'd have lost my mind." He slipped an arm around her and pulled her in closer so that their thighs and hips touched. "Although I've been losing my mind anyway."

"Why?"

He just looked at her, eyes hot.

Right. Harley: three orgasms. TJ: zero.

CHAPTER 24

Nighttime in the Sierras was impressive. High mountain peaks cast black shadows over trees, as tall as skyscrapers, that whistled softly in the dark. The moon rose, painting everything in a soft blue glow.

The coeds had long ago quieted down in their tent. All that could be heard was soft snoring. Harley still sat next to TJ, incredibly aware of his heat, his strength. The log beneath them was long and yet they sat so close she couldn't have fit a piece of paper between them.

TJ leaned forward to poke a long stick into the fire and with minimal effort coaxed the flames back to life. Sitting back, brushing against her as he did, he met her gaze.

And her body hummed. She knew his did, too. It shimmered in the night between them.

No matter what she told herself, there was something between them. Something uncontrolled, which should have scared her.

Instead, it turned her on.

He'd given her his support in Desolation, and when she'd wanted it, also his help. He'd given her a job this weekend. She knew he'd give her anything she wanted. But in that moment, all she wanted was to give *him* something.

Something of herself.

"Think they're out for the night?" she whispered.

"Christ, I hope so. Why?"

She just looked at him.

His eyes widened, and she realized she'd managed to do what few ever did—surprise him.

When he spoke, his voice was low and husky, and basically sex on a stick. "Teasing me right now is not a good idea."

"I'm not teasing."

He closed his eyes. "Harley."

She knew watching her come tended to shatter his control. She wondered if watching him come would do the same to her.

She was betting it would, since just thinking about it made her nipples hard. Without a word, she got up and walked to the tent. "You girls need anything?" she whispered through the zippered door.

No answer.

She walked back to the campfire. TJ hadn't moved. He was still sitting there, watching her, cast in the flickering light of the fire's glow. He had a few strands of sun-kissed hair falling over his forehead, curling past his collar. He'd gotten some sun, making his green eyes all the more striking.

He was so gorgeous he took her breath away.

She held out her hand.

He took it without hesitation, then raised a brow when she pulled him to a stand. She looked into his eyes for a long moment, then turned and led him away from the fire, down along the river, over bush and under trees, across a carpet of soft, giving, forest moss. Several hundred yards later they came to a small, isolated clearing, secluded and dark except for the faint glow of the stars reflecting on the water.

Without a word, she pressed on his shoulders until he obliged her by leaning back against a tree.

Looking into his eyes, she went up on tiptoes to kiss him lightly on the mouth. Then his jaw, his throat. After that she tugged on the neckline of his shirt to press a kiss to his collarbone.

His hands came up to her hips, squeezed gently, then started to slide beneath her shirt. "No," she said, squeezing her hands on his wrists, indicating he could hold her hips but nothing else.

He let out a breath and went still, silently letting her have her way. Reaching down, she skimmed his shirt up over his head and tossed it aside. She kneeled between his splayed legs to kiss him on his amazing abs, feeling the ridge of muscles leap beneath her lips. She nibbled at his belly button, then kissed the spot beneath it.

He let out a long, shaky breath, but he didn't speak and he didn't move.

She rewarded him with another kiss, right above the button on his Levi's.

And then she popped it open.

And the next.

And the next.

Beneath the Levi's was nothing but TJ in all his silky, hot, hard glory.

He shifted. "Harley."

"Shh." She set her hands on his thighs.

He let out a long, jagged breath. "I—"

Cutting him off with a shake of her head, she trailed a finger from his belly button to the opening of his jeans.

He got bigger.

And harder.

She cupped him.

"Christ, Harley," he said on a rough groan, his hands going to the thick tree trunk on either side of his hips as if he needed the leverage to hold himself up. "You have no idea what you to do me."

"No. But I know what I'm about to do to you." She looked up into his face and smiled. "Just relax. This will only take a few minutes."

He choked out a laugh at his own words being tossed back in his face, but then she tugged on his jeans so that he sprang free, and kissed him on the very tip.

"Oh, fuck." He sounded strangled. "Maybe less than a few

minutes." When she ran her tongue down his length, he gasped. "Definitely less."

Smiling at the hoarse tightness in his voice, she sat back and stared at him in all his full, magnificent glory. Lord, he was beautiful. Leaning forward again, her hands still on his thighs, she slowly drew him into her mouth.

He released a guttural noise from low in his throat and said something entirely unintelligible. She took that for "more, please," so she gave it. His fingers went to her hair, tangling in the strands as if he couldn't help himself.

She glanced up at him. Eyes closed, head back, he wore a look of such agonized pleasure it gave her a rush that was only a millimeter beneath an orgasm. When she felt him draw tight under her hands and mouth, she knew he was close, a fact that was verified when he groaned and tried to pull her away, shifting his hips backwards.

Not taking the hint, she tightened her grip and kept at him.

"Harley. God, Harley—you've got to stop, I'm going to—"

She murmured her understanding without releasing him, and just the vibration from her throat wrenched a rough groan from him. His muscles spasmed as he came, one hand still fisted in her hair, the other slapping to the trunk at his side to keep him upright.

She didn't move away until she felt him relax. He staggered, then dropped heavily to his knees. Without opening his eyes, he reached for her, pulling her into his lap as he sank all the way to the ground, sagging back against the tree, panting, boneless.

He slouched there, head back, eyes closed, wearing nothing but the opened jeans that were barely still on him.

Barefoot.

Shirtless.

Looking hot enough to spread butter on and eat up in one bite.

She smiled and curled into him, nearly purring as his hands slowly roamed her body. "Hope that helped with the tension a little," she whispered against his throat, smiling when he shivered.

"More than a little." His voice was rough, giving her a feeling of satisfaction. "In fact, I seem to be missing all of my bones."

She laughed, was still laughing when he slid his hands into her hair, tugged back her head, and kissed her long and deep. She realized he'd fully recovered, because he had his hands beneath her top, his thumbs gliding over her nipples. She moaned, and felt him smile against her neck. "I found my bones," he murmured, rocking his hips into hers.

No kidding! She snuggled in, not wanting to move, enjoying the way his heart was still pounding beneath her cheek. "We've got to go back."

"Mmmm." He took a deep breath and reached down to kiss her again. "Not yet."

"If they wake up and need anything—"

He went still, clearly thinking—fun or duty? Watching the battle was fascinating, as it took a very long few minutes.

Duty won, which only made her like him all the more.

With a groan, he climbed to his feet, reaching down to pull her to hers, holding her against him for a minute when she would have turned away. "Thank you," he murmured.

"I had a good time," she said, and made him grin.

He'd had a good time, too. It was in every line of his body, and holy smokes, that body. Milk did a body good, and sex did it better.

He hugged her hard, pressing his face in her hair. "Remember how we both said that being out here on the mountain, away from all the bullshit, made us feel alive?"

She tilted her head back and looked into his warm eyes. "Yes."

His gaze searched hers, his smile slowly fading. "I'm starting to think it's not the mountain at all, that maybe it's you. You make me feel alive, Harley."

On that shocking statement, he took her hand and led her back to camp.

* * *

The next day on the river was a rinse and repeat of the one before. Except instead of otters, they saw three huge, gorgeous bucks on one of the ridges watching them from afar. Later, they heard a pack of coyotes howling. Harley assured the girls they were not about to be coyote bait, and to distract them, told them a little about what she was doing for her internship, and from that moment on, they looked at her with what might have been respect instead of competition for TJ.

By nine o'clock that night, the coeds were once again in their tents, out cold.

"Kayaking takes it out of you," TJ said from the fire, where he was putting on more wood.

"The way you do it, it does." Harley moved toward the heat, hands out. Her legs were chilly since she was still in her bathing suit with a hoodie sweatshirt and board shorts over it. "You pushed them a little hard today."

He slid her an inscrutable glance.

She met his gaze, raised a questioning brow.

And he caved with a smile.

"I knew it," she breathed. "You did it on purpose. For a replay of last night, perhaps?"

His eyes dilated black. "I had to dunk myself in the cold water every time I thought about last night."

"I was wondering why you kept going in." She grinned. "Did it help?"

"No."

She was quiet a moment, then voiced what had been on her mind all day. "Maybe it's not the mountain?" she whispered, repeating his words from last night.

He just looked at her.

"Where did that come from?" she asked. "Because aren't you the guy who isn't into commitment. I mean, did the rules change?"

"I've never been much of a rule man."

More off balance then ever, she shook her head. "You say that like . . . like you're sure."

His gaze remained steady and thoughtful.

"But . . . you can't be sure," she whispered. "No one I've ever known is *sure*."

"Stone and Cam seem pretty sure."

She was having trouble processing the words. "But they're not playing the temporary game that we are. We have one week. Even that could be too long if you think about it. What if you get tired of being with just one person? Tired of the banality of it, tired of the daily grind? What if you get tired of sleeping with just one person, of having sex with just one person? Hell, maybe *I'll* get tired of it."

"You wouldn't get tired of the sex."

She stared at him. "Only a man would say that."

Tossing aside his stick, he rose and came toward her. Unlike her, he'd changed. His look was the usual, basic badass mountain man . . . a pair of faded blue jeans, beloved battered trainers, and a long-sleeved Henley. It was the jeans that held her attention. They were molded to him and like the night before, there was no indication of anything between him and the denim.

He got real close. "Sounds like maybe you're the one that has the commitment problem."

Before she could comment on *that*, he tugged her into him, nudging his hips to hers.

"Um, are you"—she swiveled a finger in the region of his crotch—"commando again?"

"I took a quick dip in the river to wash off." He shrugged. "Got dressed in a hurry."

"And forgot your underwear?"

Some of the tension left him, and he smiled as he nuzzled his face into her hair. "Is that turning you on?"

Duh. "Not at all."

He laughed. "Let's go for a walk so we can talk." One of his hands went to her hip, his fingers slipping beneath the hem of the sweatshirt to touch bare skin.

"Where to?" She did her best not to sound all breathy and failed. Miserably.

Taking her hand, he turned and headed out of the clearing,

away from camp. She followed him alongside the water's edge for a good quarter of a mile, even more breathless by the time they finally stopped at a small protected inlet. TJ sat on a fallen log, haloed by the moon's glow on the water behind him. "Come here."

Perfectly willing for a repeat of last night, she stepped closer, then between his long legs, but he smiled and shook his head. "Here." Tugging her into his lap, he snuggled her in.

His hand slid to the nape of her neck, his fingers in her hair as he touched his forehead to hers. After a moment, he wrapped his arms around her and kissed her, a warm, sweet kiss. *Lots* of warm, sweet kisses. He took his time, and the slow buildup was incredibly . . . hot. And she could feel that he felt . . . hot, too. "I thought you wanted to talk."

"Always." He smiled against her mouth. "But maybe not right now." He kissed her again, his fingers holding her head in place as he took the delicious buildup to the next level, still taking his damn time, but plundering now, taking what he wanted, pleasing them both with deep rhythmic thrusts of his tongue that made her think of what she wished he was doing to the rest of her body. She wanted to tell him so, but it felt so unbelievably good she couldn't speak, and when her toes curled, she began to wonder if she could orgasm from a kiss alone. When he finally pulled his mouth from hers, she heard a moan of protest and realized it was her.

Eyes still closed, she sighed. "I wish . . ." so much, she wished, but mostly that he could be deep inside, filling her.

"What do you wish, Harley?" When she remained quiet, he stroked his thumbs over her jaw. "Anything," he said softly.

She wondered at all the possibilities of *that* intriguingly wicked promise.

Still holding her face, his lips curved. "You have to be able to say it out loud. You know that, right?"

Yeah. She knew that. But she really wasn't good with voicing her needs, especially *those* kinds of needs.

A rough laugh escaped him, and he nipped her jaw. "Harley, after all we've done, what could possibly embarrass you?"

"Don't you ever lose it?" she asked, frustrated.

"I'm close now," he murmured, voice low, eyes hot, his body hard beneath hers. "Say it, Harley."

"You know what I want." She nibbled on her lower lip, watching him watch her from those heated eyes. "I want you to do what we haven't managed yet. At least not as legal adults."

He trailed a finger down her throat to the zipper on her hoodie, which he slowly pulled down. "That actually covers quite a bit of ground."

It did?

"Tell me," he coaxed. He tugged the hoodie off her arms and it fell to the ground behind her, leaving her in just her halter bathing suit top. He slipped a finger under the thin strap over her collarbone. The pad of his finger slid a little lower, heading south.

Her nipples, already hard, pebbled into two tight beads. "I want . . ."

A corner of his mouth quirked up as his finger slid even farther. "If you can't say it, how can we do it?" he asked on an amused breath.

"I'm not sure what to call it." She felt the top of her bathing suit sag a little, no longer supporting her, and she realized he'd untied it. Her breath backed up in her throat as it began to slip away from her. "Saying 'making love' seems so sappy, given the circumstances. And the other seems a little . . . coarse."

"Sex?" He was watching his finger as he slowly tugged on the suit, revealing just the very top of her breasts. "The word sex is too coarse?"

"No." She squirmed, and the bathing suit caught on her nipples. "That wasn't the word I was thinking of."

He lifted his gaze off her breasts and met her gaze, his so hot it stole her breath. "You want me to—"

"Be inside me," she whispered so softly she might have only mouthed the words. *Fuck me . . .*

Her top pooled in her lap, baring her to the waist. TJ adjusted her so that she was straddling his lap, his big, callused hands sliding down her thighs, caressing, then back up again, unbuttoning her shorts, pulling down the zipper, the rasp of the metal nearly as loud as their labored breathing. She wriggled her hips, giving him room to work. Under the shorts were her bikini bottoms, which his fingers had no problem slipping beneath.

When he touched her, the air left her lungs in a whoosh. She spread her thighs farther so that she could feel his hard sex cradled beneath her, and pressed her face into his throat. She could smell the soap he'd just used, and the man himself, and when his fingers parted her, she weaved her hands into his hair for an anchor and opened her mouth on his throat.

"God, Harley. You're wet."

At his touch, his words, she tightened her grip on his hair, biting the tendon where his neck met his shoulder without even realizing it until she heard his hiss of breath and felt him rock his hips hard into hers.

As his fingers teased her, she moaned, her mouth still on him, hips helplessly moving. She was so ready that she began whispering her plea. "Please. Please, now, TJ . . ."

Abruptly he stood her up, ripped off her shorts and bathing suit bottoms. Even before they hit the ground, his fingers slid deep inside her, his other hand cupping a breast, his thumb rubbing over her nipple in a rhythm that matched.

She lost her mind. Completely lost it. As she panted and begged softly, he met her gaze. "I know you want a quick fuck, just like we had back all those years ago, but not again. Not with what's between us now. This is more than that, Harley."

She didn't care what he called it, as long as he pulled her out of that frenzied state and filled her. Now. "TJ."

"Right here," he promised. "Harley. Look at me."

It took her a minute to calm down enough to open her eyes and meet his gaze.

"*More*," he said with that quiet intensity, and then he tugged her onto his lap, his lips taking hers hard, his tongue gliding in and out of her mouth in the same rhythm his fingers slid in and out of her body. When his thumb brushed over her very center, she threw back her head and gripped his shoulders, riding his hand, unable to hold back. She cried out his name as she burst, and he stayed with her until the last of the shudders shook her.

It wasn't enough. She reached between them to unbutton his jeans, but he stopped her. "Harley." He closed his eyes, his mouth grim. "I don't have a condom."

She pulled one out of the pocket of her shorts and held it up sheepishly. "I was a Girl Scout." she said to his soft, grateful laugh. "But for future reference, I'm squeaky clean and on the pill . . ."

"Me too. The squeaky clean part," he murmured as she slid her hands inside his jeans, caressing his hard length.

Still not enough. "Help me," she whispered, and again he lifted her, this time so she could free him and put the condom to good use. Soon as she did, she immediately sank down on him, inch by thick, delicious inch.

"Jesus, Harley," he breathed, gripping her thighs, spreading them open further, pulling her hard against him. Breathing raggedly, he held her there, giving her a minute to get used to him.

When she shifted, he growled and tightened his grip. "Christ, don't move."

Unable to help it, she rocked her hips and he swore, holding her still. "Not a muscle," he said roughly, and pressed his forehead to hers, gulping in air like a dying man. "I'm going to lose it."

Yes, but that's what she wanted, and she nipped his bottom lip, her breasts brushing his chest.

A shudder racked through him, and then went through her as well. "Please," she whispered again, and oscillated her hips.

With a groan, he brushed a kiss across her mouth, and eyes still locked on hers, he began to move. Just like on the river, he was in charge, letting her rock on him, but only as much as he allowed. He started off with glorious, agonizingly slow thrusts, but neither of them could hold to that for long, not while finally joined in the most intimate way possible. She'd never felt anything like it, and closed her eyes to savor the pleasure of having him fill her so completely.

When he said her name, she managed to open her eyes. His head was tipped down, watching as he thrust up hard into her. Then he looked up, and she was immediately lost in the dark pool of desire staring back at her. She felt like she was drowning in him, in the feel of him. She was reaching for something, needing . . . Sinking her hands in his hair, she kissed him, long and deep. With a groan, he ground his hips against hers, then stroked a thumb over where they were joined, murmuring hot, sexy things in her ear as he touched her. She burst and took him with her.

Spent, they collapsed to the ground in a pile of tangled, sweaty limbs. Either five minutes or five hours later, Harley sighed. "Okay, that was *sooo* much better than fine."

By the soft light of the moon, TJ smiled and leaned over her, kissing her jaw, each eyelid, the tip of her nose, her mouth . . . Finally, he let out a long breath and lay flat on his back. "Christ, I'm done in."

"Yes. That's what happens when you turn into a sex fiend by night."

He grinned. "It's not my fault. You keep looking at me with the eyes."

"The eyes?"

"The 'please do me' eyes. They're very distracting."

"So I should wear dark glasses, or better yet, keep my eyes closed?"

"It's possible another part of your body would call to me."

"Like?"

"Like your ass. You have a great ass, Harley."

"My ass calls to you?"

"You have no idea."

"What if I wore—"

"Let me save you some time. All of your parts call to me." His voice lowered, and his smile went from teasing to something far more devastating. "Everything about you calls to me."

Her heart pretty much turned over and exposed its underbelly. And that's when she knew she was in big trouble.

As in unless he did something fast, it'd be too late to save herself.

CHAPTER 25

Nick picked them up as planned and drove back to Wilder Adventures. Harley was quiet on the ride home, and TJ wondered what she was thinking. Back at the lodge, she helped unload, promised the coeds a disk full of pictures from her camera, and hugged Nick good-bye.

Then turned to TJ.

He smiled and reached for her, but she backed up, whispered "good-bye," and headed for her truck.

He barely caught up with her, playfully trapping her against her driver's door, pinning her hands at her sides as he leaned in and nipped at her bottom lip. "So . . ."

Closing her eyes, she let out a shaky, aroused breath at his touch. He knew the feeling. A glutton for punishment, he ran a hand down her arm for the sheer pleasure of touching her and smiled. "How about dinner?"

"I can't."

His smile faded as he took in her solemn eyes. "Okay, then how about a game of pool later?"

"I have to catch up on my research work." She shifted her gaze away. "Sorry."

"Harley."

She stared at his throat.

"*Harley.*" He accompanied the word with a finger beneath

her chin, and she finally looked at him, the emotion in her eyes nearly cutting off his air supply. "I'm leaving in five days," he whispered.

"I know," she whispered back.

"That second trip is a distinct possibility as well. If I take them both you might be gone to Colorado when I get back."

"I know that, too."

"So let's be together before I go, and say our good-bye."

Pain flickered in her gaze. "Good-bye," she whispered.

He stared at her, then closed his eyes for a beat. "Okay, now see, I meant a temporary good-bye. The kind where we get naked and sweaty, have a mutually good time, maybe multiple mutually good times, and then we say hello again the next time we see each other. But I'm thinking that you meant the kind of good-bye that doesn't come with that eventual hello."

"TJ." She let out a long, shaky breath. "I thought I could do this."

"This."

"You know. Temporary. Casual. Turns out I'm not going to be so good at it."

"Really? Because you're better at it than you think. You go through life skimming the surface, not letting anything in too deep. Hell, that's what you're doing right now, cutting this off at the knees before you get in too deep. Isn't that right, Harley?"

He heard her harsh intake of breath and knew that had been a direct hit, but before he could react, she slipped out from beneath his arm to walk away.

He barely grabbed her.

"TJ—"

"No, it's okay," he said, shaking his head. He wasn't about to beg her to want him. "I'm assuming you're heading back to Desolation sooner rather than later."

"Yes."

"Don't go alone."

"TJ, I—"

"Promise me."

She hesitated and he tightened his grip. "Promise me, Harley."

She blew out a breath. "I promise I won't go alone."

Good enough. She tugged and he let her go, standing there as she drove off, without looking back.

TJ spent the next two days running his ass ragged with short client trips. His brothers did the same. It seemed everyone wanted to get their last adventures in before the weather turned.

But even that didn't deter people from booking future trips. According to their schedule, the upcoming winter was going to be their busiest yet. The economy might have taken a hit, but there were still people willing and able to pay for their outdoor adventures.

In a few days, he was leaving for Alaska.

Normally, he'd be fine with that. Hell, he'd be great with that. But somehow this time at home, using the lodge as his home base while taking the shorter trips, felt different. It was making him want things that made no sense.

Things, and . . . people.

Harley.

He hadn't seen her since landing back at Wilder. For two days he'd gone over and over what had happened in his head, the entire kayaking trip, wondering where it had gone wrong.

Where *he* had gone wrong.

He was afraid he knew exactly—starting with when he'd said that it wasn't the mountain that made him happy, but her.

And ending when he'd forced her to face it with the sheer magnitude of their physical relationship. Even he wouldn't have called what they'd done just sex, and he doubted she could either.

Uncomfortable as it was, he was beginning to understand that this thing with her was what he wanted, that *she* was what he wanted. His error had been in thinking she might have started to feel the same.

That night he and his brothers hosted a reunion party for one of their biggest clients, a computer chip company based in San

Francisco. They'd hired a local band and hosted an open bar, and the place rocked with music and revelry. The lodge was filled with boisterous, happy computer geeks who were thrilled to be going on a mountain bike trek the next day led by Cam rather than be in their offices.

TJ walked through it, doing his job, schmoozing and wining and dining. But all he wanted was to be back out on that mountain in front of a campfire, with Harley looking at him the way she did when she thought he wasn't noticing—as if maybe he'd become as important to her as she was to him.

The next night, at the request of both her mom and dad, Harley sat at her mom's kitchen table, waiting for the "exciting" news they said they had. It had to be big. The living room was filled with their friends.

Harley had worked like a fiend the past two days, pulling two shifts for Nolan and getting data organized and sent for her internship. She'd lost no more coyotes, but was anxious to get back to Desolation to check things out, and had just gotten approval for that trip from the conservatory agency—as well as a formal offer for the job in Colorado, starting date of January 1. That was three months sooner than originally planned, and she was very happy.

Or very something anyway, but she hadn't been able to name it. "So what's up, Mom?"

Cindy Stephens was well liked, and as a result, the living room rang out with laughter and happy voices. Annie and Nick were in there.

Nolan, too.

Everyone but TJ, which Harley figured was her doing. She'd let him think she didn't want to see him. Maybe she'd even believed it as they'd come off the river, knowing that she couldn't control the slippery slide of her emotions when it came to him.

But she'd changed her mind and all she wanted was to see him.

Nolan and Skye were dancing on the patio with a bunch of

others. Nolan was laughing, his hands on Skye's swiveling hips, his eyes shining bright with warmth and affection. "Mom?" Harley asked, needing to get out of there. "The news?"

Her mom always looked twenty years younger than her real age, which was late fifties. Tonight was no different as she smiled at Harley, looking petite and willowy and pretty in a sundress. In fact, Cindy didn't look much different than she had when she'd been in the tenth grade, quitting school to run away with her high school sweetheart.

Harley's father.

She and Mark had come to the mountains, and for years had run a vitamin shop, keeping it even after they'd broken up. Then gotten back together. Then broken up again. Their friendship had lasted even when the romance hadn't.

Their business hadn't been so lucky. Her mom was dyslexic, and regularly mishandled the books. Her father, a quiet, loving, warm man who would—and had—given a stranger the shirt off his back, hadn't exactly had the temperament for being in charge. That, combined with the bad economy, and it was a wonder their shop hadn't failed long before it had.

To Harley's surprise, her dad came into the kitchen then, tall and lean and tanned, his hands going to her mother's shoulders as he bent to kiss her.

"Hey, baby," he said to Harley, lifting his face and smiling at his daughter as he leaned in to kiss her as well.

"Hey, Dad."

"We have news."

"You're kissing Mom. I think I know the news."

Her dad smiled. "More than that. We're moving back to the city."

"San Francisco?"

"Yes," her mom said with a broad smile. "San Francisco."

"Together?" Harley asked.

Her mom leaned back into Harley's dad, and they exchanged soft smiles. "Yes. Surprised?"

"Very."

Her mom smiled and hugged Harley. "I'm happy, Harley."

Well, that was good. Happy was good. Harley wished *she* could find the State of Happy herself, but she hadn't been there since TJ had been deep inside her body, his name tumbling from her lips as he'd—

"Harley?"

She forced a smile and gestured to the loud crowd in the living room. "So this is what, a good-bye party?"

"Pete wants us to work for his catering business," her mom said. "You remember Pete."

"We went to school together," her dad reminded Harley. "He wants us to run the shop. Your mom will be cooking."

"I'm so excited," her mom said. "There's a lovely apartment over the catering shop. Lots of windows. It's part of the agreement, which makes it free. We just told Skye, and she's talking about coming, too, maybe transferring to a school down there."

"It means no rent," her father said quietly, his eyes meeting Harley's, making her breath catch.

They were leaving the place they loved, for her. So she wouldn't have to help them anymore, so she could get on with her own life. Her throat tightened. "Dad—"

Her father covered her hand with one of his. It was big, warm, and callused from years of hard work. He gently squeezed her fingers. "It's a good thing, Harl. For all of us."

Her mom's smile was warm, her eyes wet. "You'll come visit. We'll have room for you. And for Skye. We'll be able to meet our own bills every month."

"Mom. Dad." She looked into their faces, needing to see a sign that it is what they really wanted, not something they felt they had to do. "I've never minded helping you. I don't want you to leave just because—"

"Not just because." Her father hugged her. "It's not just about us being a burden to you. It's that it'll give us back our lives. And more importantly, give you yours. You'll be able to finish your internship."

"Then you'll go off to Colorado," her mom said, beaming,

"and become that big, fancy research biologist. You'll be the first Stephens to have a real job, an important job. But most importantly, you'll be free to do as you want."

Harley swallowed hard. Right. Freedom to do something she loved. She'd lined it up, and it was in sight. The job. The big move. The life she'd dreamed of.

Except . . .

She squeezed her eyes shut and voiced the thought that had been haunting her for days. "What if I'm no longer sure?"

"Oh, honey." Her mom stroked her hair. "If there's one thing you've always been, it's strong as hell; mind, body and spirit. You're sure what you want. All you have to do is admit it."

Harley thought about those last words as she wandered through the party. Did she know what she wanted? Did she really know?

She headed for the food spread out on a huge table in the living room, figuring that might help. She was trying to balance a full plate and a full drink when a hand reached out to help her.

Nolan.

Though she'd worked at his garage twice in the past few days, he hadn't been there either time, having been at a business conference in South Shore. They hadn't spoken since she'd tried to kiss him and failed miserably. "Hey," she said softly.

"Hey right back at you." He lightly tugged at a strand of hair. "You caught me all up at the garage. Thanks."

She hadn't been sure he'd even want her there. "I didn't know if you—if I—" She let out a breath. "If you don't want me there anymore, I'll understand. I—"

"Harley."

She forced herself to stop talking and breathe.

"The job is yours as long as you want it," he said.

Relief and guilt swirled in her gut, and she set her plate down, suddenly not hungry. "I don't know how to do this, Nolan."

"How to be friends? That's easy enough. We call and say hi just because. We go out to lunch. We talk, smile . . ." He touched the corner of her serious mouth.

She blew out a breath. "You're going to make this easy on me."

"On both of us," he agreed. He took her drink and set it down. "Now come on. This is my favorite song. Maybe we're not going to be kissing, but we sure as hell can be dancing."

They danced for three songs, and when Harley spun off the makeshift dance floor and grabbed a soda, still smiling, she nearly plowed right into TJ.

He was wearing jeans and a soft, black sweater with the sleeves shoved up his forearms, looking big and bad and sexy as ever, and . . .

And she wished that she'd waited a few more days before taking a stand to protect her heart. She could have been with him, could have spent a few long, very hot nights together, and it would have given her memories for a lifetime.

But it was too late for regrets. They'd both made choices that were taking them away from there and from each other. His choices were far more temporary than hers, and he'd probably always be back, but never to stay.

As for her, well if she was having doubts about leaving, she'd face those without letting him complicate things.

He held out an envelope.

Her paycheck for the kayak trip, which was just about double what she'd expected. She gaped at the total. "TJ, it's too much."

"No, it's not." His warm but fathomless gaze met hers. "It's your cut of what we made. Your disk with all the pictures was a huge success. I have no idea why none of us ever thought of having a photographer around sooner. You made that trip a success, Harley. I wish you'd go on more. I think you know that." His smile held things that only made her cracked heart ache all the more. Her resolve about handling it the way she had took a further hit when he tilted his head toward the door, silently asking if she wanted to go outside.

He opened the door for her and lightly touched her back as he guided her down the porch steps. By silent, tacit agreement, they walked around the side of the house to stand at the top of the bluff at the end of the yard. They were surrounded by a 360-degree vista of sharp, rugged mountain peaks that Harley never got tired of looking at. The moon was high, casting the landscape in that iridescent pale blue glow she loved so much.

They stood there and just watched the night. Or she did. She was looking at the silhouette of the mountains and he was looking at her. "You're staring," she finally said.

"Yeah. You're so goddamn beautiful you make it hard to breathe."

"Don't."

"Don't what?"

"Don't . . . make my knees wobble." She pressed her fingers to her eyes, then dropped her hands and turned to him. "I realize my change of heart must seem sudden and ridiculous given the mixed . . . sexual messages I've sent you over the past few weeks, first at Desolation, and then in my house. And then, um, on the river as well." *For two nights running, thank you very much.*

He arched a brow at the list of places where they'd gotten quite intimately acquainted with each other's body parts. "You forgot the closet."

"Right, the closet." As if she'd really forgotten. She'd never forget any of it. Chances were those memories were going to highlight her sexual fantasies for years to come. "My point is . . ."

"You're done. You're over it."

"It's not that." As if she could be over it, over him. "It's that I can't play anymore."

"What does that mean?"

She stared up at the inky black sky, littered with stars sparkling like diamonds as far as she could see. All her life this wide, huge, gorgeous sky had given her escape and peace, and she wondered where she'd find that escape and peace once she left there. Wondered if Colorado would fulfill her the same way. "I should have stuck with my instincts, that I'm not cut out for this. If I'm going to leave here, I have to go with my head and heart clear." Although it was probably already too late for that.

"I know," he said very quietly. "You can't let an old crush get in the way of your dream."

She felt her throat tighten. "You're more than some old crush, TJ."

His eyes looked dark, so very dark.

"You are," she whispered. For so many years, she'd thought of him as big and bad and impenetrable. Invulnerable. But in fact, he wasn't a superhero. He could be hurt. She'd managed that. She hadn't expected to be able to, and the ache in her chest spread. "I'm so sorry. I shouldn't have started something I couldn't finish."

"There were two of us in this," he said. "And I'm a big boy. I knew what I was getting into. And let's be very clear. I *wanted* to get into it."

She met his steady gaze, saw the truth in it, and so much more that her throat nearly closed up. She knew he deserved more of an explanation. But could she admit that she was falling and falling hard? What good would that do either of them? She'd get over him. She had once before. She'd find her happy.

She would. Somehow. "I hope you have a great trip, TJ." She knew her eyes were suspiciously bright, that her voice was shaky. "I hope it's a good one, and that you find—" She'd been about to say happiness. After all, the mountain fueled him, made him feel alive.

But he'd told her he thought maybe *she* did that for him.

Truth was, he did it for her, too. She swallowed hard, and knew by the flash of emotion in his gaze that she'd given away her own feelings in hers.

"Harley," he said softly. "Don't do this."

"I have to. If I don't, then . . . then I won't be able to go."

He just looked at her for a long moment, and she couldn't maintain, just plain couldn't hold it in, and a lone tear escaped.

At the sight of it, a small sound of frustration came from deep in his throat as he gently rubbed his thumb over her cheek. "Doing as you want shouldn't make you cry, Harley."

She sucked in a breath, which made it sound like a sob, but

she shook her head and forced a smile. "It won't . . . I'm fine. I just . . ." *God.* "I'll miss it here, you know?"

He didn't say anything to that, just looked at her as his thumb made another swipe.

"My parents are leaving. And Skye, too. She wants to transfer. So . . ."

"So nothing holds you here," he said softly.

Actually, there was plenty holding her there. Memories. Friends. *Him.* "You should be relieved," she said, trying to tease. "You won't have to babysit me out on the mountain anymore."

She could feel the intensity of his gaze on her, but she didn't look into his eyes, didn't have the courage to face those green depths. Finally she felt him shift closer, felt the brush of his thighs to hers, and then he put a finger under her chin, waiting until she had no choice but to look at him.

"Harley," he said. "You make me laugh, you terrify me, you make me worry. Sometimes you change it up and frustrate the hell out of me, and while we're going there, I'll even tell you that you always, *always*, make me ache and want, but I've never, not once, felt like I was babysitting you."

She stared up at him, absorbing the seriousness of his voice and the look in his gaze. "Maybe," she finally said, "maybe it was just a fluke. The chemistry, the heat, everything."

"You don't actually believe that."

No. No, she didn't.

Taking her hand, he pulled her along the bluff, to the other side of a clump of Jeffrey pines, where they couldn't be seen from the house. There he molded his body against hers and kissed her. It was molten-lava hot from the get-go, and when his tongue touched hers, she heard herself moan. By the time he pulled back, she had a death grip on his shirt.

Still cupping her face, his mouth skimmed over her throat, to her ear. "Tell me again that's a fluke."

It took her a beat, but she knew him well. His voice had been low and quiet as usual, but also filled with an edge that matched the one in his eyes. "You know, you're leaving, too. You're always leaving. It's not like you're in a position to offer me—" She broke off, horrified at what she'd almost let slip, at what she'd almost asked for.

"What?" he asked. "What is it you'd have me offer you, Harley?"

When she just closed her eyes, caught between a rock and a hard spot, between her hopes and dreams, he shook his head. "You let me make love to you one night in my truck a million years ago, and it was apparently so bad that you spent the next decade avoiding me. Then I coerce you into spending time with me by following you to Desolation, where if I'm not mistaken, we had a much better than 'fine' time. Yet you back off again. So the message I'm getting is that you're going to back off no matter what, and hide behind the 'I'm leaving' thing. Do I have that right, Harley?"

"You *are* leaving!"

His eyes narrowed, dark and turbulent. "You like to throw my lack of commitment out there, but you need to be honest, at least with yourself."

She opened her mouth but he put a finger over her lips. "It's not all me," he told her. "You're holding back, too. But the difference is that *I* know we could at least try to make this work." He stepped away from her, and just like that, she felt cold and more alone than she had in a long time.

"You just don't want to," he said, and then was gone.

CHAPTER 26

TJ took his bike for a long, mind-numbing ride. On the way back through town, he refueled, and though it was past midnight, as he drove by Nolan's Garage, he saw that the lights were on.

Nolan looked up from his desk when TJ knocked on his office door. "TJ," he said, his expression carefully blank.

"You're working late," TJ said.

"Yeah."

They looked at each other a long beat.

"What can I do for you?" Nolan finally asked.

A legitimate question. They both knew that Nick handled all of Wilder Adventures' mechanical issues. And it wasn't as if TJ and Nolan were friends. Nolan was relatively new to town, and TJ was gone too much for their paths to have crossed more than a few times.

Still, there'd never been any animosity or tension between them.

Until now.

"Let me take a guess." Nolan leaned back in his chair. "This is about Harley. You should know that she dumped me."

TJ acknowledged that with a nod. "Sucks."

"I suppose you scored a date tonight."

"No. I didn't."

Nolan absorbed that, then blew out a breath. "You know, I really wanted you to be a dick so I could hate you. Or at least so *she* could hate you. Especially since then I might have had a shot."

TJ took that in a moment. Decided it wasn't entirely out of character for him to be a dick when it came to a woman. But not this woman. "Did you fire her?"

"You mean after she dumped me for you?" Nolan pushed away his laptop and rose to his feet. He came around the front of his desk, then leaned back on it, arms and ankles crossed. A casual pose. "No. She's a friend. I wouldn't do that to her."

TJ let out the breath he hadn't realized he'd been holding. "She didn't dump you for me."

Nolan raised a brow.

"She dumped me, too."

Nolan's arms dropped to his sides and his brow practically disappeared into his hairline. "No shit?"

"No shit."

Nolan thought about that a moment, then frowned. "So why are you here?"

"I just wanted to make sure you didn't fire her."

"She dumped you and you're still worried about her."

TJ scrubbed a hand down his face. "Yeah."

Nolan just stared at him for a long beat, then shook his head.

"Do we have a problem?" TJ asked.

Nolan shook his head, again. "No. Not that I haven't given thought to smashing your face in several times over the past week, but there doesn't seem to be much point in it now, other than to make me feel better."

TJ nodded. He understood the sentiment perfectly. He moved to the door. "I'm leaving town for a while. I just wanted to know that she'll have a job if she wants it."

"But you've offered her a job at Wilder."

"Yes, but I'm not sure she'll take it. She'd rather choke on her pride than admit she needs anything, especially that job."

"Yeah. She doesn't do need well," Nolan said with a small

smile. "But she does know what she wants. And if that's this job, here with me, then it's hers."

TJ nodded and turned to leave.

"That also applies to the man in her life."

At that, TJ went still.

"If you've screwed something up and the man she now wants turns out to be me, you're going to have to deal with that."

Slowly TJ turned back to face Nolan, who was suddenly looking a whole lot more alpha than his usual quiet, mild-tempered self. "I suppose I will."

And hopefully before that happened, he'd be 3,000 miles away on an ice climb, out of cell range, out of radio range, out of heart-hurts-like-hell range.

When TJ entered the lodge kitchen the next morning, his brothers were already there, mainlining caffeine. In the very center of the room, built to be huge and airy, stood a large butcher-block table, sturdy and capable of feeding the masses.

"We're working ourselves to the bone." Cam had his head down on the table. Katie was rubbing his shoulders.

Stone groaned and stretched out his long legs. "At least we're raking in the dough."

"Great." From his corner of the table, Nick looked as exhausted as the others. "We can retire early—even though we'll all be too fucking tired to enjoy it."

Emma, dressed for a day at the clinic in trousers, blouse, and doctor's coat, set a large pitcher of orange juice on the table and sank into Stone's lap, leaning into him as his arms came around her. "What are you supposed to do, turn clients away?"

"Of course not," TJ said, but they were all looking at each other, and suddenly he felt like he was watching a foreign film without the subtitles. "What?"

"We *could* cut back a little," Stone said slowly. "I'd be happy with that."

"Me, too," Cam said, giving Katie a small smile.

Nick nodded. Him, too.

"That's because *you* want to travel," TJ said to Cam, unhappy with the direction the conversation was going. "And you"—he turned to Stone—"have your house to renovate. I don't have either of those things."

"Yeah." Stone looked at him for a long moment. "I guess I assumed that you'd be happy to cut back, too."

"Yeah, well, why don't you assume my foot up your ass."

"Just think about it, TJ," Cam said quietly. "We've worked so fucking hard for so long. Hell, since we've been kids. All we're suggesting is slowing down a little, letting everyone enjoy themselves for a change. Taking the time to breathe it all in. Sleep late. Be lazy."

"Easy enough for *you* to say." TJ pushed away the food, having lost his appetite to the niggling pain in his gut. Or was that his heart? "You all have someone to sleep late with. Be lazy with."

Nothing came from the peanut gallery except the proverbial chirping crickets.

With a sigh, he took in the shocked and dismayed faces of his family. "I didn't mean that like it sounded."

"Yes, you did," Katie said gently. "We've been pretty sickening lately, I imagine."

A corner of Cam's mouth quirked. "The upcoming wedding isn't helping."

They felt the need to be nice to the poor single guy. Great. With an oath, he stood up. "Look, you guys do what works for you. Cut back. Hell, quit if that's what you want. But I'm not ready." He grabbed his keys. "I'm going for a ride."

"A ride?" Cam asked. "Or an escape?"

"Shut up, Cam."

"Oh good, a fight," Annie said entering the room. She wore her usual jeans and angry chef apron, which today read:

IN THIS HOUSE TWO RULES APPLY.
1) I'M THE BOSS.
2) SEE RULE #1.

She looked right at TJ. "Is this about Harley and whatever happened between the two of you last night at the party?"

"Nothing happened."

"Nothing made you rip out there and go for a four-hour bike ride, where, I'm assuming, you rode all sorts of stupid trails by moonlight, since you came back muddy as hell." When TJ just looked at her she lifted a shoulder. "I couldn't sleep. I was on the front porch of our cabin eating a bag of chips when you drove past me to your cabin. At four in the morning."

"Baby," Nick said to Annie. "Why didn't you wake me?"

"Because you were snoring like a buzz saw. Besides, I wanted the whole bag of chips to myself." She looked at TJ again.

Everyone did.

He sighed. "Look, I'm leaving, and then so is she." It was Harley's excuse and it was a crappy one, but it was all he had.

Just as apparently, it'd been all Harley had.

There was silence in the room as his words were absorbed.

"It can't end like this," Katie finally said. "You love her."

Stone turned to TJ. "Did you tell her you love her?"

"Jesus." TJ scrubbed his hands over his face. "We're not doing this. We're not talking about it."

Cam shook his head. "He didn't tell her."

"Look, I'll . . . work it out."

"You'll work it out?" Stone asked as if TJ was a moron. "How? What have you got?"

TJ didn't say anything. Because he had nothing. Jack shit.

Except the truth—that he was helplessly, 100 percent *gone* over Harley. Moving to the refrigerator, he grabbed a bottle of water and downed it, which did nothing to help his suddenly parched throat. Swiping a hand across his mouth, he turned and nearly plowed right into Cam, who'd somehow gotten the idea it would be okay to get all up in TJ's face. He stood so close that TJ could see the brotherly annoyance and affection swirling in Cam's green eyes. "*What?*" TJ snapped.

When Cam didn't respond, TJ nudged him for some space.

Okay, a shove. He gave him a shove.

Cam held his ground, though he did smile. "Let me guess. You're looking to kick someone's ass, and since I'm in your face and wanting to know what's wrong, it might as well be me."

Because that was true, TJ didn't bother to respond.

Cam's smile spread to a grin. "There you go with the silent shit. Man, you always had that down."

"Do you have a fucking point, or are you just enjoying the sound of your voice?"

"Actually, I have plans with the sexy woman at the table over there, so yeah, you're right, I'll get to my *fucking* point. After my accident, I lost it. Completely."

Some of TJ's irritation and frustration drained right out of him at that. "I remember." They all remembered when Cam had nearly gotten himself killed during a snowboarding race. For a long, terrifying year afterward, he'd been nothing but a shell of himself, and Stone and TJ and Annie had felt helpless watching him suffer.

"Stone tried to bully me into getting better," Cam said softly.

"Hey," Stone said from the table.

"You meant well," Cam said, eyes still on TJ. "But you were relentless. Annie, too."

Annie, looking grim, nodded. It was the Wilder way. Bully, bug, bulldoze. She hadn't known what else to do.

"Not you," Cam said quietly, putting a hand on TJ's chest. "I told you that the accident had taken my heart and soul and shredded them into pieces. I was done, man. Ready to check out, and you knew it. Do you remember what you told me?"

TJ let out a breath, his throat feeling tight. It'd been dark and terrifying times, trying to reach Cam, save him, when he hadn't wanted to be either reached or saved. "I told you that your heart and soul might be shredded, but they were still beating. They weren't destroyed."

"And?"

"And that all you had to do was take your head out of your own ass long enough to put yourself back together."

"And?"

TJ grated his back teeth together. "Gee, Cam, maybe you should tell me."

"Not as much fun that way. What else?"

TJ sighed. "And that maybe you'd have to do as you'd never done and actually work hard at something."

Cam nodded. "Because up until that moment, I hadn't had to work hard for much in my entire life. Also thanks to you, by the way. You always took care of me."

Behind them, Annie sniffed. "Goddammit. No one warned me this would be a tissue day. I'm actually wearing mascara!"

Nick pulled her into his lap, wrapping his arms around her, settling his hands on the bump of Not-Abigail.

Cam nudged TJ in the chest again. "It was good advice, Teej."

"Yeah. But my heart and soul aren't shredded."

"Maybe not, but they haven't been whole, not for a damn long time, maybe not since Sam died."

"Not the Sam card again."

"Not Sam," Cam said very quietly. "You. You're finally back to letting someone in other than us."

"This isn't about me. Harley doesn't want—" TJ broke off. She didn't want casual.

And he hadn't exactly offered her anything else, had he? At the realization, he closed his gritty eyes.

It *was* him after all.

Skye was standing at Harley's kitchen counter, slurping up a bowl of Frosted Flakes.

"Why can't you inhale the crappy cereal?" Harley asked her.

"This is the crappy cereal. I left you some."

Harley picked up the box of Frosted Flakes and shook it. Approximately three crumbs rumbled around.

"Well, you did say you didn't want to have to run today. Consider this me doing you a favor."

Harley sighed and poured herself a bowl of the healthy stuff. It had raisins. Hurray.

"You have e-mail," Skye said, and gestured with her spoon to the open laptop on the table. "Colorado wants you to respond to their job offer."

"You read my mail?"

"You have fun spam. You got two penis enlargement offers and someone named Trixie wants to meet you. What the hell's taking you so long to get back to them about the job offer? Don't you want it anymore?"

Of course she wanted it.

Didn't she?

"Harl?"

"Yeah," she said absently. "I want it."

"Good." Skye tipped her bowl up to her mouth and drank the leftover milk. "Since you'll be gone, I have a question."

"Yes, you can have my truck. I'm going to need to buy a newer one."

"Actually, I was going for something different. Something less . . . inanimate."

"Like?"

"Like Nolan."

Harley blinked.

"Are you mad?" Skye asked.

"Nolan," Harley repeated. "And you."

"I know, he seems so . . . tame for me, right? But I have a feeling that beneath that easygoing exterior beats the heart of a real tiger."

"But you're leaving, too. You're going to the city."

"Which is only like three hours away. Far enough that I have plenty of space, yet close enough for wild animal sex on the weekends. Jeez, Harley, these days no one lets long distance keep a relationship down."

TJ stood in his bedroom packing for the early morning flight to Seattle, then Anchorage. He'd made this particular Alaska trip at least a dozen times. It was a combination rock and mountain climbing/guided trek, and it required a high level of expert skill from his client. Normally for a trip like this, TJ would take clients out on a shorter trek first to prove their skills, but in this case, Colin West was a repeat client. He and TJ had taken the exact same trip three years ago.

Colin was a forty-year-old surgeon who rock climbed in his spare time. The reason the trip was so last minute was because he was supposed to be getting married to his longtime girlfriend Lydia that weekend, but he'd panicked.

And he'd needed an escape.

TJ had just had a late dinner at the lodge. Annie had cooked all his favorites, joking that by the time he got back she wouldn't be able stay on her feet that long. Hell, she'd probably not even be able to *see* her feet. When he'd laughed and agreed, she smacked him on the back of his head. Then hugged him good-bye so tight that he'd had to check his ribs afterwards for cracks. Katie and Emma had sandwiched him with hugs as well, and he pulled them both in close, smirking over their heads at his brothers when he got lots of kisses, too.

"Hands off my woman," Stone said mildly, and pulled Emma from him.

So TJ had held onto Katie, the both of them laughing when Cam yanked her free as well.

Then he'd been left alone in the kitchen with Annie and Nick, who were locked in each other's arms against the counter. Annie was nuzzling Nick's throat, and he had a hand curled low and protective on her belly, a look on his face that could only be described as bliss.

TJ walked out the back door without them even realizing he was gone. Back in his cabin, he finished packing, then stood in the middle of the living room he'd built with Cam and Stone. The place was small but the high, open-beamed ceilings made it seem much larger than it was, aided by the large picture windows. Still, it was big enough for him, and comfortable, especially since he was hardly ever home for more than a week at a time. Anyway, it'd always felt like more of a place to stay than *home*. He'd never really thought about that before. The cabin was more a part of his journey than his destination.

There came a soft knock on his door. Figuring it was someone named Wilder, he called out, "it's open," but to his surprise, Harley walked in.

And his heart kicked hard.

CHAPTER 27

Harley gave up trying to explain to herself why she needed to drive out to TJ's the night before he left. There were no words for what she needed. There were only the feelings that he'd accused her of trying to avoid.

Fat chance of truly being successful at that. She'd been feeling something for him in one form or another for too many years to count.

But apparently, for once, he didn't have words either. He stood in the doorway between his kitchen and the living room, arms up and braced on the oak doorjamb, looking dead sexy.

And dead set on letting her make the first move.

It *was* her move. She knew that.

He wore a pair of ragged old basketball shorts that fell to his knees and nothing else. His hair was in need of a trim, and it tumbled over his forehead, curling onto his neck. His expression, usually calm and easy, usually amused or getting there, was something else entirely, something she'd not seen from him before.

Hollow. Bleak.

She stepped close, her heart dropping. "What's wrong?"

He let out a low, mirthless laugh and didn't answer. Nor did he move.

"TJ?"

"Why are you here, Harley?"

Not expecting that grim, unwelcoming response, she hesitated, nearly turning tail and running. But he cared for her, she reminded herself. Deeply. He'd shown it a hundred times. In that way, maybe in all ways, he was far braver than she.

That stopped now. She became brave *now*. Stepping toe-to-toe with him, she put her hands on his chest. As his gaze met hers, she let her hands slide down his ribs, to the abs that she never got tired of touching. "Are you okay?"

"Yeah."

Her fingers got to the tie on his shorts and she saw awareness flare in his eyes.

And surprise.

She couldn't blame him. For the most part, he'd always been the first to touch. Okay, not just for the most part. Always. He'd always been the first to touch.

That had been her own stupid fear. Fear of rejection. Fear of not being enough. Of being hurt . . .

No more fear.

"Harley, why are you here?" he asked again.

"I got the job in Colorado."

"Congratulations," he said with no surprise.

"You knew I would," she breathed softly, no longer startled that he'd always had more faith in her than she had.

"I knew you would," he agreed.

"That's not why I'm here."

He didn't move, not even his hands, which were still above his head, braced on the wood as if he didn't quite trust himself to touch her. He merely stood there, arms taut, *body* taut, waiting with that endless patience of his.

Except . . . it wasn't endless. She had a feeling he'd reached his limits when it came to her. She bit her lower lip. "You said some stuff to me at my mom's party."

"Yeah."

"I know it didn't seem like it, but I heard you. I'm here for that good-bye you talked about."

"I thought you didn't do good-byes."

"I never have." Bracing her hands on his belly, she went up on tiptoes and brushed her lips across his, and when his body tensed and tightened, she did it again.

And then again.

"Until you," she whispered, nibbling at the corner of his mouth. "You, TJ Wilder, I can't seem to walk away from without one. I tried, but I can't do it." The other corner of his mouth . . . "Unless you've changed your mind."

"No." There was a faint trace of humor in his voice, but she suspected it was aimed at himself. Unfortunately, he still hadn't made a move.

"I need you, TJ."

At that, he made a low, inarticulate sound in his throat, and dropped his hands to her waist. "What?" he asked.

She stared at him. "Are you really going to make me say it again?"

"Yes."

She blew out a breath. "Fine. I need you. Okay? I. Need. You."

"Look at that, and you didn't even choke on it."

She sagged. "Give me a break. This whole thing is frustrating. I don't need people. People need me. But you, TJ"—she pressed a hand to her aching heart—"I need. And I really hope you got it that time because it doesn't seem to be getting any easier to say."

He cupped her jaw, his eyes raking over her face, searching her eyes. Whatever he saw in them softened his. "I need you, too, Harley. So much." He still wasn't pressed up against her, but she felt something in her relax anyway as his hands gently squeezed her hips.

More. She needed even more. She let her fingers skim over his chest, feeling the muscles beneath quiver as she worked her way down. Past his belly button to the waistband of his shorts, so low on his hips as to be quite, deliciously indecent. It took her breath. *He* took her breath, and her fingers kept going even lower, gliding over the erection straining against the thin material. "You're going to burst at the seams," she murmured.

He made a choked sound, half laugh, half groan, and dipped his head, nuzzling her hair as if he couldn't help himself.

"You commando again?"

"Yeah," he said thickly, and just like that, she went damp.

"Kiss me," she whispered, and then took matters in her own hands, yanking his head to hers.

With another of those rough, sexy sounds, he buried a hand in her hair, using the other at the small of her back to finally pull her in. His palm slid down to cup her butt, rocking her hard against him. She wore a flimsy little halter sundress, a gauzy number that was so comfortable. The hem was easy enough for him to bunch up in impatient fingers and then he slipped into her panties as well, holding her bare bottom in both hands.

"Christ, Harley," he gasped hoarsely against her collarbone when his fingers slipped farther down, between her thighs, finding her hot and wet. She shivered, and he lifted her, pinning her to the wall. His lips pressed to her throat and one of his hands twined in her hair, tugging her face up to his. Leaning in, until his lips almost brushed hers, he whispered, "I was going to come to you tonight."

"You were?"

"In about ten more seconds. Even knowing you wouldn't want—"

She cupped his face. "I want." There was so little space between them, her lips brushed his with each word. "I want you," she whispered. "I *need* you."

He slid a thigh between hers, lifting her up with it so that they were mouth to mouth. "Do you need this?"

"So much."

The words were barely out of her mouth before he kissed her, rough and demanding. She responded in kind, trembling, already on the very edge. He wasn't exactly steady himself, but he didn't break the kiss as he trailed his hand up her thigh.

She untied his shorts, tugging them to his thighs. Yep, he was butt-ass naked beneath, and she nearly had an orgasm on the spot. Then he ripped away her panties and suddenly she was commando, too.

Still kissing her, he shoved up her dress and pushed into her, their twin gasps of pleasure filling the room.

As wound up as she was, she came in two thrusts. He was right behind her. Unable to remain upright through his orgasm, he slid down, still holding tightly to her, still embedded deeply within her as his knees hit the floor.

Chests heaving, half dressed, half not, they stayed like that for long moments, her forehead to his shoulder, his face buried in her hair.

"Bed," he finally murmured, and somehow got them both down the hall.

He set her down in the middle of his room. Pulling back, Harley slid her hands up to the nape of her neck, untied her halter, and let it fall.

The dress slipped to her hips and caught on TJ's hands. With a flick of his wrists, the material floated to her feet. "Now you," she said breathlessly, then without waiting for him, shoved his shorts off.

Kicking free of them, he ran a finger over a breast, lightly grazing the hardened tip. "God, you're beautiful," he said, turning, nudging her onto the bed. She scooted backwards up the mattress and he followed, pinning her there with his weight. His lips went to her throat, nipping lightly until her nails dug into his shoulders. Shifting downward, he kissed her collarbone, then a breast, while she ground helplessly into him in a desperate attempt to relieve the already building pressure.

"Not fast, not this time," he murmured, kissing her belly, a hip, her thighs. He pushed them open until his shoulders could fit between, settling her legs where he wanted them.

"TJ, I need . . ."

"Anything," he promised.

You, she wanted to say. I need you to love me.

He traced a finger over her center, and she jerked and arched up for more, but he refused to be rushed. Instead, his other hand slid over her belly, holding her down for his ministrations. Bending his head, he kissed an inner thigh. His day-old stubble lightly scraped over her sensitive, quivering flesh, making her cry out. "You like that," he murmured, and did it again so that she moaned. "Yeah, I like that, too." He kissed her other thigh. And then in between. "And this," he said silkily against her. I *love* this."

"Oh, God." She couldn't put a thought together. Hell, she couldn't breathe. It was instant and hot and she was already shuddering, her body practically convulsing. "*Please.*" He was still right there at her core, lightly kissing her damp folds. She felt his breath brush over her, and even that was almost enough to do her in. "Don't stop. Don't ever stop."

His eyes flashed, something deep and meaningful, but she couldn't quite grasp it, couldn't do anything but cry out as he bent his head and sucked her into his mouth at the same time that he slid two fingers into her, rocketing her straight to the shattering climax she'd been begging for. By the time she managed to come back to herself, he was kneeling between her spread legs, eyes hot and fierce. He held her undoubtedly dreamy, enraptured gaze as he entwined their hands together beside her head and drove into her with one fierce thrust, plunging deep. Her hips arched up to meet him, their gazes still connected, their bodies connected, hell, their *souls* connected as she wrapped her legs around him. He held onto her just as tight, as if she was his lifeline.

He was certainly hers.

No matter what happened, no matter how far apart they ended up, she'd always have that. Needing even more, she pulled him down over her so she could feel his heart pounding, beating in tune to hers.

Eyes dark, he pulled nearly all the way out before thrusting back in to the hilt, making her gasp his name as the need and hunger took over, touching every part of her with every part of him. Their breathing combined, ragged and rough, shutting everything else out.

Nothing else mattered, nothing but the slow pull of their bodies, the unending kiss.

She didn't want to let him go.

Ever.

Emotion clogging her throat, she closed her eyes rather than give herself away.

"Harley."

This is just a good-bye, just a simple, easy, casual good-bye.

"Harley, look at me."

She forced her heavy eyelids open and somehow managed to meet his gaze, knowing by the look in his that yep, she'd given herself away.

Seemed she needed some practice on multitasking orgasms and heartbreak.

Gently, so gently it brought tears to her eyes, he swept her hair back from her face. "I love you," he said, the words causing her to spiral and shudder as she burst.

And took him with her.

When TJ woke up, he knew even as he reached out that Harley was gone. He almost believed he'd imagined her, except for the bite mark on his shoulder.

And what felt like nail indentations in his ass.

But the amusement drained quickly, because last night, hot and amazing and heart wrenching as it'd been, had been his good-bye.

Two days later TJ was in Anchorage, preparing to take a charter with Colin into their drop zone when his cell phone rang.

"TJ," a voice breathed softly in his ear, sounding relieved to get him.

"Harley?"

"Yeah."

For a moment they did nothing but breathe. He wasn't sure

what to say that hadn't already been said, but he was happy as hell to hear from her. "You okay?"

"Yeah. I'm fine."

Silence.

Memories.

Longing.

He recovered first, or at least put up the pretense of it. "Where are you?"

"Desolation. And no, not by myself." She paused. "Nolan and Skye are with me."

Nolan. TJ pinched the bridge of his nose and took a breath.

"He's here with Skye. And to protect me, of course."

"He's with Skye?"

"They're beginning a . . . mutual affection."

Suddenly he could breathe. Breathing was good. "Any problems?"

"Actually earlier we heard a gunshot."

Christ. "How close?"

"Couple miles. We called it in. By some miracle, the rangers located two guys exiting out of the east entrance, without a permit of course, and loaded with unregistered shotguns and ammo."

It could have been worse, he told himself. "Arrested?"

"Yep. I don't think I'll be losing any more of my coyotes."

"*Your* coyotes?" He felt himself smile in spite of the lingering fear for her. "You're leaving, remember?"

"Yeah. TJ . . . any regrets?"

"None," he said firmly, then paused. "You?"

When she was quiet, he shook his head at himself. Obviously she had regrets, she'd sneaked out in the middle of the night.

"None," she finally said, then hesitated. "Well, maybe one." She paused again and just about killed him.

Had his phone died? "Harley? You still there?"

"Yes." She inhaled deeply. "It's you, TJ. You're my regret. I regret not telling you sooner, like years sooner, how I felt about you."

He heard the click, telling him she was long gone before he

found his words and could point out that she *still* hadn't told him.

Twenty-four hours later, TJ and Colin were at 15,500 feet in a tent smack in the middle of a windstorm that was threatening to rip them right off the side of a mountain.

It wouldn't happen. TJ was pretty sure.

Well, at least 80 percent sure.

Colin lay flat on his back staring up at the ceiling of the tent. "I'm a fucking screwup. I should be in front of the pastor tomorrow, saying 'I do' with Lydia at my side. Sex for the rest of my life, guaranteed. Man, what the fuck was I thinking?"

TJ didn't know. Guaranteed sex sounded pretty darn good. But then again, suddenly so did waking up every day wrapped in the same woman.

Christ. It'd gotten to him, all of it; laughing at karma, watching his brothers fall in love.

Being with Harley.

Falling for Harley.

"You ever screw up?" Colin asked. "I mean really screw up?"

TJ thought about how he'd let Harley think all he wanted was a casual, temporary thing, how he'd said he loved her but without the other words she'd needed to go with that love. "Yeah."

"How did you fix it?"

"Still working on that."

Colin thought about that, then shook his head. "This is all wrong. I changed my mind. I want to get married tomorrow." Colin closed his eyes, then opened them again, and they were damp. "How fast can you get me home?"

"Are you kidding me?"

"Look, I let her think I love my adventures more than I love her. I have to tell her that's not true. That I'd rather be with her than on a damn mountain. It's cold here, man. I should be in my warm bed with my warm almost wife."

"You could call her."

"No, we're going in person and tell her I'm an ass. I want to see if she'll marry this ass. On Squaw Peak like we planned. Take me home, man."

TJ let out a breath and pulled out his phone to make the calls necessary to get them out of there. Because home sounded like a damn fine place to be.

CHAPTER 28

Two days later, Skye was mooching breakfast while Harley was still looking at her e-mail, specifically the one asking her to confirm she wanted the job.

She really needed to respond.

She'd actually started to a hundred times, pressing REPLY, then typing "yes, thank you!" but then her finger would hover over the SEND.

And then it'd hit DELETE instead.

But the truth was, there was only one thing she really wanted to type and that was, "I can't take the job because there's no TJ Wilder in Colorado!"

Sitting back, she closed her eyes and let it all wash over her, giving herself permission to listen to her gut instincts, her emotions, the truth . . .

"Are you meditating?" Skye whispered.

"Shh."

"You're supposed to be sitting cross-legged and chanting 'ohmmmm.'"

"Quiet. I'm listening to myself."

"Are you asking yourself for guidance about the job, or about how you let the hottest guy on the planet get away?"

"Skye!"

"Sorry." Skye spooned in another bite. "Carry on."

Harley closed her eyes again. Turned out her heart did have something to say. It said that she already had her answers, that possibly she'd *always* had her answers, from way back since that long ago night in the back of TJ's truck. She stared off into space as she let that terrifying and life-altering realization echo through her.

She wanted him. She needed him.

She loved him.

She always had. Suddenly it wasn't so confusing after all. Not when she added everything up, including some of the things he'd said to her.

Sometimes you have to take a risk.

There are all kinds of love.

You make me feel alive.

I love you.

She stood up and paced the length of her kitchen.

"You okay?" Skye asked.

"Yeah. I just realized I left something unfinished."

"One of your reports?"

"Something bigger."

Much bigger.

Skye stared at her, and then let out a slow smile. "You're going for it."

"I'm going for it." Harley pulled out her phone and tried TJ's cell. It went directly to voice mail. She wondered what message to leave. *I forgot to mention that I don't need you for just one night, but for all my nights?*

She laughed a little softly at herself. "Hey," she said. "I . . . ah, hell. I've had an epiphany, I guess you'd call it. Painful sucker, too. Call me."

Now she just had to be patient.

Problem was, she'd never really mastered the act of patience. So she called Stone. "I need a favor."

"Good," he said. "So do I."

* * *

Harley's conversation with Stone rang in her head for the rest of the day. They'd made a deal. She'd take a temporary job with Wilder until she figured out what the hell she wanted to do with her life, but she wanted to start by going to Alaska to meet up with TJ. Unpaid, of course.

Stone had countered her offer. He was hiring, temporary as she insisted, but she would be paid starting immediately, and she had to trust him because there was a quick little trip she had to help him out with first.

She was taking a small group up Squaw Peak for an impromptu sunset wedding. Her job was to get the bride and the pastor there and be the photographer for the happy event. Nick flew them up and landed on Eagle Rock, a gorgeous plateau, then flew off again to go pick up the groom at some undisclosed location.

Harley led Lydia—the bride—and the pastor to a higher, smaller plateau, where watching the sun set would be like sitting on top of the world. There she sat on the five-hundred-foot-high cliff and fiddled with her camera as she absorbed the view.

Behind her, Lydia was sitting, chatting quietly with her pastor. Harley had already taken several nice shots of them. She heard the chopper and knew Nick was back with the groom. It would take them thirty minutes or so to climb up there.

Harley took some shots of God's glory spread out before her, then slowly lowered the camera as the truth hit her. She'd heard people talk of life-altering decisions before, but until that moment, sitting in the late afternoon sun with the whole world at her feet, she'd never really gotten it.

She belonged there.

She belonged there with TJ.

Even more of a revelation—she was irrevocably, desperately, 100 percent in love with him.

And he hadn't called her back.

To be fair to him, he *was* out in the middle of nowhere, literally, no doubt with absolutely zero reception. He probably didn't even know she'd called him yet. "You are such an idiot," she said out loud. "A very *slow* idiot."

Just then, a set of unbearably familiar battered boots and two long, denim-covered legs appeared in her field of vision. "If I agree, are you going to argue with me?"

With a gasp, she looked up and faced . . . who else . . . the only man who'd ever stopped, and then kick-started, her heart with a single look. "TJ! What are you doing here?"

He squatted in front of her. "Thought I'd drop by, say hi."

She choked out a shocked laugh. "But your client—"

"He's the groom. He decided he was crazy not to follow his heart."

She felt her heart surge. "I know the feeling."

His eyes warmed. "Yeah?"

"Yeah." She drew a deep breath. "I missed you. I'm so sorry I left your cabin like I did. I shouldn't have done that."

"You mentioned an epiphany."

"I don't want to say good-bye."

He nodded, and ran a finger over her jaw. "Is there anything you do want?"

"You."

"You already have me."

"No, I mean . . . more than just . . ."

"Casual?"

"Yes," she whispered, talking fast, as if that could help her make him understand. "Here's the thing. I can't seem to breathe without you. And I really need to breathe, TJ."

His lips twitched, his eyes warmed. "Harley," he said very softly, and she nearly lost it.

"No, listen," she said. "I know you didn't want—that we said—"

He took one of her waving hands in his and pressed it to his chest. Beneath, she could feel the steady beat of his heart, and it helped calm hers. "Me too, Harley. All of it. I want you so damn much. I want to be with you, only you. I want everything that you can give me."

"What about your trips?"

"I can take 'em or leave 'em. What I can't do without is you."

She felt the smile and the tears rush together, and she became utterly and completely sure of at least one thing. "*Not* casual."

He shook his head solemnly. "There's nothing casual about how I feel about you."

She lurched up and pretty much threw herself at him, crawling up his body. Rising to his full height, he had one arm beneath her butt, the other across her back and right there on top of the world he kissed her, *claimed* her. In response, she sank her fingers into his hair, pouring out everything she had, all the heat, affection, frustration, fear, *love* . . . all of it into that one kiss.

"Ahem," Nick said from behind them. "The pastor said we're on the five-minute countdown."

They kept kissing.

Nick sighed. "You two do realize there's no closet door this time, right? That we can all see you?"

TJ slowly let Harley slide down his body, taking a minute to scrape his teeth over her jaw, and when she moaned, he let out a low growl of appreciation and bent his head again, but Nick stepped close and slapped a hand on his chest.

Without taking his eyes off Harley, TJ said, "We have five minutes. You just said so yourself."

Nick shook his head and walked away.

Grinning.

TJ pulled some papers out of his pocket. Harley's employment papers, the ones she'd filled out earlier for Stone. "I found these."

"Stone told you."

"That you want to temp for us as our new outdoor specialist and photographer? Yeah."

"Are you okay with that?"

"Do you really have to ask?"

"Actually . . ." She held her breath, then bent and opened her backpack, pulling out a pencil. "Can I see those? I have a change to make."

He peeked into her well-organized pack. "Wow. Impressive."

"You like? A good friend taught me how to organize it."

His eyes were quiet and assessing. "A good friend?"

"The best kind of friend. My *everything* friend." She flipped through the pages to the end. "It occurred to me that I've always had a lot of temporary stuff in my life. I'm hoping to change that, and upgrade to a more permanent status." She erased the "temporary" on her application, then leaned in and wrote *permanent*. She looked up. "If there's still a place for me."

"There will always be a place for you, at Wilder, and in my heart. Turn it over, Harley."

She felt a little dizzy from his words, and the deep meaning behind them. "What?"

"The application. Turn it over."

She flipped the pages over. He'd written her name at the top, and then a list of qualifications:

Pro—makes me hot
Pro—makes me smile
Pro—makes me hot
Pro—accepts me as is
Pro—makes me hot
Pro—makes me feel whole

Con—makes me hot

She burst out laughing. "Makes you hot is a con?"

"I couldn't think of anything bad."

"Liar."

He smiled and ran his thumb over her jaw. "Okay, maybe I just like you how you are, faults and all."

Her breath caught. "Even though I have a hard time putting how I feel into words?"

"You've shown me how you feel. In actions."

Her throat caught. He got her, really got her. She closed her eyes and opened her heart, and for the first time in her life, took a *real* risk. "You once asked me what was going on between you and me. I never answered you."

"I know. We've been waiting for you to decide."

"I've been a little slow on the uptake," she admitted. "I didn't have the words then, but I have the words now."

He reached for her hand and brought it to his mouth. "Do you?"

"I love you, TJ." She was a little startled at how easily the words came. "I think I always have."

He looked stunned, and she took a moment to realize that he hadn't been sure exactly what she was offering him. And with that, she faced something else. All along she'd understood that she was out of her element, far from her comfort zone when it came to him, but the truth was, he was just as far out of his comfort zone, and just as off balance.

She'd rendered him speechless. Before the smug smile could spread across her face, he'd grabbed her in a crushing hug, burying his face in her neck. There was no sly teasing, no sexy innuendo, nothing but him holding her like he planned to never let her go. "I wasn't happy in Alaska," he whispered. "For the first time, I needed out of there." He pulled back a step and slid his hands up to cup her face so she could see his tender smile. His voice, when it came, was low and gruff with emotion. "It wasn't home."

"You've been gone from Wishful for much longer before."

"No. Well, yeah. But that's not what I'm getting at. I missed you next to me."

Undone, throat tight, heart pounding, it took her a moment to respond. "Home is being next to me?"

"Now you're getting there." His smile warmed her from the inside out. "Yeah, home is being next to you. And on top of you. And underneath," he murmured. "And buried deep inside . . ."

With a laugh, she walked back into his arms. And found her own sense of home.

Epilogue

Four months later

Harley sat at one of the many decorated tables arranged across the lodge's expansive back deck. Cam's and Katie's wedding reception was in full swing. Guests were dancing, eating, talking, laughing.

It was a beautiful January evening, a cool thirty-four degrees, but there were freestanding heaters at every corner, and no one felt the chill.

Least of all Cam and Katie, locked in each other's arms in the center of the makeshift dance floor. Stone and Emma weren't too far away, swaying to the music as well.

Harley sighed in pleasure, enjoying the sense of . . . peace. She and TJ had just come back from co-guiding a three-week bike trip in Costa Rica. She could still feel the warmth from the long days in the sun.

And the longer nights in TJ's arms. Oh yeah, that was definitely her favorite part. The way he looked at her, held her, touched her.

As she smiled with the memories, he came back to the table. He'd ditched his tux jacket and tie, had untucked his white shirt, and looked good enough to finish unwrapping and eat for dessert.

He held two flutes of champagne, smiling as he handed her one, his eyes filled with heat and affection.

There were no more long treks on the schedule. If any booked, Harley and TJ would probably take them, but for the time being they were back in Wishful. She'd moved into his cabin. During the days, he was working the shorter adventures with his brothers, and she joined in when needed. She was also working for the local forest service on a part-time basis as their wildlife biologist liaison.

But the favorite part of her life was sleeping next to TJ every night. They'd not talked about the next step, but her heart was so full she knew it would all come.

"Here. Hold this."

Harley blinked as Annie gently shoved a pink bundle in her arms.

Not-Abigail.

Who'd turned out to be Abigail after all. Eight pounds of pure, beautiful, tyrannical joy. She was a real Wilder-in-training, too. At two weeks old, she had every single person in her orbit wrapped around her cute little pinky finger.

Harley was terrified of her. "Annie, I—"

Annie was gone, on the dance floor with Nick.

Oh, God. Harley stared down in terror at the infant, who yawned and stared back, smacking her perfect little heart-shaped mouth before letting out a shuddery sigh of contentment.

Or gas.

And Harley's heart, frozen in terror only a moment before, did the oddest thing. It completely softened, and she turned to look at TJ in marvel. She actually . . . wanted one. Not that she'd say that out loud, never, but—

"You want one," he whispered.

"God. I think I do."

TJ laughed softly and slipped an arm around Harley, reading her mind as easily as he always read her body. "Okay," he murmured, letting his mouth brush her ear. "But first things first."

Her breath caught. "Like?"

"A wedding."

Her heart swelled until she could hardly breathe. "Really?"

"Really." He pulled her in a little closer, and with his other hand, gently stroked a finger over Abigail's soft cheek. "And then all the practicing required for one of these. Lots of practicing, Harley."

She laughed, her heart so full it actually hurt. "We've been doing that, every night for months."

"You can never practice enough."

She actually glanced back at the lodge, thinking of the closet. TJ grinned. "I love how you think, Future Mrs. Wilder."

She grinned back, then squealed in shock as Annie took Abigail back and yelled in happy surprise, "*Future Mrs. Wilder?*"— repeating TJ's words. "Did you just get *engaged?*"

In no time, the whole family moved close to hear more, and it was an entire case of champagne later before TJ got Harley in the closet to begin their practicing.

If you liked this book, try LOVE, UNEXPECTEDLY
by Susan Fox . . .

"Merilee said I could bring a date to the wedding, then got in this dig about whether I was seeing anyone, or between losers. I'd really hate to show up alone."

He'd learned not to trust that gleam in her eyes, but couldn't figure out where she was heading. "You only just broke up with NASCAR Guy." Usually it took her two or three months before she fell for a new man. In the in-between time she hung out more with him, as she'd been doing recently.

Her lips curved. "I love how you say 'NASCAR Guy' in that posh Brit accent. Yeah, we split two weeks ago. But I think I may have found a great guy to take to the wedding."

Damn. His heart sank. "You've already met someone new? And you're going to take him as your date?"

"If he'll go." The gleam was downright wicked now. "What do you think?"

He figured a man would be crazy not to take any opportunity to spend time with her. But . . . "If you've only started dating, taking him to a wedding could seem like pressure. And what if you caught the bouquet?" If Nav was with her and she caught the damned thing, he'd tackle the minister before he could get away, and tie the knot then and there.

Not that Kat would let him. She'd say he'd gone out of his freaking mind.

"Oh, I don't think this guy would get the wrong idea." There was a laugh in her voice.

"No?"

She sprang off the washer, stepped toward him, and gripped the front of his rugby jersey with both hands, the brush of her knuckles through the worn blue-and-white-striped cotton making his heart race and his groin tighten. "What do you say, Nav?"

"Uh, to what?"

"To being my date for the wedding."

Hot blood surged through his veins. She was asking him to travel across the country and escort her to her sister's wedding?

Had she finally opened her eyes, opened her heart, and really seen him? Seen that he, Naveen Bharani, was the perfect man for her? The one who knew her perhaps better than she knew herself. Who loved her as much for her vulnerabilities and flaws as for her competence and strength, her generosity and sense of fun, those sparkling eyes, and the way her sexy curves filled out her Saturday-morning sweats.

"Me?" He lifted his hands and covered hers. "You want me to go?"

She nodded vigorously. "You're an up-and-coming photographer. Smart, creative." Face close to his, she added, eyes twinkling, "Hot, too. Your taste in clothes sucks, but if you'd let me work on you, you'd look good. And you're nice. Kind, generous, sweet."

Yes, he was all of those things, except sweet—another wimp word, like doll. But he was confused. She thought he was hot, which was definitely good. But something was missing. She wasn't gushing about how *amazing* he was and how *crazy* she was about him, the way she always did when she fell for a man. Her beautiful eyes were sharp and focused, not dreamy. Not filled with passion or new love. So . . . what was she saying?

He tightened his hands on hers. "Kat, I—"

"Will you do it? My family might even *approve* of you."

Suspicion tightened his throat. He forced words out. "So I'd be your token good guy, to prove you don't always date ass-holes."

"Ouch. But yes, that's the idea. I know it's a lot to ask, but please? Will you do it?"

He lifted his hands from hers and dropped them to his sides, bitter disappointment tightening them into fists.

Oblivious, she clenched his jersey tighter, eyes pleading with him. "It's only one weekend, and I'll pay your airfare and—"

"Oh, no, you won't." He twisted away abruptly, and her hands lost their grip on his shirt. Damn, there was only so much bat-tering a guy's ego could take. "If I go, I'll pay my own way." The words grated out. He turned away and busied himself heaving laundry from his washer to a dryer, trying to calm down and think. What should he do?

Practicalities first. If he agreed, would it affect the exhibit? No, all she was asking for was a day or two. He could escort her, make nice with her family, play the role she'd assigned him. He'd get brownie points with Kat.

"Nav, I couldn't let you pay for the ticket. Not when you'd be doing me such a huge favor. So, will you? You're at least think-ing about it?"

Of course he'd already accumulated a thousand brownie points, and where had that got him? Talking about *roles*, she'd cast him as the good bud two years ago and didn't show any signs of ever promoting him to leading man.

He was caught in freaking limbo.

The thing was, he was tired of being single. He wanted to share his life—to get married and start a family. Though he and his parents loved each other, his relationship with them had al-ways been uneasy. As a kid, he'd wondered if he was adopted, he and his parents seemed such a mismatch.

He knew "family" should mean something different: a sense of warmth, belonging, acceptance, support. That's what he wanted to create with his wife and children.

His mum was on his case about an arranged marriage, sending him a photo and bio at least once a month, hoping to hook him. But Nav wanted a love match. He'd had an active dating life for more than ten years but, no matter how great the women were, none had ever made him feel the way he did for Kat. Damn her.

He bent to drag more clothes from the washer and, as he straightened, glanced at her. Had she been checking out his ass?

Cheeks coloring, she shifted her gaze to his face. "Please, Nav? Pretty please?" Her brows pulled together. "You can't imagine how much I *hate* the teasing." Her voice dropped. "The *poor Kat can't find a man* pity."

He understood how tough this wedding would be for her. Kat had tried so hard to find love, wanted it so badly, and always failed. Now she had to help her little sister plan her wedding and be happy for her, even though Kat's heart ached with envy. Having a good friend by her side, pretending to her family that she'd found a nice guy, would make things easier for her.

Yes, he was pissed that she wanted only friendship from him, but that was his problem. He shouldn't take his frustration and hurt out on her.

He clicked the dryer on and turned to face her. "When do you need to know?"

"No great rush, I guess. It's two weeks off. Like I said, I'll probably leave Monday. I'll take the train to Toronto, then on to Vancouver."

"It's a long trip."

"Yeah." Her face brightened. "It really is fun. I've done it every year or so since I moved here when I was eighteen. It's like being on holiday with fascinating people. A train's a special world. Normal rules don't apply."

He always traveled by air, but he'd watched old movies with Kat. *North by Northwest. Silver Streak.* Trains were sexy.

Damn. He could see it now. Kat would meet some guy, fall for him, have hot sex, end up taking him rather than Nav to the wedding.

Unless . . .

An idea—brilliant? insane?—struck him. What if he was the guy on the train?

What if he showed up out of the blue, took her by surprise? An initial shock, then days together in that special, sexy world where normal rules didn't apply. Might she see him differently?

If he analyzed his idea, he'd decide it was crazy and never do it. So, forget about being rational. He'd hustle upstairs and go online to arrange getting money transferred out of the trust fund he hadn't touched since coming to Canada.

It had been a matter of principle: proving to himself that he wasn't a spoiled rich kid and could make his own way in the world. But now, principles be damned. Train travel wasn't cheap, and this was a chance to win the woman he loved.

Unrequited love was unhealthy. He'd break the good buddy limbo, stop being so fucking pathetic, and go after her.

But first, he had to set things up with Kat so she'd be totally surprised when he showed up on the train. "Yeah, okay." He tried to sound casual. "I'll be your token good guy. I'll fly out for the wedding."

"Oooeeee!!" She flung herself into his arms, a full-body tackle that caught him off guard and almost toppled them both. "Thank you, thank you, thank you." She pressed quick little kisses all over his cheeks.

When what he longed for were soul-rocking, deep and dirty kisses, mouth to mouth, tongue to tongue. Groin to groin.

Enough. He was fed up with her treating him this way. Fed up with himself for taking it. Things between them were damned well going to change.

He grabbed her head between both hands and held her steady, her mouth inches from his.

Her lips opened and he heard a soft gasp as she caught her breath. "Nav?" Was that a quiver in her voice?

Deliberately, he pressed his lips against hers. Soft, so soft her lips were, and warm. Though it took all his willpower, he drew away before she could decide how to respond. "You're welcome," he said casually, as if the kiss had been merely a "between friends" one.

All the same, he knew it had reminded her of the attraction between them.

She would be a tiny bit unsettled.

He had, in a subtle way, served notice.

Token good guy? Screw that.

He was going to be the sexy guy on the train.

You won't want to miss Karen Kelley's THE JAGUAR PRINCE, the first in her new series, in stores now!

This wasn't happening. Callie closed her eyes and took a deep breath. "You're not real," she repeated over and over until she could feel herself beginning to relax.

The naked hottie was only the last fragment of a delicious dream she'd been having. Right before she went to sleep, hadn't she wished he would magically materialize in her bed?

She relaxed and smiled. It had been a great dream. The way he touched her, nuzzled her neck, pressed his naked body against hers. It had been one long sensuous dream. That was probably why she'd apparently gotten rid of her hot granny gown sometime during the night. Okay, now she was back to normal. No more fantasies that a hot sexy man was in her bed. The idea was ludicrous.

Deep breath. Inhale. Exhale. She was wide awake now. She opened her eyes.

He was still there, sitting on the end of her bed, staring at her with what appeared to be . . . amusement? He laughed at her! He was in her house, her bed, and he laughed at her!

Callie sat up, and the cover fell to her waist. His gaze dropped. She grabbed the sheet and pulled it against her chest. "Get out! Who are you? How did you get into my house? Where's my gown?"

One eyebrow arched. "Are you always this emotionally unstable?"

"Emotionally . . ." she sputtered.

"Unstable," he slowly and distinctly repeated.

"I am not emotionally unstable!" Oh God, she was arguing with the serial killer. She took another deep breath, then exhaled once more. She needed to stay calm. "If you don't leave right now, I'm going to call the police."

Oh, yeah, now he really looked nervous—not! He didn't even flinch. Just sat there staring at her. And why wouldn't he? He probably weighed around one-eighty. She would be no match for him.

Maybe if she kept him talking, he wouldn't kill her right away. She'd once read somewhere that if you could befriend your abductor, then he would be less likely to kill you. Not that he'd abducted her, but he had apparently broken into her home. God, she hoped this worked.

"How . . . uh . . . did you find me?" Surely someone would've noticed a naked man following her car. For the first in her life, Callie wished her rattletrap car went faster.

She frowned. How had he followed her? Her car wasn't that slow. He probably had his own car. He'd waited for her to leave, then followed.

So, he drove around naked. And no one noticed this?

"Does it matter how I came to be here?" he asked.

"I guess not." If she knew where he came from, then maybe she could talk him into going back, though. "Where are you from?"

"New Symtaria."

"Never heard of it. Is that a suburb of Dallas?" New ones were cropping up all the time.

"It's in another galaxy."

Alrighty. "Another planet?"

He nodded, still looking amused about something.

"And you are?"

"Prince Rogar."

She nodded. Delusional. Probably escaped from the state hospital. This was worse than she ever could have imagined. Not only was he naked, but he was a nut. Automatically, her eyes strayed downward. She swallowed, then quickly jerked her gaze to a safer place. She had to stop looking . . . looking at him . . . down there. It wasn't like she'd never seen a naked man before.

This was ridiculous. She needed help and all she could think about was staring at his . . . his nakedness. She had to call the police or something—911. Her cell phone was in her purse. From now on, she was keeping it on her bedside table. If there ever was a from-now-on in her future. Okay, keep him talking.

"And why are you here?" She smiled. At least she tried to pull it off as a smile, even though her stomach rumbled, her hands were sweating, and she was probably going to throw up any second.

"To take you home."

She looked around "I am home, so . . . bye-bye."

He grinned and she noticed his teeth were pearly white, and he had a nice smile. Ted Bundy probably had a nice smile, too.

"You're part Symtarian," he continued.

"Okayyy . . ." He thought she was from another planet, too. This was worse than she could've imagined.

"When our planet was dying, some of the people were sent to other places. An expedition went in search of a new planet to call home. Some of our people were forgotten, and became integrated with the aliens. Now we're searching for them so we can bring them home."

"And you're doing it without clothes."

"It happens when I shape-shift."

"Well, of course, I should have guessed." The guy was a raving lunatic. "And what form do you take?"

A fog began to roll across her bedroom. She glanced nervously around, then looked at her crazy guy. Her mouth dropped open as he slowly began to change.

The prince dude gritted his teeth and lowered his head. His skin changed from flesh to short black hair with visible spots. He stretched out across her bed, his hand curling into a fist, becoming a paw.

Oh, God, she was crazy. Now she would never get her chance to work with the big cats—except in her warped mind. It wasn't fair.

The fog rolled in thicker until all Callie saw were patches of black fur, a glimpse of golden eyes boring into her. She couldn't move. She tried, but her legs wouldn't budge.

The fog slowly dissipated.

A black jaguar from last night lay across the end of her bed, panting slightly. It met her gaze, and seemed as though it was gauging her reaction.

She opened her mouth, then closed it when no words came out. The cat purred from deep in its throat. She swallowed past the lump in hers. What if the jag was real? Oh, yeah, now she felt better. She was going to die. Then again, she might already be dead and this was hell.

Whatever it was, the jaguar was still stretched across the foot of her bed.

The room began to tilt, then grow dark, and she knew without a doubt, she was about to faint. She'd never fainted in her life.

And here's a sneak peek at UNDONE, the historical romance anthology featuring Susan Johnson, Terri Brisbin, and Mary Wine. Turn the page for a preview of Susan's story, "As You Wish."

Fortunately for the earl's pressing schedule, the night was overcast. Not a hint of moonlight broke through to expose his athletic form as he scaled the old, fist-thick wisteria vines wrapped around the pillars of the terrace pergola. The house to which the pergola was attached was quiet, the ground floor dark save for the porter's light in the entrance hall. Either the Belvoirs were out or already in bed. More likely the latter, with only a single flambeau outside the door.

He'd best take care.

Kit had described the position of Miss Belvoir's bedchamber—hence Albion's ascent of wisteria. Once he gained the roof joists of the Chinoiserie pergola, he would have access to the windows of the main floor corridor. From there he could make his way to the second-floor bedchambers, the easternmost that of Miss Belvoir. Where, according to Kit, she'd been cloistered for the last month, being polished by her stepmother into a state of refined elegance for her bow into society a few weeks hence.

Which refinements, in his estimation, only served to make every young lady into the same boring martinet without an original thought in her head or a jot of conversation worth listening to.

Hopefully, there wouldn't be much conversation tonight. If he had his way there wouldn't be any. He hoped as well that she wouldn't prove stubborn, but should she, he'd stuff his handkerchief in her mouth to muffle her screams, tie her up if necessary, and carry her down the back stairs and out the servants' entrance. It was more likely, though—with all due modesty—that his much-practiced charm would win the day.

Pulling himself over the fretwork balustrade embellishing the pergola, he stood for a moment balanced on a joist contemplating which window would best offer him ingress. His mind made up, he brushed himself off, navigated the vine-draped timbers, and reached the window. Taking a knife from his coat pocket, he snapped open the blade, slipped it under the lower sash, and pried it up enough to gain a fingerhold.

Moments later, he stood motionless in the dark corridor. The stairs were to the right, if Kit's description was correct. After listening for a few moments and hearing nothing, he quietly made his way down the plush carpet and up the stairs. A single candle on a console table dimly illuminated the hallway onto which the bedrooms opened. Pausing to listen once again and distinguishing no undue sounds, he silently traversed the carpeted passageway to the last door on his right.

It shouldn't be locked. Servants required access if the bell pull by the bed was rung. For a brief moment he stood utterly still, wondering what in blazes he was doing here, about to abduct some untried maid in order to seduce her. As if there weren't women enough in London who would welcome him to their beds with open arms. Considerable brandy was to blame, he supposed, along with the rackety company of his friends who had too much idle time on their hands in which to conjure up wild wagers like this.

Bloody hell. He felt the complete absence of any desire to be where he was.

On the other hand, he decided with a short exhalation, he'd bet twenty thousand on this foolishness.

Now it was play or pay.

He reached for the latch, pressed down and quietly opened the door.

As he stepped over the threshold he was greeted by a ripple of scent and a cheerful female voice. "I thought you'd changed your mind."

The hairs on the back of his neck rose.

His first thought was that he was unarmed.

His second was that it was a trap.

But when the same genial voice said, "Don't worry, no one's at home but me. Do come in and shut the door," his pulse rate lessened and he scanned the candlelit interior for the source of the invitation.

"Miss Belvoir, I presume," he murmured, taking note of a young woman with hair more gold than red standing across the room near the foot of the bed. She was quite beautiful. How nice. And if no one was home, nicer still. Shutting the door behind him, he offered her a graceful bow.

"A pleasant, good evening, Albion. Gossip preceded you." He was breathtakingly handsome at close range. Now to convince him to take her away. "I have a proposition for you."

He smiled. "A coincidence. I have one for you." This was going to be easier than he thought. Then he saw her luggage. "You first," he said guardedly.

"I understand you have twenty thousand to lose."

"Or not."

"Such arrogance, Albion. You forget the decision is mine.

"Not entirely," he replied softly.

"Because you've done this before."

"Not this. "But something enough like it to know."

"I see," she murmured. "But then *I'm* not inclined to be instantly infatuated with your handsome self or your prodigal repute. I have more important matters on my mind."

"More than twenty thousand?" he asked with a small smile.

"I like to think so."

He recognized the seriousness of her tone. "Then we must come to some agreement. What do you want?"

"To strike a bargain."

"Consider me agreeable to most anything," he smoothly replied.

"My luggage caused you certain apprehension, I noticed," she said, amusement in her gaze. "Let me allay your fears. I have no plans to elope with you. Did you think I did?"

"The thought crossed my mind." He wasn't entirely sure yet that some trap wasn't about to be sprung. She was the picture of innocence in white muslin—all the rage thanks to Marie Antoinette's penchant for the faux rustic life.

"I understand that women stand in line for your amorous skills, but rest assured—you're not my type. Licentiousness is your raison d'être, I hear: a very superficial existence, I should think."

His brows rose. He'd wondered if she'd heard about Sally's when she mentioned women standing in line. She also had the distinction of being the first woman to find him lacking. "You mistake my raison d'être. Perhaps if you knew me better you'd change your mind," He suggested pleasantly.

"I very much doubt it," she replied with equal amiability. "You're quite beautiful, I'll give you that, and I understand you're unrivaled in the boudoir. But my interests, unlike yours, aren't focused on sex. What I do need from you, however, is an escort to my aunt's house in Edinburgh."

"And for that my twenty thousand is won?" His voice was velvet soft.

"Such tact, my lord."

"I can be blunt if you prefer."

"Please do. I've heard so much about your ready charm. I'm wondering how you're going to ask."

"I hadn't planned on asking."

"Because you never have to."

He smiled. "To date at least."

"So I may be the exception."

"If you didn't need an escort to Edinburgh," he observed mildly. "Your move."

"You see this as a game?"

"In a manner of speaking."

"And I'm the trophy or reward or how do young bucks describe a sportive venture like this?"

"How do young ladies describe the snaring of a husband?"

She laughed. "Touché. I have no need of a husband, though. Does that calm your fears?"

"I have none in that regard. Nothing could induce me to marry."

"Then we are in complete agreement. Now tell me, how precisely does a libertine persuade a young lady to succumb to his blandishments?"

"Not like this," he said dryly. "Come with me and I'll show you."

"We strike our bargain first. Like you, I have much at stake."

"Then, Miss Belvoir," he said with well-bred grace, "if you would be willing to relinquish your virginity tonight, I'd be delighted to escort you to Edinburgh."

"In the morning. Or later tonight if we can deal with this denouement expeditiously."

"At week's end," he countered. "After the Spring Meet in Newmarket."

"I'm sorry. That's not acceptable."

He didn't answer for so long she thought he might be willing to lose twenty thousand. He was rich enough.

"We can talk about it at my place."

"No."

Another protracted silence ensued; only the crackle of the fire on the hearth was audible.

"Would you be willing to accompany me to Newmarket?" he finally said. "I can assure you anonymity at my race box. Once the Spring Meet is over, I'll take you to Edinburgh." He blew out a small breath. "I've a fortune wagered on my horses. I don't suppose you'd understand."

This time she was the one who didn't respond immediately, and when she did, her voice held a hint of melancholy. "I do understand. My mother owned the Langley stud."

"That was your mother's? By God—the Langley stud was legendary. Tattersalls was mobbed when it was sold. You *do* know how I feel about my racers, then." He grinned. "They're all going to win at Newmarket. I'll give you a share if you like—to help set you up in Edinburgh."

Her expression brightened, and her voice took on a teasing intonation. "Are you trying to buy my acquiescence?"

"Why not? You only need give me a few days of your time. Come with me. You'll enjoy the races."

"I mustn't be seen."

Ah—capitulation. "Then we'll see that you aren't. Good Lord—the Langley stud. I'm bloody impressed. Let me get your luggage."